**Also available from
Shannon Stacey**

*Undeniably Yours
Exclusively Yours*

shannon stacey

yours to keep

HQN™

ISBN-13: 978-1-61793-752-1

YOURS TO KEEP

This edition published by arrangement with Harlequin Books S.A.

Printed in U.S.A.

Thank you so much to my readers.
So many of you have told me you love
the Kowalski family and want more,
so I hope you enjoy meeting Sean Kowalski,
as well as revisiting the rest of the family.
As always, thank you to Angela James
and the Carina Press team, as well as the HQN team,
for your dedication and enthusiasm.
And to my husband, whom I love madly
even though he never lets me drive.

Yours to keep

CHAPTER ONE

"STILL AS UGLY AS EVER, I see."

Sean Kowalski flipped the bartender the bird and dropped his duffel on the floor next to an empty stool. "Runs in the family, cousin."

Since they both stood a hair over six feet, they were able to exchange a quick hug over the bar, and Kevin thumped him on the back. "Damn glad you made it home."

"Me, too." Sean sat on the bar stool and took a long swig of the foamy beer Kevin put in front of him. "Sorry I missed your wedding. And Joe's, too."

"You were getting your ass shot at in Afghanistan. We won't hold it against you. Much."

"Still can't believe you both found women willing to be your Mrs. Kowalskis. What's wrong with them?"

Kevin flashed him a grin. "It's the dimples, man. Women can't resist them. Too bad for you we got 'em from Ma and all you got are the blue eyes from the old man's side."

"They do me well enough. How are your parents doing?"

"Good. They're looking forward to seeing you, and Ma made lasagna for tonight."

Sean grinned and patted his stomach. "I didn't stop for lunch, so I've got plenty of room. There are a lot of things I miss about my mother, God rest her soul, but her cooking isn't one of them. Aunt Mary, though? Damn, that woman can put a meal together."

Kevin nodded, then stepped away for a minute to grab a water. "So, you've got no job. Gonna mooch food from Ma and bum an apartment from me. The army was supposed to make you a man, not a useless son of a bitch."

"Twelve years was enough. Don't know what I want to do now, but I know it's not more of that."

"No interest in going back to Maine and helping your brother run the lodge?"

Sean shrugged. It had come up—especially when he'd told his brothers and sister he was going to hang out with the New Hampshire branch of the family for a while. But spending the rest of his life at the North- ern Star Lodge wasn't something he wanted to do. As a child, he'd hated strangers making themselves at home in his house, and he'd never outgrown it. He just wasn't cut out to be an innkeeper.

"It's a plan B," he said.

Kevin took a swig off the water bottle, then

screwed the cap back on. "You know I'm just giving you shit. You can crash here as long as you want."

"Appreciate it. Once I've had my fill of Aunt Mary's cooking, I might go home or…hell if I know." It was one of the reasons he'd decided to leave the army. There was nowhere he had to be tomorrow. Or the day after that.

A tall, busty redhead stepped out from a back room and Kevin waved her over. "This is my cousin Sean. Sean, this is Paulie Reed, my head bartender, assistant manager and all-around right-hand man. Woman. Person. Right-hand person."

"Nice to meet you," Sean said, shaking her hand. She had one hell of a grip.

"I've heard a lot about you. Welcome home. My fiancé, Sam, and I live in the apartment below yours, so give a shout if you need anything."

"Will do." He watched her walk away because she had a hell of a swing, but—whether it was the mention of a fiancé or the fact she just wasn't his type—it didn't do much for him. "Jasper's Bar & Grille, huh? Interesting name."

"It came with the place and I'm too cheap to buy a new sign. Finish that beer and I'll take you upstairs now that Paulie's off break."

Sean knocked back the rest of the suds and picked up his duffel. He followed his cousin to a back hallway, then up two flights of stairs to the apartment

Kevin was letting him use for the duration of his visit. It was a decent place and clean, with an over-size leather couch and a big-screen TV. All good, as far as he was concerned.

"So this is it," Kevin told him when he was done showing him around and had given him the key. "You've got all our numbers, and Paulie's usually in the bar if you need anything."

Sean shook his hand. "See you at dinner, then. Looking forward to meeting Beth and that baby girl of yours."

"Lily's a firecracker. Had her first birthday a week ago and loves terrorizing the shit out of her cousins." He whipped out his wallet, and it fell open to a picture of a feisty-looking little girl with one of those palm-tree-ponytail things on the top of her head, bright blue eyes and devilish dimples.

"She'll break some hearts someday," Sean said, because that's what men seemed to say when shown pictures of other guys' daughters.

"And I'll break open some heads. Joe's Brianna looks a lot like Lily, but without the dimples. She's four and a half months now and loud as hell." Kevin headed for the door. "I told Beth I'd be home by three so she can make something to bring to Ma's without tripping over Lily, who doesn't stay where we put her anymore. I'll see you about six."

When he was gone, Sean dropped onto the couch

and closed his eyes. It was good to be home, even if home was a borrowed apartment. For the first time in twelve years he could go wherever he wanted. Do whatever he wanted. The army had given him a good start in life and he didn't regret the years he'd served, but he was ready to be his own man again.

The first order of business as his own man? A power nap.

A knock at the door surprised him, jerking him out of a light sleep. It wasn't as if he was expecting company. As far as he knew, the only people who'd be looking for him were family, and he was meeting them at his aunt and uncle's. Still, he pulled open the door expecting to see one of his cousins.

He was wrong. His unexpected guest was definitely *not* related to him, which was a good thing considering his body reacted as though it was his first time seeing a pretty woman. She had a big curly mass of dark hair full of different colors—almost like a deep cherrywood grain—and whether she'd be a brunette or a redhead probably depended on the lighting. Her eyes were even darker, the color of strong black coffee, and just the right amount of curves softened a taller-than-average, lean body.

A body that made his body stand up and take notice in a way the sexy bartender downstairs hadn't. This woman wasn't too top-heavy and the way she took care of her body made him think if they wrestled under the sheets, she'd make it one hell of a good match.

Okay, he really needed to get laid if he was going to start imagining sex with any random stranger who knocked on his door.

"Can I help you?" he prompted when she just stood there and looked at him.

She picked at the fraying wrist of a navy sweatshirt that had Landscaping by Emma written across the front in fancy letters. "Are you Sean Kowalski?"

"Yup."

"I'm Emma Shaw...your fake fiancée."

"Say what?"

EMMA SHAW SURE KNEW how to pick a fake man. The real Sean Kowalski was tall, had tanned and rugged arms stretching the sleeves of his blue T-shirt, and dark blond hair that looked as if it was growing out from a short cut. A little scruff covered his square jaw, as if he'd forgotten to shave for a couple of days, and even squinting at her in a suspicious manner, his eyes were the prettiest shade of blue she'd ever seen.

Okay, maybe it wasn't all suspicion. His expression implied he was afraid she was some crazy woman who'd gone off her meds and was going to start speaking in tongues or show him the handmade Sean doll she'd crafted to sleep with.

"Lady, I've never had a fiancée, fake or otherwise,"

he said in a low voice that made her knees weaken just a little. "And it's been a while since I've gone on a decent bender, so if I'd asked you to marry me, I'm pretty sure I'd at least remember your face."

That would have been hard to do. "We've never actually met."

He stopped squinting at her and snorted. "Let me guess—this is some joke my cousins thought would be a funny way to welcome me home? Okay, so… ha-ha. I've got stuff to do now."

He started to close the door, but she slapped her hand against it. "I'm a friend of Lisa's. Your cousin-in-law, I guess she'd be."

"Mikey's wife?" He pulled the door open when she nodded. "Maybe we should start this conversation in a different place. Like the beginning."

She took a deep breath, then blew it out. "My grandmother's raised me since I was four."

"Maybe not *that* far back."

"She retired to Florida a couple years ago with some friends, and I take care of the house I grew up in. But all she was doing was worrying about me, and when she started talking about moving back so I wouldn't be alone, I told her I had a boyfriend. Then I told her he'd moved in with me. And, because I would only date a super-great guy, after a while he proposed and naturally I accepted."

"And I got dragged into this how?"

"I had just gotten home from having lunch with Lisa and she'd mentioned sending you a care package. Your name just popped into my head when Gram asked what my boyfriend's name was."

He shook his head. "Let me get this straight. You told your grandmother that a guy you've never met is your boyfriend?"

"I just wanted her to worry less."

"Maybe she's right to worry about you."

Ouch. "I'm not crazy, you know."

He folded his arms across his chest and looked down at her. "You made up an imaginary boyfriend."

"You're not imaginary. Just uninformed."

He didn't even crack a smile. "What do you want from me?"

And here came the crazy part—the *more* crazy part, anyway. "Gram's coming home. She wants to check on the house and…she wants to meet you."

As she spoke, Emma made sure none of her body parts were breaking the plane of the doorway, just in case he slammed the door in her face. It was something she might do, if some strange guy showed up on her doorstep and told her they were in a deep, meaningful relationship.

"So…what? You want me to have dinner with you guys? Pretend I'm your fiancé for a few hours?"

"She'll be here a month."

He laughed at her then. A deep, infectious laugh

that made her want to join in even though he was laughing at her. Not that she could blame him. Even her best friend had laughed, although that might have been because Lisa thought she was joking. And she had been at the time. But as Gram's arrival grew closer and she still couldn't work up the nerve to tell her she didn't really have a fiancé, the idea didn't seem as funny.

Sean obviously disagreed, since he laughed long enough so she shifted her weight from one foot to the other before clearing his throat. "Since I know you didn't come here thinking I'd move in with you and pretend to be your fiancé for a month, what is it you want?"

"Actually, I did come here to ask you if you'd move in with me and pretend to be my fiancé for a month." And, no, it didn't sound a whole lot more sane than when she'd practiced saying it in the mirror.

"Why would I do that?"

Good question. "Because you're not really doing anything else. I'd pay you. And you're a nice guy?"

"Lady, you don't know anything about me."

"I know you just got out of the army, so you don't have a permanent home. I know you don't have a job yet. And I know you're a really good guy."

"I know somebody in my family has a big mouth."

"Lisa's proud of you. She talks about you a lot."

He sighed and ran a hand over his hair. "Look,

I'm not an actor for hire. I think, if you're not willing to tell her the truth, you should just tell your grandmother you broke up with your...me."

She wanted to argue with him—to make him understand she just wanted her grandmother to be happy—but it had been such a long shot, anyway, and she didn't have the heart to keep at it.

"Well," she said in a voice that only trembled a little, "thanks for your time. And welcome home, too."

"Thanks. Take care of yourself."

Even after he'd disappeared back into the apartment and closed the door, Emma managed not to cry.

It wasn't the end of the world. She'd have to tell Gram they'd broken up, and that would be the end of it.

It wouldn't be the end of the worrying, though. If anything, it would be worse. Now Gram would not only worry about Emma being alone and taking care of the house and a business, but she'd think her granddaughter was nursing the heartbreaking loss of a broken engagement, too. Even if Gram could bring herself to return to Florida, she'd do nothing but fret again—the very thing Emma was trying to put a stop to.

Emma crossed the street and happened to glance up as she climbed into her truck. Sean Kowalski was watching her from his apartment window, and she forced herself to give him a friendly smile and wave before she closed her door and slid the key into the ignition.

It was too bad, she thought, and not just for Gram's sake. That was a man any woman would want to be pretend-engaged to, even if only for a month.

IT WAS A GOOD TEN MINUTES after walking through the Kowalskis' front door before Sean could even get his coat off. The whole gang was there, but his aunt could throw some mean elbows and got to him first.

"Sean!" She threw herself at him and he caught her up in a big bear hug.

He'd missed her more than he'd imagined he would while he was overseas. After his mom died unexpectedly the year he was nine, Aunt Mary had managed— from a state away and with four kids of her own—to step up and be a mother figure to her four nephews and one niece. It had been good to see his siblings, but being squeezed by his aunt while her tears burned his neck was like coming home.

He got a little choked up himself when Uncle Leo pulled him into his arms and gave him a few solid thumps on the back. Though Leo was shorter than his brother, Frank, he was close enough in looks and mannerisms to remind Sean of his dad, who'd passed away nine years ago.

"Your old man would have been proud," Leo

barked and Sean nodded, not trusting himself to speak.

Then came a gauntlet of cousins and their families. Joe, with his pretty new wife, Keri, who was holding rosy-cheeked baby Brianna. Terry and Evan with Stephanie, who, at thirteen, was growing into a pretty young woman. Kevin introduced him to Beth, who only managed a quick "nice to meet you" since she was wrangling Lily.

Mike and Lisa's family was a lot taller than the last time he'd seen them. He managed to find out Joey was now fifteen, Danny twelve, Brian nine and Bobby seven, before Mary started hushing the kids and herding them all toward the dining room.

"Dinner's ready to come out of the oven," she said. "Let's eat while it's hot."

As he'd expected, the massive dining room table was practically groaning under the weight of his welcome-home feast. She'd even made garlic bread that was soft and buttery on the inside and crusty on the outside. A far cry from his own pathetic efforts to re-create it by sprinkling garlic salt on a buttered slice of white toast.

"I swear, Aunt Mary, the whole time I was in Afghanistan, the only thing I could think of was your lasagna. Except for when I was thinking about your beef stew. Or your chicken and dumplings."

She gave him a modest *tsk,* but he could tell by

the slight blush on her cheeks she was pleased by the compliment. "You always did have a good appetite."

The company was as good as the food, and stories flowed like the iced tea as they plowed through the lasagna. He told a few watered-down tales of Afghanistan. Joe told the story of blackmailing Keri into joining the entire Kowalski family on their camping trip. Mike told him about Kevin fainting like a girl the day Lily was born.

He laughed at the description of his cousin going down like a cement truck that blew a hairpin turn and crashed through the guardrail, holding his stomach because he hadn't been able to resist the third helping his aunt had pushed on him.

"It's game night," nine-year-old Brian told him when the talk had died down and they were clearing the table. "Are you going to stay and play?"

"Sure." It wasn't as if he had anything better to do. "Just give me a few minutes to let my dinner settle, okay?"

"Sean's playing," the kid bellowed as he raced back to the others. "He's on my team!"

"We don't even know what we're playing yet," Danny pointed out.

"Don't care. He's on my team."

While the family debated which board games to drag out with the ferocity of a cease-fire negotiation, Sean stepped onto the back deck for a little fresh air.

When he closed the sliding door and stepped to the left—out of view of people in the house—he almost bumped into Lisa.

Sean had always liked Mike's wife. She was on the shorter side of average—maybe five-three—but she had six feet of attitude and didn't let anybody push her around.

"Ran into a friend of yours today," he told her.

"Oh, yeah?"

"Tall. Hot. Batshit crazy?"

It was a few seconds before understanding dawned in her eyes, followed by a hot blush across her cheeks. "She didn't."

"Oh, she did. Knocked on my door and told me she was my fiancée, and that you knew she was throwing my name around."

She put her hand on his arm. "It was harmless, Sean. Really. She was just trying to make her grand-mother feel better about being in Florida."

"Did she tell you her grand plan?"

The flush deepened. "Oh, no. Tell me she didn't."

"She did."

"I thought she was only joking."

"I thought it was a prank your husband and his cohort brothers cooked up, but she was serious."

Lisa shook her head, but he could see the amuse-ment tugging at the corners of her mouth. "What, ex-actly, did she tell you the plan was?"

"What did she tell *you* it was?"

"She was kind of hinting around that maybe you could pretend to be the boyfriend."

"That almost sounds sane." He gave a short laugh. "The plan's now evolved into me moving in with her and pretending to be her fiancé for an entire month."

She didn't meet his eyes. "Maybe she did mention that, too, but she laughed, so I thought she was kidding."

"Nope." Sean folded his arms across his chest and leaned against the house. He should go back in and see if there was any blueberry cobbler left. Emma Shaw was nothing but a weird blip on his radar and he should forget her. But it didn't seem she was a forgettable woman. "So what's her deal, anyway?"

"Her grandmother kept talking about selling the house because she's afraid it's too much for Emma. Emma doesn't want a different house, so she made up a guy."

"Making up a guy would almost be normal. She made up an imaginary life for *me*. That's not normal."

"It's a really nice house." He just looked at her until she laughed and shrugged. "Okay, it's crazy, but—"

"But it's all out of love for her poor, sweet grandmother. Yeah, I got that part."

The look she gave him let him know she hadn't missed his less-than-flattering tone. It was a look that probably would have cowed him if he had to live with her, sleep beside her and depend on her for a hot meal. But he didn't, so he grinned and gave her a wink.

She blew out a breath and then her face grew serious. "Emma's parents were killed in a car accident when she was four, on their way to do some Christmas shopping. Her grandmother, Cat, and her grandfather, John—who died about ten years ago—were watching Emma. When the state police gave them the bad news, they didn't even consider giving her up. They were all she had, and as their friends enjoyed their empty nests and started traveling and retiring, the Shaws started all over with a grieving four-year-old."

"I'm sure they're nice people, Lisa, but come on."

"Cat tried to hide how much she wanted to go down to Florida with her friends, but Emma knew. And it took an entire year for Emma to convince her grandmother it was okay to go. And even then, every time they talked on the phone, Cat talked about moving back to New Hampshire because Emma was alone and the house was too big for one person and there was too much lawn to mow and this whole list of stuff. So Emma made up a man around the house and Cat was free to enjoy her book clubs and line-dancing classes."

Sean was going to point out the rather significant difference between lying about having a boyfriend and asking a stranger to move in for a month, but at that moment his aunt stepped outside and closed the slider behind her.

"I knew I'd find you out here." She smiled to let him know she wasn't offended he'd try to sneak a few quiet minutes away from his own welcome-home dinner. "What are you two talking about?"

"I ran into a friend of Lisa's today," he told her, enjoying the way Lisa's eyes got big and she started trying to communicate with him by way of frantic facial expressions behind her mother-in-law's back. "Emma Shaw."

"Emma Shaw... Oh! The one who does the landscaping, right?" Lisa nodded. "She's such a nice girl, but I haven't seen her in ages. Not since I ran into you two at the mall and overheard you talking about her engagement. How are she and her fiancé doing?"

Lisa opened her mouth, but closed it again when Sean folded his arms and looked at her, waiting to see how—or even if—she was going to get out of the conversation without lying outright to Aunt Mary.

"I...think they're having some problems," she finally said. Nice hedge, if a bit of an understatement.

"Oh, that's too bad. What's her fiancé's name? I meant to ask that day, but you started talking about some shoe sale and I forgot."

It was a few seconds before Lisa sighed in defeat. "Sean."

"Isn't that funny," Mary said, smiling at him before

turning back to her daughter-in-law. "What's his last name? Maybe I know his family."

That was a pretty safe bet.

"She told her grandmother she was dating our Sean," Lisa mumbled.

When his aunt pinned him with one of those looks that made grown Kowalski men squirm, Sean held up his hands. "I had nothing to do with it. I didn't even know."

"How could you not know you were engaged?"

"I was in Afghanistan. And I met her for the first time a few hours ago."

Her eyebrows knit. "I don't understand."

"It's nothing, really," Lisa said. "She didn't want her grandmother to worry about her, so she told her she had a boyfriend, and Sean's name was the first one that came to mind."

"That's crazy."

Sean grinned at Lisa. "Told ya."

The slider opened and Joey's head popped out. "Sean, you got drafted for Monopoly, and they're going to start cheating if you don't get in here and take your turn."

Since he'd rather go directly to jail and not pass go than listen to Lisa try to explain Emma Shaw to Aunt Mary anymore, he gave the women a whaddya-gonna-do shrug and followed Joey to the family room. He was late to the game, so he got stuck being the stupid thimble, but he just grinned and pulled up some floor next to the oversize coffee table.

He then proceeded to have his ass handed to him by his cousins' kids, who had the real estate instincts of Donald Trump and the sportsmanship of John McEnroe facing off against a line judge. A guy's attention couldn't wander to a mass of dark curls and pleading brown eyes for a few minutes without hotels popping up all over the damn place. One moment of distraction, remembering the way his body had responded to hers, and he found himself promising Bobby a trip to Dairy Queen in exchange for the loan of a fistful of paper money.

He didn't fare any better at Scattergories, though he did come up with *landscaper* when the letter was *L* and the category was occupations. Stephanie smoked them all, managing to find alliterative adjectives to go with her answers. *Prissy professor.* For an *F* fruit, she came up with *fresh figs.* Sean's answer space for that one was blank.

After the scores were tallied, he scratched down a few adjectives for his occupations pick. *Lovely landscaper. Lush landscaper.* Or maybe...*lusty landscaper?*

"The grown-ups are breaking out the cards for

some five-card stud," Kevin told him. "We don't take checks."

Shit. At the rate he was going, he'd be bankrupt by the third hand.

CHAPTER TWO

A CLEANING SERVICE, Emma thought as she attacked another nest of rapidly procreating dust bunnies with the vacuum wand. That's what she wanted the birthday fairy to bring her.

Actually, she really wanted Sean Kowalski for her birthday, but he'd scratched himself off her wish list, leaving her with nothing to do but take out her frustrations on the dark, dust-bunny-breeding recesses of her house. No. Her grandmother's house.

Should she tell Gram over the phone that she and Sean had broken up, or wait until she got there?

It was a question she'd been asking herself since leaving his apartment the day before, but she still didn't have an answer. Gram would be heartbroken for her. And she'd want to fix it, which she couldn't do from 1,531 miles away.

Her phone vibrated in her back pocket, so she slapped the off button on the vacuum and tugged the phone free. A picture she'd taken of Lisa at Old Orchard Beach the previous summer filled the screen and she seriously considered hitting the ignore button.

Lisa never called her in the morning because Emma was usually working and, as far as she knew, didn't know she'd rescheduled some appointment to free up time to obsess about the house before Gram arrived. That meant something was going on, and she had a gut feeling that something was Sean Kowalski.

After a bracing deep breath that didn't do much to brace her, she hit the talk button. "Hey, Lisa."

"Did you seriously ask Sean to move in with you?"

Emma groaned and sank onto the couch. "I really did."

"Did he shut the door in your face?"

"No, he was very polite and careful not to make any sudden moves."

"I think the phrase he used was 'batshit crazy.'"

Ouch.

"But hot," Lisa said. "'Tall, hot and batshit crazy' was his exact description."

The hot part made her feel a little better, but in remembering his expression, she didn't think hot meant hot enough to overcome the batshit-crazy part. "I guess I'll wait until Gram gets here to tell her my fiancé and I called it quits."

"That sucks. If you say it just happened, she'll wonder why you're not broken up about it. But if it happened long enough ago so you're over it, she'll be upset you didn't tell her."

"Last week, when she said she was looking forward to meeting him, I said he felt the same way." She needed something hard to beat her head against. "How did I get myself into this?"

"Your mouth's quicker than your brain."

"Gee, thanks."

"So what did you think of him?" Lisa asked, her voice dropping down into the "let's dish" range.

It should have been an easy question to answer since she'd been thinking about him pretty much non-stop—except when she was obsessing about Gram—since she left his apartment yesterday. "I don't know. Tall, hot and, unfortunately for me, not batshit crazy. But it's not like I haven't seen his face before."

"Pictures don't do that man justice. Even a very happily married woman like me can see that."

No, they didn't, Emma thought, her gaze drawn to the ridiculous photo of Sean hung above the wing-back chair. It was ridiculous because he'd had his arm around Lisa's niece Stephanie at a family barbecue, but, in response to a request from Gram, Lisa had helped her insert herself into the picture instead. She didn't even want to imagine what Sean would think of that.

"I wouldn't throw him out of bed," she admitted when Lisa waited for her to say something.

Maybe it was for the best that he'd said no. Her sleeping on a couch a few feet away from Sean Kowalski sleeping in her bed had seemed like a fine idea in theory. But, after meeting the man, being that close to him when the lights went out and not being *in* the bed with him wasn't a fine plan at all.

Work kept her pretty busy. She wasn't one for hanging around in bars, and none of the guys she already knew really got her motor running, so she'd been in a bit of a drought. Based on her reaction to simply meeting the man, Sean had the potential to rev her engine as if she was nosed up to the start line of a quarter-mile run.

"Crap, I've gotta run," Lisa said. "The boys all have dentist appointments in an hour and I just saw my youngest run by with a handful of Skittles."

"Have fun with that." Emma wasn't sure how her friend did it. If Emma had four boys, she'd spend her days in the bathroom, taking nips off the bottle of NyQuil in the medicine cabinet.

"If I don't talk to you again before your grand-mother arrives, good luck."

"Thanks." She'd need it.

After shoving her phone back in her pocket, Emma dragged the couch away from the wall, revealing a new nest of dust bunnies to vent her frustrations on.

She used her toe to turn on the vacuum, hoping the drone of the motor would drown out the no-longer-quiet purr of her own neglected engine.

SEAN MATCHED THE NUMBER on the directions to the middle of nowhere Lisa had given him to the number on the mailbox—it had daisies painted on it, of all things—and turned his truck onto Emma Shaw's driveway.

The massive, traditional New England farmhouse at the end of the driveway was a thing of beauty. White siding—painted clapboards, not vinyl—with dark green shutters painted to match the metal roofing. A farmer's porch wrapped from the front around one side to what he assumed was the kitchen door, and hanging baskets full of different-colored flowers hung on either side of every support post.

There was an eclectically painted grouping of wooden rockers and side tables on the porch, inviting him to sit and chat awhile, and flower beds surrounded the sides of the house he could see. Not surprising, he guessed, as he parked alongside a pickup bearing magnetic signs with the same Landscaping by Emma logo she'd had on her sweatshirt.

After climbing out of his own truck, he climbed the steps to the front door, and after taking a deep breath—which didn't help because oxygen didn't cure insanity—he rang the doorbell.

It was almost a full minute before Emma opened the door. She looked cute as hell, with her hair scraped into a sloppy ponytail and a streak of dust down her nose. He stuck his hands in his pockets so he wouldn't reach out and wipe it away.

Her eyes widened when she saw him. "Hi."

"Got a minute?"

"Sure." She stepped back and let him into the foyer. Immediately to the left was a good-size living room, and all the furniture was dragged to the center of the hardwood floor. The air was thick with the scents of Murphy Oil Soap and Lemon Pledge. "Getting ready for the white-glove inspection?"

She grimaced and swiped at her face, but she only made it worse. "Gram's not like that. I just have a lot on my mind, and when that happens, I clean. It's a sickness."

He wasn't sure where to start. "I had dinner at my aunt and uncle's last night."

"How are they doing? I haven't seen Mrs. K. in ages."

"They're good. Got a chance to talk to Lisa, too. She says you're not crazy."

"I already told you I'm not crazy."

"Crazy people don't always know they're crazy."

She blew an annoyed breath at the wisps of hair escaping the ponytail. "Trust me, I know the *circumstances* are crazy. But I'm not. Do you want a drink or something? I have lemonade. Iced tea. I think I'm out of soda, which explains the frenzied, caffeine-fueled cleaning spree."

"I'm good, thanks." He didn't expect to be there long enough to drain a glass. "So let me see if I've got this straight. This all came about because your grandmother moved to Florida and couldn't have a good time because she was too worried about you?"

She nodded and perched on the arm of the couch. "Instead of enjoying herself, she was constantly worrying about me. About me being alone in this big house. Worrying that I won't remember to change the batteries in the smoke detectors or that I'll fall off a ladder trying to clean out the gutters. It seemed harmless at the time to tell her there was a man around the place."

"Why not tell her you'd hired a handyman or something?"

She laughed and he tried to ignore how much he liked the rich sound of it. "And have her frantic I'd managed to hire some transient serial killer? No, a boyfriend was better. Especially one whose family I know so well. You're my best friend's husband's cousin. How bad could you be?"

"What did you tell her I did before I became your imaginary boyfriend?"

"I told her you were in the army and that we met when you came home on leave to visit your family." She shrugged. "And that when you came home for good, we started dating. It was easier to remember if I tried to stick close to the truth. The timeline's off, of course. She thinks you got out of the army before you really did."

He shoved his hands in his pockets, pretty certain

he must be losing his mind. "What would I get out of the deal?"

She looked as startled as he felt at the possibility he might actually be considering the plan. "A temporary job—landscaping, not just living here—and a place to stay."

"I have a place to stay. And guys like me can always find a temporary job."

"Guys like you?"

He smiled and raised an eyebrow at her. "Guys with strong backs who aren't afraid to get their hands dirty. What else?"

"Nothing, I guess. There's really nothing in it for you." Her shoulders slumped for a moment, but then she straightened her back and laughed. "It was crazy, anyway. I just wanted Gram to stop worrying about me and get on with her life. She loves it there—I can hear it in her voice—but she's torn."

"Did you think she wouldn't come home for your wedding?"

"I didn't think it would get that far. I assumed at some point I'd meet a nice guy—you know, one who actually knew I existed—and we'd start dating. I'd tell her you and I broke up, and after a little while tell her about my new boyfriend. The real one."

"But you haven't."

She shrugged and shook her head. "No. To be honest, I haven't really been looking. I want to grow my company enough so I can leave the heavy lifting to somebody else and do the design part-time before I get married and have kids."

He should get in his truck and drive away. He had his own life to sort out, and spending a month playing house with Emma would be a weird detour to take. Staying over Kevin's bar and finding a job pounding nails somewhere would give him everything he needed, but without the soap opera.

But she really did seem like a decent woman who'd gotten herself into one hell of a situation. Not to gain anything for herself, but so her grandmother could relax and enjoy her bingo games. Lisa liked her, of course, but so did his aunt Mary, and she was a pretty shrewd judge of character.

He cleared his throat. "Between graduation and signing my name on the army's dotted line, I wrecked a motorcycle. I messed myself up pretty bad, but when Aunt Mary called because she never went more than a few weeks without talking to us, I told her I just had a little road rash and a bruised elbow. I made my family lie for me, too."

Emma nodded. "Because there was nothing she could do and the truth would have worried her sick."

"Yeah. So I get it, I guess. Where you're coming from, I mean, and how you got to this point."

"It started out a harmless white lie, but then it got away from me. And I'm afraid if she comes home and

I'm alone, she might not go back. She loves it down there and both of her best friends are there now."

He must be as crazy as she was. "If I do this, what's your endgame?"

"My endgame?" She shrugged. "I'm hoping before she leaves she'll agree to sell me the house. And then I'll wait awhile and tell her we broke up."

"Wait a minute. You're going to get her to give you her house under false pretenses?"

She shook her head, the ponytail swinging. "Not give. *Sell*. Her reasons for not selling to me are ridiculous, and before you proposed to me—" He tried not to react to her words, but it was damn weird when she talked about him like that. As if he had a double life he couldn't recall. "—she kept talking about putting it on the market because she didn't want this big old house tying me down and holding me back."

He looked at her, and her dark-coffee eyes met his with an intensity that almost made him take a step back. It sure seemed as if she was telling the truth. "If I start thinking you're just some deadbeat looking to scam Granny out of her house, I'm done."

"Are you seriously going to do this for me?"

"I guess I am." He pulled the cheap department-store diamond he'd picked up that morning from his pocket and held it out to her.

"Wait." There was a faint thread of panic in her voice. "What are you doing?"

"There's hedging and then there's outright lying. I'd like to keep the latter to a minimum, so I'm going to propose to you, and you're going to accept."

"Oh. Okay."

"So how about it? Wanna be my fiancée?"

When she blushed and nodded, he slid the ring on her finger. He had to wiggle it a bit to get it over her knuckle, but it fit better than he'd expected. It got a little awkward then, because it seemed as if *something* should follow a marriage proposal. A kiss. A hug. Hell, even a handshake.

Then she shoved her hands, ring and all, in the front pockets of her jeans. "Thank you. For doing this, I mean. And for the ring. I can pay you for it."

"Don't worry about it." False intentions or not, no woman of his—more or less—would pay for her own jewelry. "So, do we share a bedroom in this fairy tale of yours?"

He liked the way a slow blush burned her cheeks and had an urge to brush his thumb over the spot, to see if her skin felt as heated as it looked. "She knows we live together. Theoretically, of course. So she probably assumes we're sleeping together, yes."

Now, *that* was a plan he could get behind. "And how would you propose to handle that?"

"I put a sofa in the bedroom. For reading and watching TV…and for me to sleep on. You can have the bed."

They could discuss that later. "So what now? When does she get home?"

"In three days."

"Wow. Short notice."

"Maybe we should have dinner or something so we can talk and get to know a little about each other. I've got a full day tomorrow, but I could grab a pizza on the way home if you want to come over."

A first date with his fiancée, Sean mused. Life after the army wasn't turning out to be quite as boring as he'd feared it might be. "Sounds good. I like anything on my pizza that's not classified as a vegetable. What time?"

"About six? I'll be knee-deep in fertilizer tomorrow, so I'll need to shower first."

Since that was a visual he didn't need any more detail on, Sean nodded, then turned toward the door. "I'll see you at six, then."

He was almost free, when she called his name. "You won't change your mind, will you?"

"Like I said, if I think you're scamming her for anything but her emotional welfare, I'm gone. Otherwise, I gave you my word and I'll see it through."

He could almost see the tension easing from her body. "Thank you."

"Before I go, you need any help putting this furniture back?"

"No, but thanks. I'm not done scrubbing the base-board trim yet."

He lifted a hand in farewell and let himself out. They had three days to become intimately acquainted enough to pass themselves off as a cohabitating engaged couple.

Mentally, he backspaced out the word *intimately*. There wouldn't be anything intimate about their relationship, despite the close quarters. They'd be playing a role, with stage kisses and fake affection. Once the curtain dropped—or the bedroom door closed, as the case may be—so would the act.

"You're going to what?"

It wasn't anything Sean hadn't asked himself every five minutes or so since getting sucked into Emma's plan, but it sounded different when his cousin said it. Or maybe it was Kevin's subsequent pointing and laughing his ass off that changed the tone.

"It's only a month," Sean said, maybe a little defensively. The shorter, dark-haired waitress—Darcy, he thought her name was—put a beer in front of him and he took a long pull. He'd been looking forward to it all day.

Kevin looked skeptical. "A month of living with a total stranger, pretending you're so madly in love with her you're going to marry her? For real?"

"No, not for real, moron. For pretend. That's the point."

His cousin laughed some more, then pulled out his cell phone and started texting. Sean craned his neck, but couldn't see the screen.

"What the hell are you doing?"

Kevin chuckled. "Telling my wife."

"You could have waited until I went upstairs."

"No, I really couldn't."

Kevin shut his phone, but it was only a few seconds before it chimed. He looked at the screen, chuckled, then was texting again.

Sean pulled out his phone and opened a new message to Kevin. I'm still here, asshole. Send.

A couple minutes later, Kevin grinned and slid his phone back in his pocket. "Beth wants to know the sleeping arrangements since there's no way even a grandmother will buy a separate-bedrooms story."

"Beth wants to know, huh?"

"Trust me, by now the whole family wants to know."

Sean was tempted to bang his head against the bar, but he wouldn't be able to knock himself out, so he didn't waste the effort. "There's a sofa in the bedroom. She'll sleep on it and I get the bed."

"Chivalrous."

"I'm too tall for a sofa."

"I don't know Emma well, but I seem to recall she's

not exactly short." Kevin gave him a knowing look. "Not exactly hard on the eyes, either."

That she wasn't. But the last thing Sean wanted to do was get tangled up with a woman. Tangled up in the sheets? Usually okay, but that, along with playing house, could give Emma the wrong idea. Permanence wasn't in his current vocabulary. Not that it was necessarily in hers, either, but no sense taking any chances.

"When does your future grandmother-in-law arrive?" Kevin asked when he finally caught the hint Sean wasn't going to discuss his fake fiancée's easiness on the eyes.

"Saturday. We're supposed to have dinner together tonight and get to know each other, I guess."

"You think you're going to get to know each other well enough over a meal to fake out her grandmother?"

"She thinks we can do it."

"What do *you* think?"

Sean shrugged. "I told her I'd do it, so I'll do my best to make sure we pull it off."

"Does Ma know about this yet?"

"Not yet," he said, grimacing. He wasn't looking forward to telling her, either. Assuming Beth wasn't on the phone with her already, giving her the big news.

Sean stood and picked up his beer, intending to

take it upstairs with him. He could return the empty mug later. "I know as soon as I walk away you're going to call Joe and Mike, so I'll just leave it to you to spread the word."

Kevin laughed. "Don't forget Mitch. And Ryan and Josh and Liz."

Sean froze, beer halfway to his mouth. Shit. He hadn't even thought about his brothers and sister and what they might think. Thinking he'd lost his mind was a given, but if one of them got to thinking he needed saving from himself and made the drive over, it would blow everything all to shit.

"Do me a favor," he said, "and let me give them the heads-up. And try to keep your half of the family in check."

"I'll try, but don't put off calling them too long. Once Ma hears about it…"

Yeah, that's what he was afraid of. He'd have to talk to Aunt Mary soon, and as much as he didn't want to, he'd have to have that discussion in person. Hopefully, her wooden spoon wouldn't be close at hand. That sucker hurt.

He went up to the apartment that was supposed to be a temporary home, but was now going to be nothing more than a motel stop, and sank onto the couch. He hadn't unpacked much yet—not that he had a lot to unpack—so the physical act of moving into Emma's house wouldn't be difficult.

And he didn't think he'd have too hard a time pretending to be attracted to her. Batshit crazy or not, she was tall—which he liked in a woman—and hot, which he *really* liked. And that hair... She had the kind of hair a man could bury his face in or plunge his hands into, capturing the thick, dark cloud in his fingers.

Sean shifted on the couch, muttering some choice words under his breath. It had been a long time since he'd buried his face in any woman's hair, and now he'd be stuck sleeping in the same room with a woman it would be a bad idea to touch. He'd be close enough to smell her shampoo. To hear the whisper of breath and skin as she sighed and shifted in her sleep. But too far away to run his hand down the long, warm curve of her back and turn that sigh into his name on her lips.

Groaning, he hit the TV power button on the remote control next to his leg, looking for some distraction. A movie. An old fight rerun. Hell, a Three Stooges marathon would do. Anything to get his mind off sex. He couldn't be thinking those kinds of thoughts.

He was an engaged man now.

CHAPTER THREE

EMMA CHANGED HER MIND about Sean Kowalski at least a dozen times over the course of her workday, but she never got as far as calling Lisa to ask for his cell-phone number—which she'd stupidly forgotten to get—before she remembered what was at stake.

Peace of mind for Gram. Freedom from worrying about losing her home for herself. Pretty much everything, as far as she was concerned.

So at six o'clock, she opened the door to Sean with her hair still damp from the shower and a smile on her face. "I wasn't sure you'd come."

He shrugged and held up a six-pack of bottled Budweiser. "I told you I would. I wasn't sure what kind of wine you'd like, or even if you like it at all, so I brought beer."

"Sounds good. Come on in. The pizza's in the kitchen. I'm starving, so I got a Meat Lover's."

"Beer was probably a better choice than wine, then. Not sure if you serve red or white with pepperoni, ham, sausage, hamburger and bacon."

She laughed and led him into the kitchen, but the

amusement died in her throat when he reached for the fridge door, presumably to keep the beer cold, then stopped. He frowned and leaned closer. Peered at the photograph held in place by a brown-eyed-Susan magnet. This one showed Emma at a Red Sox game with Sean's arm draped around her shoulder and the green field of Fenway Park behind them.

He was still frowning. "This creeps me out a little. Isn't that supposed to be Lisa? I'm pretty sure I was at that game with Mikey and his wife."

"It was Lisa who did the manipulating, not me, if that makes it any less creepy."

"Not really. Just how many of these fake pictures do you have?"

"A couple dozen, I guess, that Lisa's done for me over time. We're not really photograph happy, which helps, but I've got enough so it looks like we're a couple, at least. And I needed some to take with me when I flew down to visit her."

"Where was I when you went to Florida?"

"You couldn't get away."

"From what?"

She shrugged. "You happened to have a family wedding going on during the only weekend I could spare from work. You're a busy guy, really."

He looked as if he was going to say something else, but then he shook his head and stuck the six-pack in the fridge, pulling out two bottles before closing the door. After twisting off the caps, he set one down by each plate.

"Anything I can help you with?"

She shook her head. "Everything's on the table. Go ahead and dig in."

It didn't escape her notice that he placed a slice on her plate before serving himself, and it gave her hopefulness a little boost. Obviously he'd been raised with good manners, which would not only help him win Gram over, but make him more apt to stick to his word.

Before she sat, she grabbed the spiral-bound journal she'd been jotting down notes in since she'd first joked about her plan to Lisa, and set it on the table. "I wrote down a few things. You know, about myself? If you skim through it, it'll help you pretend you've known me longer than two days."

Instead of waiting until they were done, he set down his slice, picked up the notebook and opened it to a random page. "You're not afraid of spiders, but you hate slugs? That's relevant?"

"It's something you would know about me."

"You graduated from the University of New Hampshire. Your feet aren't ticklish." He chuckled and shook his head. "You actually come with an owner's manual?"

"You could call it that. And if you could write

something up for me to look over, that would be great."

He shrugged and flipped through a few more pages of the journal. "I'm a guy. I like guy stuff. Steak. Football. Beer. Women."

"One woman, singular. At least for the next month, and then you can go back to your wild pluralizing ways." She took a sip of her beer. "You think that's all I need to know about you?"

"That's the important stuff. I could write it on a sticky note, if you want, along with my favorite sexual position. Which isn't missionary, by the way."

It was right there on the tip of her tongue—*then what* is *your favorite sexual position?*—but she bit it back. The last thing she needed to know about a man she was going to share a bedroom with for a month was how he liked his sex. "I hardly think that'll come up in conversation."

"It's more relevant than slugs."

"Since you'll be doing more gardening than having sex, not really."

"Wait a minute." He stabbed a finger at one of the notes in the journal. "You can't cook?"

"Not well. Microwave directions help."

"I'd never marry a woman who can't cook."

"I'd never marry the kind of man who'd never marry a woman who can't cook, so it's a good thing we're just pretending."

He closed the journal and set it aside to return to his pizza. But before he bit into it, he looked across the table at her. "You told her we met while I was home on leave, but did you tell her *how* we met?"

"It's on page one of the journal."

"Paraphrase it for me."

She really didn't want to. Somehow the idea of him reading her lies seemed less directly humiliating than her reciting them out loud. But he cocked an eyebrow at her as he chewed, clearly waiting for her to tell the story. "We met at Jasper's Bar & Grille."

"Kevin's bar?"

"You were home on leave and he hadn't owned the place long, so you stopped in to check it out. Lisa and I had been shopping in the city and stopped in for a Jasper burger." She felt her face flush and stared down at her plate. "It was love at first sight."

She heard him chuckle and wanted to glare at him, but she had a feeling that would only turn his chuckle into a full-fledged laugh. "So you wrote to me and I wrote back and then I left the army and here we are."

"In a nutshell." She let him swallow his mouthful of pizza, then asked, "You have plans for tomorrow?"

He shook his head. "Not really."

"Want to start work? Just a half day, over on the big lake. And then we could do some shopping. Stock up on food and get some stuff so it looks like you actually live here."

"Sounds good. What time?"

"I usually leave here at seven-thirty. I can probably meet you somewhere so you don't have to get up even earlier to drive over here."

"I'll be here. I never sleep past six, anyway."

"Never?" She was up at six on weekdays, but on weekends she liked to sleep in a bit.

"Never. And I like a big breakfast, so I hope you're a morning person."

He kept a straight face, but Emma could see the amusement in his eyes. "You can get two doughnuts at the coffee shop drive-through, then."

When the amusement spread to his mouth, Emma took a long swig of beer and looked anywhere but at the curve of his lips. He had a nice mouth. A *really* nice mouth that looked as if it knew its way around a kiss, and since the thought of kissing Sean gave her a need to squirm in her chair, she looked at the clock over the stove. And at the grocery list stuck to the fridge.

But, dammit, right next to the grocery list was the picture of her and Sean, and the grin didn't lose its potency in two dimensions. Thank goodness he had those good manners and wasn't the kind of guy to plant one on her in front of her grandmother.

The discussion turned to first-date small talk while they ate. They both liked cheesy action movies and preferred home-style diners to fancy restaurants.

Emma read romance and Sean read horror and bi-
ographies. They both preferred half-hour sitcoms
to hour-long dramas or reality shows, and they both
hated shopping for clothes.

It was a start, she told herself as she walked him
to the door. Hopefully, he'd look through the notes
she'd written for him, and she knew a lot about him
already, thanks to Lisa. It would have to be enough.

AS SOON AS EMMA OPENED the door at twenty after
seven, Sean could see she had spent as much time
tossing and turning the night before as he had. She
looked tired and her mouth was set in a way that made
her look a little cranky.

"I'm running a few minutes behind," she said.
"You want a coffee?"

"Sure." He followed her into the kitchen, and when
she waved in the direction of the coffeemaker before
sitting at the table, he assumed he was on his own.

Maybe it was a test, he thought as he opened the
cabinet over the coffeemaker in search of a mug.
Luckily, she organized her kitchen in a way that made
sense to him, so he didn't have to rummage through
drawers looking for a spoon. He could almost pass for
somebody who lived there.

Once he'd put the half-and-half back in the fridge,
he pulled up a chair across from her. She ignored
him, sipping her coffee while she flipped through an

enormous leather-bound organizer. Then she pulled out her phone and hit a button.

"Hey, it's Emma," she said after a pause. "The Duncans decided they don't like the black mulch, after all. Or Mrs. Duncan did, rather. She thought it would be artsy, but it—and I quote—'swallows up the accent lighting.'"

Another long pause while she rubbed her forehead. "I can use most of it to touch up for my other clients with the black, but I'll need three yards of the gold cedar for the Duncans. And, yes, she knows how much it will cost."

Sean tuned her out, then picked up his coffee mug and wandered out of the kitchen. It seemed a little rude to go roaming around her house, but her grandmother might suspect something was up if Sean had to ask her for directions to the bathroom.

In the living room he found another picture of himself and Emma. It took him a few minutes to figure out it was Stephanie who'd been replaced that time, and only because a balloon was barely visible along one edge. He'd been home on a short leave and took the time to drive over from Maine for Stephanie's birthday because her long, funny letters meant the world to him during deployment.

Besides a half bath and a boring formal dining room, he found her office on the ground floor. It wasn't a big room, but bookshelves full of romance novels lined the walls. In one corner, a fat easy chair begged to be relaxed in and a gas parlor stove stood across the room. A desk sat under the window, holding a fairly new computer and piles of paper threatening to slide off in every direction. He wondered if the filing cabinet next to the desk was full or if she just ignored it.

He could still hear her voice coming from the kitchen, so he set his coffee down on an end table and made his way up the stairs. All the doors stood open, so he peeked his head in each room as he walked down the hall.

The first room he looked in had to be her grandmother's, judging by the photos and decor. A lot of crocheted things, too. Not the room he was looking for, so he kept going.

He found what looked like a combination guest room and storage closet, so he guessed she didn't have a lot of overnight company. The bathroom was big and had been updated in the last decade or so. Hiding behind a set of louvered doors was a state-of-the-art washer-and-dryer set, which wasn't surprising considering what Emma did for a living.

Finally, at the end of the hall on the right, he found what had to be Emma's bedroom. His bedroom.

Judging by the long arch meant to disguise a weight-bearing beam, it had started life as two smaller bedrooms, but at some point the wall had been removed to make a master suite. Besides a bed that looked queen-size and the usual bedroom furnishings, there was a sitting area. End table with a lamp surrounded by more books. A small flat-screen TV mounted to the wall. And the couch she'd be sleeping on for the next month.

Even with the room's expansion, he figured there was only about ten feet between the bed and the couch. Despite the fact he'd learned over the years to sleep through any conditions, this arrangement was going to be a little awkward. Intimate.

There was a door to the left of the sitting area, and he poked his head through to find a three-quarter bath—toilet, sink and a shower. It'd do.

Aware of how many minutes he'd burned exploring, Sean went back down to the kitchen, grabbing his coffee along the way. He could see by the tension in her shoulders she didn't really care for him being so free with her home, but she'd probably come to the same conclusion he had.

"I just want to finish this coffee," she said. "Rough night."

He splashed the little bit of hot coffee left in the pot into his mug and leaned against the counter, watching her make a few more notes in her organizer.

"So…landscaping, huh?" He'd pushed a few mowers in his time. "Don't you think having *Emma* in the business name's a bad idea, though?"

She set down her pen and narrowed her eyes at him. "What? Girls can't be landscapers? You've heard we're allowed to vote now, right?"

"I just think if I want my lawn mowed or my weeds whacked, I'm more likely to call Bob or Fred."

"And that's fine. If you want somebody to mow your lawn or whack your weeds, call Bob or Fred. But if you want an artist to design the beautiful, virtually maintenance-free landscaping for your summer cottage or lake house, you call Emma."

Her defensive tone made him want to chuckle and poke at her some more, but he stifled the urge. "So you specialize in design, then?"

"Yes, but I do the labor, too." She smiled. "Except for the next month, of course. I'll have you to do the heavy lifting."

"Not afraid of a little hard work." He was looking forward to it, actually. His body was accustomed to a little more physical activity than it was currently getting. If he got too soft, his cousins would wipe the grass with him during the annual Fourth of July family football game.

Emma looked at her watch and then stood to rinse her coffee mug. "Time to hit the road."

It wasn't until she'd climbed behind the wheel of her truck and was watching him expectantly that Sean realized he couldn't remember a time he'd ever ridden shotgun to a female driver. Call him old-fashioned, but he liked to be the one in control.

But she'd be signing his paychecks for the next few weeks, so she was the boss. He slid in on the passenger side and closed the door, only to find himself white-knuckled by the time they reached the highway. She didn't drive any better than she claimed she cooked.

They spent the morning at a three-million-dollar summer home on the shores of Lake Winnipesaukee, where he had the joy of turning a pile of rocks dumped next to the house into stone walls outlining what would be the perennial beds, whatever the hell that meant.

It was good physical labor that worked up a sweat, but it didn't make him nearly as hot and bothered as watching Emma work. She didn't whine. Didn't worry about breaking a nail. She just worked alongside him, humming country tunes under her breath, and he found out the hard way how attractive a hardworking woman could be.

Ten feet, he thought. Ten feet between his bed and hers. A few steps.

Then she bent over in front of him to adjust a rock, and he dropped the one he was holding onto his toes, which made a dozen curses echo through his head, though he managed not to say them out loud.

Thirty days with Emma was shaping up to be one hell of a job.

CHAPTER FOUR

"IT'S NOT WALT DISNEY WORLD, Sean. You get in, you get what you need and you get out." If Emma had known shopping with him was going to be like this, she would have hidden a cattle prod in her purse.

"I'm shopping."

"No, you're meandering."

He stopped the cart—again—to look at something on the shelf and then resumed walking at a snail's pace. "I might see something I need."

"I have a list. See?" She held it up. "I know what we need."

"That's *your* list. Do you have salt-and-vinegar chips on it?"

"No. I don't like salt-and-vinegar flavor. Makes my tongue burn."

"See? If we sprint through the store, just getting what's on your list, I won't have any salt-and-vinegar chips."

"Maybe if you'd written down a few notes about yourself, I would have put them on my list."

He shook his head. "*I* don't come with an owner's manual. Sorry."

She pulled on the end of the cart, trying to make him move a little faster. "The store closes in six hours. You might need to pick up the pace."

He stopped so abruptly the cart jerked her arm. "You need to relax."

"No, I need to get the shopping done so I can move on to the next thing." She glared at him, willing him to shut his mouth and move his feet.

"You know, for a long time I've had what Uncle Sam saw fit to issue me and what my family could send in a care package," he said quietly, and her impatience fizzled and died like a match dropped in a puddle. "When I got back stateside, I bought some necessities, but not a lot because I was on the move. I'd like to browse a little bit."

"I'm sorry." She let go of the cart and blew out a breath. "Here you are doing me a huge favor and I'm being all…intense."

"Bitchy," he muttered, not quite under his breath.

"I prefer *intense*."

"Intensely bitchy."

Between the amusement lurking at the corners of his mouth and the fact he was right, Emma decided to let it go. Not only his less-than-flattering assessment of her mood, but the stress of her grandmother's impending arrival. What was the worst that could happen if this plan didn't work? Gram would be angry and see this little escapade as proof it was all too much for Emma. She'd sell the house and Emma would rent an apartment and life would go on.

And that thought made her want to cry, so she shook it off and tried to be patient as they very, very slowly made their way up and down the aisles.

"What the hell is this?" Sean picked up a box from the shelf and showed it to her. "It looks like a cheese grater for your feet."

"Women like having smooth heels."

"Do you have one of these?"

"Hell, no. It looks like a cheese grater."

They laughed as he put it back and moved on to the next thing that caught his fancy. Between the department store and the grocery store, they managed to almost fill the bed of his truck, but an hour later when everything was all put away, it didn't seem to make much of a difference.

"It still doesn't look like you've lived here for a year," Emma said.

Sean shrugged and sat backward on a kitchen chair, folding his arms across the back of it. "She won't think much of it. Single, former army guys aren't really known for dragging around domestic clutter."

"It just seems like you should have more…stuff. Pictures and sports trophies and stuff like that."

"It's all in boxes in the attic back home. If she says something, which she won't, I'll just tell her I haven't gotten around to getting them yet."

She grabbed a couple of sodas out of the fridge and set one in front of him. "Lisa told me a little bit about your family. She said you're all really close to Leo and Mary, even though you were all in Maine."

"My mom died when I was nine. It was an aneurysm, so we didn't even see it coming, and everything would have gone to shit, including my dad, if not for Aunt Mary and Rosie. Rosie's the housekeeper at the lodge, but really she's more than that. On top of raising her own daughter, she stepped up and helped my dad raise the five of us. He died nine years ago, but Rosie's still there, helping Josh run the lodge. But without Aunt Mary backing her up, I don't know how we would have turned out."

She loved the way his face softened when he talked about his family. And the way the muscles in his arm flexed as he lifted the soda to his mouth. And the way his throat worked as he swallowed. And...

And nothing, she told herself. She needed to think of him as an employee...kind of. Except for the whole sharing-a-bedroom thing.

"So tomorrow's the big day," he said, and she wondered if he was just trying to change the subject away from his family. "Are you ready?"

"As ready as I can be, I guess. I can't wait to see

Gram, of course. I've missed her so much, but a month is a long time."

"It'll fly by once we settle in and you two start catching up on lost time."

She twisted the ring on her finger, watching the stone catch the last rays of the late-day sun. "For something I've obsessed about right down to the last detail, I can't help but think I should have thought it through a little more."

"You can still change your mind."

She shook her head. "No, we're committed."

"Or we should be," he said, and they both laughed.

Then he drained the last of his soda and stood. "I'm going to hit the road. Gonna relax and get a good night's sleep before the big show starts."

"Okay. If you bring your stuff over by ten, you'll have time to put it away before I have to leave for the airport."

"I'll be here."

After he was gone, Emma collapsed on the couch in a bundle of raw nerves. Starting tomorrow, she was going to have to start convincing her grandmother she was in love with Sean Kowalski. And tomorrow Sean would be moving into her house. Into her bedroom. Into her life.

A good night's sleep was out of the question.

AFTER A FEW HOURS of hard deliberation, Sean decided to call his oldest brother, Mitch. He was a rolling stone, too, never staying in one place too long or spending too much time in one woman's bed. He, of all the siblings, was the least likely to think Sean had left his marbles overseas and needed an intervention.

"Hey, little brother," Mitch said after the third ring. "How's it going?"

"Good." Weird, but good. "You got a minute?"

"Five or six, even. I'm in Chicago, getting ready to drop an old office building, but we're waiting on paperwork right now." Mitch's childhood obsession with wrecking balls had led to his being one of the more respected controlled-demolition experts in the country. "What's up?"

"I've got myself into a little situation here, and since I don't have time to explain it over and over, I thought maybe you could spread the word."

"In other words, you don't want to tell Liz."

"Pretty much." *Fierce* was a good word to sum up the only girl of the five kids. "I don't want to be the one to tell Rosie, either."

"Does it involve bail money?"

Sean laughed. "No."

"A shotgun wedding?"

"Um…not exactly."

He told Mitch the story, starting with Emma knocking on his door and leading up to the present—

him at Kevin's apartment to grab his few belongings and make the dreaded phone call.

"Holy shit," Mitch said when he was done talking. "That definitely qualifies as a *situation*. Is she hot?"

"Very. But she can't cook worth a damn."

"That's what takeout's for." His brother was quiet for a few seconds, then chuckled. "So this hot chick's going to pay you to be her man for a month. Is that legal in New Hampshire now?"

"Screw you, Mitch. She's paying me to do landscaping. The fiancé thing is…whatever. She'll be sleeping on the couch in the bedroom. I'll be in the bed. It's strictly hands-off."

"My money's on a week."

His brothers would have the betting pool in place by the end of the day, no doubt. "Throw me in for making the whole month. Got no problem taking your money."

"She's hot and single. You're a guy. Sleeping in the same room? You're as good as half in the sack already."

Not a chance. "Look, I've got to get going. Get my toothbrush in her bathroom before we head to the airport and all that."

"I think I'll call Liz first," Mitch told him. "I might even record the conversation."

"The important thing is that you get the story

straight. If any of you come over for the Fourth of July, you need to have your shit together."

"Oh, I'll be there. You can bet your ass on that. And speaking of the Fourth, what do Uncle Leo and Aunt Mary think of all this?"

Sean winced. "I don't think they know yet. The rest of them do, though, so it's only a matter of time before Aunt Mary comes after me. I've been putting it off."

"That only makes it worse."

"I know. But if it's already a done deal by the time she finds out, maybe she'll go along."

That made Mitch laugh out loud again. "Sure, buddy. You keep telling yourself that."

"I'm hanging up now."

"Good. I've got phone calls to make."

Sean shoved his phone in his pocket and made one last trip around the apartment. Since everything he owned fit in his duffel and he'd only been there a few days, it didn't take long to make sure he had everything.

Five minutes later, he was on the road, and it wasn't long before he was turning in to the driveway. He glanced at the mailbox and shook his head as he parked in front of his temporary home. The one with daisies on the mailbox and Emma under the same roof.

It was just a month, he reminded himself. One

month and then he'd be on his way, with his brothers' money and a few paychecks in his pocket and no strings trying to hold him back.

EMMA KNEW A FEW THINGS about Sean Kowalski. She knew he was tall and outrageously handsome and liked salt-and-vinegar potato chips. She knew he had a body designed to trigger female double takes everywhere he went. She knew he'd served his country, wasn't afraid of a day's work, loved his family, played with his cousins' children and was, no doubt, though she hadn't seen it yet, kind to animals.

What she hadn't known was how much impact seeing him stretch out on her bed and tuck his hands under his head would have on her. And she certainly hadn't anticipated the heat that curled through her body and settled in a place she'd been neglecting for a while.

"A little soft," he said, squirming against the mattress in a way that made her hips want to wiggle along for the ride. "I like it harder."

Emma coughed to cover the little squeaking sound she made, as if announcing her hormones' state of libidinous distress. "I like to nestle."

"It's a girlie bed."

Not with him sprawled across it, it wasn't. "I'm a girl."

"I noticed." When he turned his head and winked

at her, she swallowed hard and glanced at her watch in what she hoped was an obvious gesture. She just wanted him off her bed.

Which wasn't going to help, of course, because he was going to be sleeping in that bed for the next month. And she'd be about ten feet away, tossing and turning on the couch. Great plan. Inspired, really.

"Time to go?" he asked.

"Yeah." They'd done everything they could. What little he owned had been moved in. The biography of Ulysses S. Grant he was reading was tossed on the coffee table in the living room. A battered and over-size coffee mug emblazoned with the army logo was upside down next to her favorite mug in the dish rack. She'd found it at the Salvation Army store, along with a few other things that might help give the illusion he'd been living there for a year. It was showtime.

"Okay. Gimme a few minutes and I'll meet you outside."

"Wait. You're going, too?"

He snorted and swung his feet to the floor. "Of course I'm going with you to pick up your grand-mother at the airport. What kind of jerk did you think you were marrying?"

"This is insane."

"Pretty sure I already told you that." His eyes grew serious. "This is your last chance, you know. I can be out of here in a half hour. You can still tell her we broke up and you must not have loved me as much as you thought because you're not all broken up about it. She'll be so thankful you came to your senses before marrying me, she won't even ask too many questions."

She knew he was right. It was insane. And this *was* her last chance to back out. Once she introduced him to Gram at the airport, they were all in. For a month.

Then she shook her head. "No. We can do this and then Gram's mind will be at ease and she can finally enjoy her retirement so I can move on with my life."

Sean walked over to her, so close she wondered if he was going to try to shake some sense into her. "Then there's just one more thing to do."

"Oh, crap. What did I forget?" Considering how much time she'd spent going over everything in her mind instead of sleeping, she couldn't imagine what it would be.

When he rested his hand at her waist for a few seconds before sliding it around to the small of her back, she felt her muscles tense and her cheeks burn.

"You can't be doing that," he said in the same low, husky kind of voice a man would use to tell a woman he wanted to take off her clothes.

Her mind was frozen, all of her attention on that warm pressure against her T-shirt, and it took a few seconds to form a coherent sentence. "Doing what?"

"You're as jumpy as a virgin at a frat party." He

ran his fingers up over her spine until he reached the small bump of her bra strap, and then back down to her waist. "We've been dating a year and a half, and living together for a year of it, but you still blush and tense up when I touch you?"

He had a point, but there was no way to fix that before Gram got off her plane. "Maybe you're just that good."

It was the wrong thing to say if she was trying to back him off and settle her overheating nerves. The grin he gave her would have been potent enough to get her out of her clothes if the situation was different.

"That's a story I can get behind," he said.

"Thought we were trying to keep the lies to a minimum."

The grin only widened. "Who says it's a lie?"

She rolled her eyes and tried to step back—really needing to put a little space between them—but he held her close. "We're going to be late."

"No, we're not. But don't you think we should at least have a practice kiss first?"

Almost against her will, her gaze focused on his mouth. Yes. Yes, they should. "If Gram asked, I was going to tell her you have a thing about public displays of affection."

"This isn't public. This is your—*our*—home."

"Public as in with an audience." She needed to look

away from his mouth, especially since it was getting closer, but she couldn't.

When his face got close enough so she registered his intent, she raised her gaze to his, but it was too late. Before she could react, his lips met hers, his hand still on her back to hold her close, and she closed her eyes.

Practice. That's all it was. And if her body started tingling and her fingers itched to run through his hair and her body wanted to melt against his...well, that just boded well for a month of pretending they were into each other, didn't it?

The jolt of heat that ran like an electrical shock through her body could be an unwelcome complication, but she'd worry about that later. Like maybe when she wasn't too busy thinking about pushing him back onto that soft, girlie bed he'd complained about and proving women liked it a little harder, too.

It took every ounce of self-control she could muster not to whimper in protest when his lips left hers. She wanted to take his head in her hands and drag his mouth in for another kiss. Maybe slip her hands under the back of his T-shirt so she could glide them over the warm flesh of his back and feel his muscles twitch under her fingertips.

"Not bad for a practice kiss," he said in a casual voice that pissed her off. No way could he have felt nothing while her senses sizzled like a drop of water on a hot, oiled skillet.

"And the Oscar goes to," she muttered when he winked and walked out of the room.

She was about to swear and take a kick at the coffee-table leg when she spotted him in the full-length mirror on the closet door standing ajar. He'd stopped just outside in the hall, and she watched his reverse image as he pulled at the fly of his jeans, no doubt adjusting for the evidence he wasn't as unaffected as he wanted her to think he was. Then he rolled his shoulders and kept walking.

Despite the fact both of them being affected would be an even greater complication, Emma was smiling when she met up with him again in the front hall.

"We can take my truck," he told her in a terse voice that made her have to smother a bigger and much more smug smile.

"No, we can't. I have the extended cab and it might rain. We can't throw Gram's luggage in the bed to get wet."

"I'm driving."

She paused halfway out the front door. "Excuse me?"

"You drive like a girl." He held out his hand, presumably for her keys.

"You're an ass."

"We can stand here and argue about it. I'm sure your grandmother will understand."

"A sexist ass, no less."

He grinned and snatched her keys out of her hand before she could react. "Next time, you might want to actually meet the man you're going to marry before you tell your family about him. Get in the truck. *Honey.*"

CHAPTER FIVE

Catherine Shaw, who preferred to be called Cat, stepped off the plane in Manchester and quickly retrieved her luggage. It was good to be back, if only temporarily. There was a time she might have thought it was good to be *home,* but she considered herself a Floridian now.

It had cost her a little extra to fly into New Hampshire, rather than to Logan Airport, but Emma was picking her up and she didn't want her granddaughter bothered with Boston, even if her fiancé was driving.

They'd arranged to meet by the small food court and she spotted Emma immediately, standing next to a tall, good-looking man who was scanning the airport, watching people. A year and a half of civilian life hadn't taken much of the edge off the soldier.

Emma hadn't seen her yet, and she took a few minutes to give her granddaughter a good looking over.

She was thinner, which wasn't surprising since the girl couldn't cook worth a darn. Her work was so physical she was burning through her steady diet of takeout and microwave meals. She'd have to put some meat on the girl's bones while she was there.

Emma looked so much like her mother at first glance, but it was mostly the hair. In the lines of her nose and mouth and the dark brown of her eyes, Cat could see glimpses of the son and husband she'd lost. As always, she felt the pang of grief like a constant and unwelcome companion, but it was overshadowed by her gratitude for the blessing that was her grand-daughter.

Then Sean's eyes met hers and he obviously recognized her—no doubt from the photos she sometimes remembered to email from Florida. He touched Emma's arm and Cat didn't miss the way she jumped, her cheeks flushing pink.

Then Emma was running across the lobby and Cat opened her arms for a fierce hug. "Gram!"

She squeezed Emma, rocking a little, until she caught sight of her future grandson-in-law through the corner of her eye. He looked anxious, shifting his weight from foot to foot while he watched their reunion.

Cat let go of Emma and turned to him, extending her hand. "You must be Sean."

He had a decent grip. She didn't trust men with weak handshakes. "It's nice to meet you, Mrs. Shaw."

Lovely manners, too. "Please, call me Cat. Being called Mrs. Shaw makes me feel old."

He grinned, a naughty grin that probably weakened her granddaughter's knees. "Anybody can see you're anything but that...Cat."

"I think you and I will get along just fine."

"How was your flight?" Emma asked as Sean relieved Cat of her luggage and began herding them toward the exit.

"Uneventful, which is never a bad thing."

When they made their way through the parking lot, the first light drops of rain were falling, so Sean put her luggage in the backseat of the truck and Emma climbed in after it. Cat was impressed when he took her elbow to help her into the passenger seat before closing her door and going around to his own side. He was a nice boy.

"So you have family around here, Sean?" she asked when they were on the highway, heading north.

"Yes, ma'am, I do. My aunt and uncle live about fifteen minutes from...home, and I've got four cousins and their families nearby."

"Oh, good. I can't wait to meet them all."

He turned his head and gave her a quick glance before looking back to the road, and she wondered why it would come as a surprise his fiancée's grandmother would want to meet his family.

"They're always pretty busy," he said, "what with all the kids and everything, but I'll see what I can do. Maybe a barbecue or something soon."

It was a little over an hour's ride, giving Cat plenty of time to not only listen to Emma's constant chatter about the house and work, but to feel the anxiety in the truck. Her granddaughter's voice was a little too chipper. Sean's fingers kept tightening on the steering wheel, then he'd flex them and relax, but they'd tighten again. She'd almost think they'd had a fight before her arrival, but there wasn't any anger simmering between them. Just nervousness.

Cat stopped worrying about them when Sean turned onto the driveway and drove up to the beautiful old house she'd called home since she was a young bride of nineteen. She and John had borrowed down-payment money from his father to buy it when she got pregnant, expecting to fill it with a large and noisy, but loving, family.

They had no way of knowing at the time Johnny would be their only child or that the two of them would end up spending several years rattling around the place alone until tragedy gave them Emma. The girl had not only brought joy back into their lives, but had breathed life back into the house.

It was the joy Cat chose to remember as Sean hopped out of the truck and jogged around to open her door. She smiled when he offered his hand to help her down. And she watched as he did the same for Emma.

Her granddaughter hesitated for only a second, but

Cat didn't miss it. Then she put her hand in Sean's, clearly flustered, and hopped out of the truck. Her feet had barely hit the ground before she pulled her hand away and turned to grab the luggage.

It was going to be an interesting month. Cat wasn't sure exactly what was going on, but she knew one thing for sure—whatever they were up to, Emma and Sean hadn't been sharing a bed and a bathroom for the past year.

SEAN DIDN'T THINK it was going too badly…until Emma set a steaming glass dish on a trivet in the middle of the table. It was a casserole. One with tufts of little green trees sticking up out of some kind of sauce.

Broccoli. He hated broccoli. Loathed it.

"Chicken Divan," Emma said, and only an idiot could have missed the note of pride in her voice as she put her hands on her hips, oven mitts and all. "It's my best dish—okay, my only real baked dish—so I made it as a welcome-home meal."

Cat smiled and Sean forced his lips to move into what he hoped was a similar expression. A woman who was sleeping with and living with and planning a future with a man would know he didn't like broccoli. And it was his own damn fault for laughing off her suggestion he write an owner's manual of his own.

She served him first, maybe because he was the

fake man of the house, plopping in front of him a steaming pile of perfectly good chicken and cheese ruined by the green vegetable. He smiled at her—or maybe grimaced—and took a sip of iced tea.

He could do this. He'd survived boot camp. He'd survived combat and the harsh weather of Afghanistan. He could survive broccoli. Probably.

"It looks wonderful," Cat practically cooed, and Sean's stomach rumbled. Whether in hunger or protest he couldn't say.

Emma, of course, flushed with pleasure at the compliment. With a few wisps of hair framing her pink cheeks and her eyes sparkling, she was beautiful. Not beautiful enough to merit eating broccoli, but beautiful enough so he watched her for a minute as she served herself and sat down across from him.

Then he made himself look back to his own plate. He'd given his word he'd make this charade work, and Cat wanting to know why Emma fed her fiancé his least favorite food wasn't a good way to start.

He put it off as long as he could—picking out mouthfuls of cheesy chicken that weren't too bad—but he couldn't leave behind a pile of uneaten broccoli.

Suck it up, soldier. The broccoli's tree trunk or stalk or whatever people called it squeaked between his teeth, a little undercooked. Or maybe it was supposed to feel like that. Either way, he didn't like it, so he chewed and swallowed as fast as he could. Then he dug up another forkful and did it again.

He'd gotten through basic training by putting one reluctant foot in front of the other, and that's how he got through Emma's Chicken Divan. One squeaky, nauseating bite after another.

"Sean, you said your aunt and uncle live near here," Cat said in between a bite, "but Emma told me you have two older brothers and a younger brother and sister in Maine?"

Silently thankful for any excuse to put down his fork, Sean gulped down some iced tea and wiped his mouth. "That's where we're from, but only Josh still lives in Whitford. He runs the lodge for the family."

"A lodge for snowmobilers, I think Emma said?"

"Any winter activities, actually, but primarily sledders." He was trying to get used to it, but it was bizarre how much these two women knew about him. "My great-grandfather started the Northern Star Lodge as an exclusive hunting club, but by the time my dad took it over, nobody was doing that much anymore and the clientele changed. It's right on the sled trails, so it does okay."

"What do the rest of them do?"

He might have resented the Twenty Questions game if not for the fact it gave him an excuse to ignore the green tree trunks left on his plate. "The oldest, Mitch, runs a controlled-demolition company. It's based out of New York, but he hotel hops mostly. Then there's Ryan, who builds custom homes in the Boston area. I'm in the middle and then there's Liz, who lives out in New Mexico, of all places. Josh is the youngest."

"Do you see them often?"

It was pretty benign, as questions went, but Sean took another sip of his drink to buy himself a few seconds. He'd seen them all but Liz a few days ago, when they'd gathered at Ryan's place in Mass for a welcome-home party. With the lodge a five-hour drive from Boston's Logan Airport on top of the flights and busy schedules, it had made more sense to gather at Ryan's. And since he wasn't quite ready to settle down and commit to anything, Sean had decided to spend some time in New Hampshire before heading home.

But, as far as Cat knew, he'd been out of the army for two years, not less than two weeks.

"I see them often enough to not miss them too badly," he said, "but not so much we get on each other's nerves."

Emma cleared her throat. "Do you want some more Chicken Divan, Sean? There's plenty."

Hell, no. "No, thanks. It was good, though."

Her smile brightened, causing him a pang of guilt for the lie. Or maybe the pang was the broccoli. "I have an apple pie for dessert. Store-bought, of course, since I wanted it to actually taste good."

Cat laughed. "I did everything I could to teach her how to cook. Lost cause, I guess. She'd rather play in the dirt. Do you cook, Sean?"

"I grill. We grill a lot." He didn't miss the way Emma's eyes widened.

"At least you won't starve. I've taken to grilling a lot in Florida because it's better than heating up the house. More often than not, we end up gathering at one person's grill and throwing something on it, like a potluck. Maybe tomorrow I can make you my famous honey-ginger grilled salmon."

Emma gave him a quick shake of her head, panic in her eyes. Shit. She didn't own a barbecue grill. "It's… uh. We had to scrap it."

Cat's eyebrows rose. "Scrap it?"

"I blew it up," Emma said in a rush. "And we haven't bought a new one yet. I mean, not a big explosion, of course, but I did something wrong with the propane tank and…I broke it."

"And you wonder why I worry about you."

Sean smothered a chuckle with his napkin. Way to convince somebody you can be left unattended, he thought.

"Of course, I worry a lot less now that you have Sean."

The look she gave him—all sweet and trusting and gooey with gratitude—made him feel like a heel. No.

Wrong body part. He felt like an ass and he had to grit his teeth to keep from spilling everything.

Then he looked at Emma and the urge receded. She was watching her grandmother and it seemed as if some of the tension eased out of her body. Her expression was full of love and relief, reminding him of why they were in this position—to ease Cat's mind so she could enjoy her retirement. At least it seemed to be working.

The store-bought apple pie went a long way toward making him more comfortable, but at the first opportunity, he excused himself. "I need to make a few phone calls, so I'll leave you ladies to catch up."

It was a lie, but, hell, what was one more? On his way out, he ducked into Emma's office and grabbed one of the umpteen pads of sticky notes she had scattered on the desk and rummaged around until he found a Sharpie marker.

Once upstairs, he went straight into their shared bathroom. He peeled the top sticky note off the pad and stuck it to the mirror, and then pulled the cap off the Sharpie.

EMMA STARED AT THE NOTE stuck to the mirror, her fingers curled over the edge of the sink. Her face was washed. Hair and teeth brushed. It was time to go out and curl up on the couch and try to sleep.

I hate broccoli. And peas.

Great. So he wasn't a fan of green vegetables. Where was the information she really needed to know—namely, whether or not he wore pajamas? It hadn't occurred to her to worry about it before, but, holy hell, she was worrying about it now.

She was wearing pajamas, of course. Or what passed for them in her world. A well-worn and oversize University of New Hampshire T-shirt over soft flannel boxers. She'd considered buying something prettier and a little more feminine, but she didn't want to send mixed messages to the man who'd be sleeping in her bed.

All she could do was hope Sean had put the same consideration into his sleeping attire. He probably didn't sleep in the buff, despite the deliciously vivid visual of that her imagination had no trouble conjuring. He'd been in the army for twelve years—a good chunk of that deployed overseas—and surely they weren't in the habit of sleeping nude.

Flannel would be nice. And not battered shorts, like hers. Long pants and a long-sleeved shirt buttoned up to his throat would be nice, like something Ward Cleaver would have worn to bed in his 1950s sitcom.

When she finally dropped the curtain on the mental drama and left the bathroom, she was a little disappointed he was already asleep. Clearly he wasn't struggling to hold back the reins of runaway sexual attraction the way she was. He'd dimmed the over-head light, but she could hear him softly snoring and make out the sheet pulled halfway up his stomach. His *naked* stomach, which led her gaze to his naked chest and then to his naked shoulders, the muscles nicely highlighted by the way he slept with his arms raised over his head.

Was the rest of him naked, too?

"When you stare at somebody who's sleeping," he mumbled without moving or opening his eyes, "they usually wake up."

Busted. Her face burned as though his words were a blowtorch and she rushed across the room to slap the light switch off. In the faint glow of moonlight penetrating the curtains, she went to the couch and tried to get comfortable. It wasn't quite long enough, but she curled up under the light cotton blanket and closed her eyes.

Getting caught staring on the first night was em-barrassing, but at least he wasn't a mind reader. There was no way he could guess she'd been wondering what he wore from the waist down.

"Good night, Emma."

The quiet, husky voice in the darkness made her shiver. "Night, Sean."

A little less than seven hours of tossing and turn-ing later, Emma's question was answered—much to the detriment of her recently revived libido.

At some point during the night, Sean had thrown off the sheet. Probably right around the time he rolled onto his stomach. With his hands shoved under his pillow and one knee drawn up a little, she had a clear view of his ass—showcased perfectly in dark blue boxer briefs.

Even though she was careful not to look directly at the ass in question, Sean stirred. He shoved his face a little deeper into the pillow and stretched one of those not-quite-awake stretches that made his entire body— and hers—vibrate and the muscles of his back ripple.

Since there was no way she couldn't stare directly at that view, but she didn't want to get caught looking again, Emma scrambled off the couch. Grabbing the stack of clothes she'd put out the night before, she went into the bathroom and closed the door against temptation.

When she emerged a while later, refreshed and dressed and ready to face the day, Sean was sitting on the edge of the bed, scrubbing his face with his hands. He'd thrown on a pair of jeans, but she noticed immediately he hadn't done up the fly.

"Good morning," she said, injecting a little more cheer into her voice than she felt.

"Morning."

So, not a morning person, then. Since, unlike her, he hadn't had any problem falling asleep, she didn't think he was still tired. "If I know Gram, she's already working on breakfast, and I didn't get my lack of cooking ability from her."

"I'll be down in a few minutes."

He didn't seem inclined to make conversation, so she left the room and followed the heavenly scent of coffee and bacon to the kitchen. "Morning, Gram."

Cat paused in stirring a big batch of scrambled eggs in her favorite cast-iron skillet, which had been sadly neglected in her absence. "Morning, sweetie. Is Sean up?"

"He'll be down in a few minutes." Figuring it was something a domesticated woman would do, she fixed him a cup of coffee along with her own. "You didn't have to go to all this trouble for us."

"Don't think I didn't see the boxes of doughnuts and instant oatmeal in the pantry. And cooking for one isn't any fun."

Emma didn't think cooking for any number of people was fun, but she wasn't going to turn down a homemade breakfast. "I was able to rearrange a few things to get a couple of days off, but Wednesday I have a job I have to do. And Sean, of course."

"I knew you'd be busy this time of year, so I wasn't expecting you to keep me company every minute. I'll probably go into town and see some old friends."

Emma smiled, but a slight tremor racked her insides. The nearest town, where they'd always gone and Emma had attended school, wasn't a small town, but it wasn't big, either. Knowing Gram was probably in contact with old friends, she'd been pretending she was engaged there, too. Her own friends knew the truth, but anybody in Gram's circle was convinced Emma was engaged, even though they'd never met the lucky fellow.

It had been a careful balancing act. Sean tended to travel to the town where his family lived so he could visit them at the same, she told people. And sometimes they'd just missed him. Or he'd gone back to Maine for a visit but work had kept her from accompanying him.

Hopefully, all her groundwork wouldn't crumble under Gram's scrutiny.

"Something smells good," Sean said as he walked into the kitchen. And like any good fiancé, he slid an arm around Emma's waist and leaned in for a quick morning kiss, smelling of shampoo and shaving cream and toothpaste.

It was over almost before she registered his intention, but she managed not to jump back like…how had he put it? A virgin at a frat party?

"You're in for a treat," she said in a surprisingly normal voice. "Gram's scrambled eggs are to die for."

"So what's the plan for today?" Gram asked while dishing up the eggs and bacon.

"Whatever you want to do." Emma handed Sean his coffee cup.

"We should go buy a new grill," Gram said. "And I'll see if there's any decent salmon to be had."

Emma nodded. At least grill shopping meant going to the city rather than into town. One step at a time. One day at a time. That's how they'd get through the month.

And, God help her, one kiss at a time.

CHAPTER SIX

SEAN GOT THE SUMMONS he'd been dreading in the form of a voice mail left on his cell phone while they were struggling to get the new grill out of the back of the truck.

"Sean, it's Aunt Mary." As if any other woman in his life ever used that tone of voice with him. "I don't know what kind of game you're playing, but I want to see you. Today. Alone. Don't make me come looking for you, young man."

Yeah, he was in trouble. And it was his own damn fault because he should have known his cousins couldn't keep their mouths shut. They never had. Especially Mikey. He was always the rat growing up.

He gave Emma and Cat a song and dance about promising his uncle he'd give him a hand changing the oil in his riding lawn mower and made the drive over like a criminal being marched into the courtroom to face the judge. This judge, though, would whack the shit out of him with kitchen utensils if she didn't like his answers.

He was already exhausted and a confrontation with

his aunt was the last thing he wanted. The clock on Emma's bedside table had read one in the morning when a sound had penetrated his sleep. A sleepy, sexy and definitely feminine moan wasn't a bad thing to wake up to, except when the female was sleeping on a couch across the room. Alone.

She'd quieted after that single sound, but his body sure as hell hadn't. As a result, he'd drifted in and out of a tortured sleep and woken up on the wrong side of the bed.

Aunt Mary was in the kitchen—as usual—when he arrived, and right after pointing him in that direction, Uncle Leo disappeared into the den and closed the door. Chicken.

She started in on him the second he crossed the threshold from the living room. "I was wrong about you all these years. I always thought you were a smart boy, but you don't have the brains God gave a jackass."

"Aunt Mary, I—"

"Don't you Aunt Mary me, Sean Michael Kowalski. I should go get my wooden spoon and thunk some sense into that thick head of yours."

Sean sighed and tried to school his expression into something closer to contrition than belligerence. Not that she wouldn't see through it, but he made the effort regardless. "I'm just helping her out for a few weeks so that—"

"Helping her lie to her grandmother, you mean."

"I know it sounds bad, but—"

"Because you were raised better than that."

He'd known this wouldn't be easy, but he'd been hoping to at least finish a sentence or two. "Can I talk? Please?"

"When you have something sensible to say."

He gave himself a few seconds so none of his frustration would show in his voice. Hopefully. "Remember after high school when I dumped my bike and I told you I had a bruised elbow and a little road rash?"

She pinned him with a look that made him want to squirm. "Yes."

"Well, I dumped my bike because a truck hit me. I also had a bad concussion. And four broken bones."

Her expression froze for a few seconds, but then he saw the comprehension in her eyes, followed by an unholy gleam of pissed off. "You little bastard. Why would you do that?"

"I didn't want you to worry. You wouldn't have believed I was okay without leaving your family to come take care of me, and Lisa was so pregnant she was going to pop any day."

"You're my family, too, and don't you forget it."

"You would have been stressed out for no reason, because there was nothing you could do. I didn't want that for you, so I talked the others into lying for me.

It's the same situation Emma found herself in, more or less."

She glared at him, her arms folded across her chest. "Protecting weak old women from the truth, you mean?"

Oh, hell, no. "You are not weak or old, Aunt Mary, and neither is Emma's grandmother, Cat. I know you're upset about this, but I bet you've hedged around the truth a time or two to keep somebody you love from being unhappy."

When she didn't respond right away, he thought maybe she was softening. "I don't like this at all, Sean."

"I gave Emma my word." That was the bottom line.

Her mouth tightened. "And?"

"And…" He took a deep breath. "If you can't back me up on this, I'll have to keep Cat away from here. And she knows you're nearby, which means I'll have to say we had a falling-out."

"Don't threaten me, young man," she said, but her tone was a little softer. She, of all people, knew Kowalski men were stubborn and meant what they said.

But the last thing he'd ever want to do was have conflict with this woman. He loved her too much. "I've seen them together and Emma was right. Cat's a lot happier now, thinking we're engaged, and that's all Emma's trying to do. Please, Aunt Mary. I gave her my word."

She sighed—the deep, meaningful sigh only a mother could really master. "What is it you want me to do?"

"Cat wants to meet you. Maybe have dinner. I was thinking...*hoping* you and Uncle Leo could have a barbecue."

She was still considering the idea when Joe walked into the kitchen and stopped. Sean watched him take in his mother's body language and turn to retreat.

"Joseph, did you know about this craziness Sean's involved with?"

The guy gave him a look promising retribution in the near future and turned back to his mom. "Yes, I did."

"And you didn't tell me?"

"It wasn't my place, Ma. And they're not hurting anybody."

"It's wrong."

Joe smiled what was probably supposed to be a placating smile, but his obvious amusement at Sean's predicament was ruining it. "It's wrong that Emma wanted her grandmother to enjoy her new life in Florida?"

"Don't get wise with me, Joseph. That's not the issue here."

"It *is* the issue," Sean said, drawing his aunt's gaze

back to him. "Her grandmother's peace of mind is exactly the issue."

She stared at his face intently, for what seemed like forever, and he hoped like hell none of his own doubts showed there. "Saturday. Anytime after three and we'll fire the grills at five."

"Thank you, Aunt Mary."

"I'll keep my mouth shut and play along, but if she asks me outright if you two are up to no good, I won't lie."

He couldn't see why Cat would ask a question like that. "I'll make it up to you. I promise."

"Go before I change my mind."

He went, Joe on his heels, and didn't stop until he was safely in the driveway. "Your mother can be a scary lady sometimes."

Joe leaned against the fender. "How the hell did you talk her into it?"

"I told her I'd have to stay away—claim we had a falling-out—if she didn't."

"Ouch. But I hope you realize Ma was the easy part."

That was the easy part? He didn't think so. "What do you mean?"

"What are you going to do about the five kids who know that not only were you not engaged last week, but that they haven't been writing letters for Lisa to send to you at Emma's house for the last year and a half?"

"Shit." Every time he thought he had his eye on the ball and could smack it out of the park, it curved on him again. "I didn't even think of them. Dammit."

Joe laughed and slapped him on the back. "We'll take care of the kids. Don't worry."

"Thanks, man." He started to climb into his truck, then stopped. "Look, I know this is funny to you guys, but don't forget it's not a joke to Emma and Cat. If we blow this, her grandmother's going to be really upset."

Joe grinned and slapped the side of the truck. "Come on, cousin. You know we've always got your back."

"Yeah, that's where you usually stick the kick-me sign." His cousin was still laughing when he backed out of the driveway.

"I NEVER WOULD HAVE GUESSED something with orange juice *and* soy sauce in it could taste so good," Emma said, leaning back in the lawn chair with a sigh. They'd demolished Gram's honey-ginger grilled salmon in record time and she had no desire to move.

"I'll write the recipe down for you."

"I'll just screw it up, anyway."

Gram laughed. "All you do is mix the ingredients together, pour it in a bag with the salmon and half an hour later give it to Sean to throw on the grill. He cooked the salmon to perfection tonight."

Of course he did. As he'd told her earlier, she had nothing to worry about because the Y chromosome came with an innate ability to master the barbecue grill.

"The salad was good, too," Sean said.

"Thanks," Emma muttered. "Even I can't screw up shredding lettuce."

The man looked incredibly relaxed for somebody who'd probably been raked over the coals by his aunt and was now relaxing with two women he barely knew. She, on the other hand, felt as if she was detoxing. Jumpy. Twitching. A trickle of sweat at the small of her back.

Sean stood and started gathering dishes, but held out a hand when Emma started to get up. "You ladies sit and visit. I'll take care of the cleanup."

Once he was inside, Gram smiled and raised her eyebrows. "He does dishes, too? No wonder you snapped him up."

It was tempting to point out a few of his less attractive traits, like the fact he was a sexist baboon who wouldn't let her drive. But he was doing a good job of convincing Gram he was Emma's Prince Charming, which was the whole point, so she bit back her annoyance with the Saint Sean routine. "He's a keeper."

"Something's bothering you. Tell me what it is and you'll feel better."

Emma really doubted that. She made a conscious effort to relax her face. "It's nothing, really. Work stuff."

"Really, Emma, I won't be bothered if you and Sean have to work tomorrow. I understand you're very busy. And I'm proud of the fact your business is doing so well."

"It *is* going well." Emma gave her grandmother a genuine smile. "The summer people love to show off my work, and then all the other summer people just have to have me, too."

"That's wonderful, dear." Gram took a sip of her iced tea, then set the glass on the patio table. "But I want to hear more about Sean."

"Um...like what?" She knew he didn't like broccoli or peas.

"Oh, I don't know. How does he like working for you? Since you're the owner, will he be a stay-at-home dad once you have children?"

Emma was pretty sure Sean's ideal wife would be barefoot and pregnant in the kitchen with a baby on one hip and a laundry basket on the other, but she didn't say so. "His working for me isn't really long-term. He's just not sure what he wants to do yet. And we'll figure out the baby thing when the time comes."

In other words, she had no clue, but she hoped

Gram wouldn't figure that out. Maybe if she was vague enough, whatever Sean said about the subject wouldn't contradict her. She sipped her iced tea and concentrated on not looking stressed-out.

Gram reached over and touched her hand. "Are you happy?"

And there it was—the million-dollar question. Everything she and Sean were going through was meant to convince Gram the answer to that question was a resounding *yes*.

"I'm happy, Gram. I really am. My company's thriving and I...have Sean. And, even though I miss you, I love knowing you're having a great time in Florida with your friends."

"You should see us down there. That warm sunshine does wonders for the body, and we feel ten years younger, at least. You should see Martha line dance! That woman can shake and shimmy like a twenty-year-old."

Emma laughed, trying very hard not to visualize Martha—who could only be described as stout—shaking and shimmying. "I loved the pictures of you swimming with the dolphins."

"That was amazing! You wouldn't believe how friendly they are." And, as Gram started telling her the story, Emma felt the tension easing out of her body.

At some point Sean joined them, bringing a fresh

pitcher of iced tea with him, and they sat on the deck listening to Gram talk about frolicking in sunny Florida until long after the sun had set. And then, once Gram had gone up to bed, Emma and Sean faced each other across the patio table.

"I like Cat," he said, once her grandmother was safely out of earshot. "This isn't quite as hard as I thought it would be."

"It's going better than I thought," she agreed. "I'm still having a hard time believing the ploy might actually work."

"She sure does love Florida."

"I could tell that even over the phone. When she started talking about moving back, I knew I had to do something."

He smiled, his eyes warm. "Even if it was crazy."

"I think the words you used were *batshit crazy*." She watched his brow furrow for a moment, as though he was trying to remember saying it. "But Lisa also told me the tall-and-hot part of it, so I didn't take it personally."

"Maybe we shouldn't talk about the hot part right before we go to bed."

Good point. "You think you can stick this out for a month?"

"Told you I would."

"And you've got Gram wrapped around your little finger already. I'll have to start complaining about

you once in a while, or when it comes time to tell her
I broke up with you, she'll never believe it."

"True. Maybe you should tell her *I* broke up with
you."

Emma tossed a balled-up napkin at him. "Funny."

"You can worry about that later. For now, your
grandmother believes you're madly in love with me
and that's all that matters."

"So you're telling me Emma's grandmother actually fell for it?" Kevin dredged a fry through a puddle
of ketchup and popped it in his mouth. "I don't believe it."

Sean shrugged. "I'm tellin' you. She doesn't give
us funny looks or anything."

He'd taken off midmorning to give Emma and her
grandmother some time alone, since he and Emma
would be working the next day, and because, after
three days of pretending, he needed a break. He'd
done some errands and then showed up at Jasper's Bar
& Grille to see what was going on. He'd gotten there
just as Kevin's wife and daughter had arrived to visit
him during his lunch break, and they'd invited Sean
to join them.

Beth slid Lily's high chair closer to her seat and
farther from Kevin's. The tot was trying to trade her
cut-up banana for her daddy's fries, not that Sean

blamed her. "I have to admit, I didn't think it would work."

"Neither did we," Sean told her and they all laughed.

"Isn't it weird?" Beth gave Kevin one of those wifely looks when he slipped Lily a fry, then looked back at Kevin. "I can't imagine living with somebody I don't know."

"Yeah, it's weird. Maybe being in the army helped. I'm used to living with whoever came along. And it's not so bad. Cat's a wicked-good cook."

"Takes so little to make a Kowalski man happy," Beth mused.

Her husband smiled and leaned across the high chair to kiss her cheek, slipping the kid another fry. "I seem to recall winning your heart with my Jasper burgers."

"Among other things. And when Lily has a belly-ache later, you're dealing with it."

Sean turned his attention from the domestic bliss to his fish-and-chips basket. He was happy for his cousins—all paired off and doing the parent thing—but it wasn't for him. Maybe in a few years when he'd found a place he wanted to stay in and a woman he wanted to stay there with. But for now, he wasn't even looking.

When Lily decided she'd had enough of her high chair and started making her displeasure known rather loudly, Beth packed up all her baby debris and kissed her husband goodbye. "Good luck, Sean. I'll see you Saturday."

"So," Kevin said when they were alone, "how are those sleeping arrangements going?"

"She's still on the couch."

"I think Josh took two nights for the pool. He's out."

Sean shook his head, a little disgusted by his youngest brother's lack of faith in his self-control. "You'll all be out when the month's over. Out money, that is."

He said it as though he believed it, but he was on shaky ground. Three nights of sleeping in the same room as Emma was playing hell on his sleep cycle. And when he'd dreamed of her last night—naked and hot for him, with her dark cloud of hair tickling his chest—and woken sweaty and hard and aching, not crossing that ten feet of bedroom had almost killed him.

Going to work tomorrow would be a good thing, he thought. Even though he'd be alone with her, a little physical labor would do his body good. Maybe if he tired himself out, he could sleep through the night without his dick trying to lead the way to her like some kind of damn dowsing rod.

"I've gotta get back to work," Kevin said, breaking

into thoughts he was better off not having, anyway. "Your lunch is on the house today."

"Thanks, man." He stood and shook his cousin's hand before polishing off the rest of his lunch.

On a whim, he took the scenic route to Joe and Keri's house, and since both their vehicles were in the driveway, he pulled in and got out.

Keri answered the door, looking frazzled and not having the best hair day he'd ever seen. "Hi, Sean. I was just thinking, gee, I need more Kowalskis in my life right now."

He laughed and stepped into the big foyer. "Baby acting up?"

"I thought the Kowalski men were royal pains in the ass—no offense—but you guys have nothing on the girls."

"Joe writing?"

She blew out a sharp breath and put her hands on her hips. "No. Joe is *pretending* to write so I won't dump Brianna in his lap, but he's probably playing some stupid game."

From the other room came a pissed-off howl that Sean hoped was their daughter and not a wild animal foraging for table scraps. "So he's in his office?"

Keri nodded and waved a hand in that direction before making a growling sound and heading off to appease her daughter. Welcome to the jungle, he mused before heading to Joe's office. He rapped twice on the door, then let himself in.

Joe looked up with a guilty start and Sean knew his wife had him all figured out. "She knows you're only pretending to write so you don't have to deal with the kid."

"You know what *really* sucks? Everybody keeps saying to just wait till she's older. Like it gets worse. How can it get worse?" Sean lifted his hands in a "don't ask me" gesture. "For years I've been writing about boogeymen and the evil that lurks in the hearts of men. I had no idea there's nothing scarier than a baby girl."

Sean laughed. "She can't be that bad. What does she weigh? Ten pounds?"

"Fifteen. But it's fifteen pounds of foul temper and fouler smells. Trust me."

"I'll take your word for it."

Joe leaned back in his leather office chair and sighed. "Let's talk about your life. She still on the couch?"

"Yes, she is."

"Good. I said you'd last three weeks."

Maybe, but Sean wouldn't bet on it. Or he *shouldn't* have bet on it, anyway. Especially a whole month. His balls ached just thinking about it. "You guys come up with a plan for the kids for Saturday yet?"

"Yeah, but it's going to cost you."

"Not a problem. I'll just take it out of all the money I'm going to collect from you idiots at the end of the month."

Joe grinned. "You keep telling yourself that, buddy."

He was. With as much oomph as he could muster. And he'd probably keep telling himself that right up to the minute he got Emma naked.

CHAPTER SEVEN

"If I'd known we were just going to sit around and watch the plants grow today, I would have brought my book."

Emma jerked her attention from the columbine plants she'd been checking on and back to Sean. "Sorry. Zoned out for a minute. Did you get the weed blocker done?"

"Yeah. I don't get why they want the pathway to the beach done in white stone. Don't you usually walk back from the water barefoot?"

"Not this couple. It doesn't matter how practical it is. All that matters is how it looks."

"Whatever. It's going to take the rest of the day to get all that stone down, so stop mentally tiptoeing through the tulips and let's go."

Emma wanted to tell him to shove his attitude up his ass, because she was the boss, or at least flip him the bird behind his back, but she didn't have the energy. Living a fake life was a lot more exhausting than she'd anticipated.

She didn't even want to think about what it was

like trying to sleep every night with her boxer-brief-clad roommate sprawled across the bed only ten feet away, so she thought about Gram instead. Gram, who was, at that very moment, on her way into town. The town that had heard the rumors of her engagement, but never actually seen her fiancé.

If Gram returned from town still believing Emma and Sean were headed to the altar, it would be a miracle.

"You look beat," Sean said, and she barely managed to restrain herself from whacking him with the shovel. He, of course, looked delicious with his muscles rippling and a light sheen of sweat making his tanned arms gleam as he shoveled stone.

"The couch is shorter than I thought. But I'm getting used to it."

"There's room in the bed."

She forced herself to keep shoveling stone into the wheelbarrow. If she didn't look at him, she didn't have to see on his face whether or not he was serious. If he wasn't, she might whack him with the shovel, after all. If he was...

"That's a bad idea."

He laughed. "So is filling your wheelbarrow so full you can't move it, but you did it, anyway."

"Crap." She'd mounded the stone so high she'd have to dump half of it out to budge the damn thing.

"I'll wheel it down for you." He winked at her. "This time."

Her mouth went a little dry when he stepped between the handles and hefted the wheelbarrow as though it was a sack of groceries, but she followed him to the area he'd already prepped with weed-blocking fabric, where she'd be spreading the first batch of white stone chips. And she managed to make most of the walk without ogling his backside.

"How have you managed to do this on your own for so long?" he asked once he'd set the wheelbarrow in place for her.

"I don't usually fill the wheelbarrow all the way to the top."

He pulled off his leather work gloves and shoved them into his back pocket. "I'm serious. This is…"

He let the sentence trail away and Emma rolled her eyes. "Not women's work?"

"I was going to say it's pretty demanding, physically."

"It takes me a little longer than it would a man, but I chip away at it. And sometimes I'll pay Joey and Danny to give me a hand."

"So Mike and Lisa's kids know you pretty well, then?"

"Yeah. If I didn't have you today, I probably would have brought all four boys. Brian and Bobby can spread mulch and stone and they make a few bucks under the table. It usually takes me longer to fix what they did than to do it myself, but they get jealous if it's only the older two all the time."

"Do you think they can really handle a secret like this?"

Emma sighed and leaned on her shovel. "I don't know. I hope so."

It was a two-part plan, though shaky at best. Part one was to keep the kids away from Cat Shaw as much as possible. Part two of the plan was to make it a game. With prizes. Terry's daughter, Stephanie, and Lisa's four boys had been given the backstory and issued the challenge. All children who didn't blow the secret would earn cash and video-game time at the end of the month, with hefty bonuses going to teens who helped coach the younger kids.

From what Sean said, it was surprising Mrs. Kowalski's head hadn't exploded, but she seemed reluctantly willing to comply. For now.

"I can't tell you how much I appreciate what your family's doing for me," she said, pulling her gloves back on. "I know they must think I'm crazy."

"A little." But he smiled, which kept her from focusing too much on his words. "But they're trying."

Because he'd asked them to, she thought. And she knew it wasn't just a matter of asking them to. He'd probably had to fight for their cooperation, trying to convince them to go along with something he himself wasn't sure about. Or hadn't been sure about.

There had been another sticky note on her bathroom mirror that morning. *I think you're doing the right thing.*

It wasn't a lot, but it was enough to get her through one more day. And, assuming Gram didn't come home from town demanding answers, another after that.

CAT TOOK HER TIME wandering down the main street of town, enjoying a perfect New England early-summer day.

She had some old friends to look up and a few groceries and other things to buy, but for now she just walked. Walking helped clear her mind, a state she hadn't achieved since arriving back in New Hampshire.

Something just wasn't quite right about Emma and Sean's relationship. She'd felt it in the airport and the feeling had only grown stronger after living under the same roof with them for a few days.

At first she'd tried to excuse Emma's reaction to Sean's touches as the embarrassment a well-raised young woman would feel about public displays of affection in front of one's grandmother. But really, it was so obvious to her they hadn't been dating for the past year, never mind living together, that she wondered if she should be offended by their drastic underestimation of her intelligence.

What she couldn't wrap her head around was the why of it.

A banner advertising a going-out-of-business sale caught her eye and she stopped on the sidewalk. Walker Hardware had been selling household, gardening, animal and building supplies since Isaiah Walker first hung out the sign in 1879, and Russell Walker had been the guy behind the counter since 1983 when his father had passed away. Actually, he'd been behind the counter helping his dad since he was barely tall enough to see over it, and she couldn't imagine how hard losing the store would be for him.

He'd lost his wife about six years before. Flo Walker had a heart attack hanging out the laundry and she'd lain in the grass until she didn't show up for knitting club. A friend had called the house and then Russell. He'd called out the rescue squad, but he'd beat them there only to find she was already gone. Cat had had just a passing acquaintance with Flo, who was originally from Connecticut, but she'd gone to school with Russell. They'd never been chummy, but they'd known each other their entire lives.

She walked up the wooden steps and smiled as the familiar bell jangled to announce her entrance. No annoying buzzers for Walker Hardware.

Russell was behind the counter, studying a news-

paper through reading glasses perched on the end of
his nose, but he looked up when the bell sounded. He
took the glasses off as a smile warmed his face, which
was still handsome under a full head of silvery hair.

"Cat! I heard you were coming home for a visit."
He rose to his feet and closed the newspaper with a
snap. "Florida obviously agrees with you."

He'd always been a charmer, but at sixty-five she
thought she'd have built up an immunity. She was
wrong. "Thank you, Russell. How have you been?"

He shrugged, waving a hand at the nearly empty
shelves bearing red going-out-of-business discount
signs. "I still have my health."

"I'm sorry."

"Bound to happen. Can't compete with the big-
box stores. People tried, of course. If they just needed
a roll of tape or a fuse or a pair of garden shears,
they'd come here. But times are tough and I can't be-
grudge them wanting to save what money they have.
Glad now I didn't fight too hard when my daughter
wanted to go off and be a vet instead of taking over
the place."

"What will you do?"

"The building's for sale to help pay off some debt,
so I'm on the waiting list for an apartment in senior
housing." He paused, sorrow shadowing his features.
"A hundred and thirty–some odd years my family's

kept this place going, and a couple months from now, I won't have a pot to piss in."

She didn't know what to say. There really wasn't much she *could* say. "Let me take you out to lunch. We'll have something full of fat and cholesterol and sodium because why the hell not?"

The invitation appeared to take him by surprise, but he recovered quickly enough. "I had to let my part-timer go last year. I can't leave."

"What are the customers going to do if you take an hour for lunch? Take their business elsewhere?"

His laugh was rich and echoed through the barren store. "I guess you're right about that. And I sure could use a smiling face right now."

"Then stick a sign in the door, lock up and let's go."

They walked down to a café at the end of the street, which happened to be the only one in town, and snagged a table in a relatively quiet corner. They both ordered coffee and Russell got the fried-chicken special while Cat ordered a hash-and-cheese omelet.

"How's Emma doing? I haven't seen her in a few weeks, but you must be happy she's finally heading toward the altar."

"She's doing great. And Sean's a very nice young man." She took a sip of her coffee, considering. "Have you met him?"

Russell frowned for a few seconds, then shook his head. "No, I don't think I have. I guess she keeps him pretty busy, and when she shops, he usually heads down to the city so he can visit his family at the same time."

"Have you heard of anybody meeting him?"

"That's an odd question. You just said yourself he's a nice young man, so he must exist."

It did sound crazy, but she couldn't let go of it. "Oh, he exists. But I don't think he's been dating my granddaughter for a year and a half, or living under the same roof for a year."

He looked confused. "Why would they lie?"

"That's the question I can't answer." She took another sip of her coffee. "But you can tell when two people are in love. And when they've...well, you know."

His slow smile warmed his eyes, which were the same blue as his shirt. Funny how you could know a man sixty-odd years and never know what color his eyes were. "It's been a while, but, yes, I know."

When Russell looked at her like that, she could remember so clearly how she'd felt during that headlong rush into love with her husband and how much she missed him. But sometimes she wondered if she was missing him so much as just missing having somebody, and she wondered if Russell ever felt the same way.

She smiled back at him, trying to think of something to say, but coming up empty. It had been a

long time since she'd had a flirtatious conversation
with a man.

That thought brought her up short. Was that what
was going on? Was he flirting? Or was he simply
being kind and she was latching onto it as though it
was the last lifeboat off her AARP-eligible sinking
ship?

Thankfully, the waitress—who was a young
woman Cat didn't recognize—brought their meals
and she was saved by digging into her forbidden feast.

"I don't think I've had real fried chicken since I
turned fifty and Flo dragged me in to have my cholesterol numbers checked," Russell said.

"We've only got so many years left, so I intend to
enjoy them. If I can't have eggs and hash and cheese
once in a while, I might as well lie down and start decomposing."

"I like that about you."

"But only once in a while," she said again. "If you
eat like this all the time, you won't have enough life
left to worry about it."

Russell set down his fork to wipe his mouth, then
took a sip of coffee. "I remember being at the store
when I still needed a stool to reach the cash register,
ringing up a customer. I knew from the time I could
walk that hardware would be my whole life and that
if Dani hadn't been so stubborn, it would have been
hers, too. But I've got to admit, there's a little part

of me that's not sorry to see the store go. And, sitting here with you smiling at me, and a pile of fried chicken on my plate, I guess I've still got enough life left in me to try to enjoy myself."

For the first time in her sixty-five years, Cat decided to be forward with a man. "You got enough life in you to take an old woman dancing?"

"Well, if I should come across any old women, I'll have to give that some thought. But in the meantime, I'd like to dance with you."

When she blushed like a schoolgirl, Cat supposed she should at least be grateful she didn't giggle like one. "You're a charmer, Russell Walker. I think I'll have to keep an eye on you."

He just grinned and bit into a big, greasy hunk of fried chicken.

SEAN JOGGED PAST the mailbox, glancing at the daisies, and turned down Emma's driveway. He'd have just enough time for a quick shower before Emma's alarm went off and another day of crazy started.

When four in the morning rolled around and he'd spent more time tossing and turning than sleeping because his aching body was keeping him awake, he'd eased out of bed and sneaked out of the house for a run. It worked in boot camp—crush disobedience and rebellion with grueling physical punishment. He wasn't sure if the same principle would work on his dick, but it was worth a shot.

Slick with sweat and slightly winded, he crossed the porch and sneaked back into the quiet house. After kicking his sneakers off, he went up the stairs— remembering just in time where the squeaky spot was—and let himself back into Emma's room. *Their* room. She was still snoring, so he went into the bathroom and closed the door.

He ran the shower hot, washing the sweat away, and then slowly turned the dial toward cold until he was wide-awake and his body was beaten into submission. Then he toweled as much of the water out of his hair as he could, dried himself off and wrapped the towel around his waist.

He had a mouth full of toothpaste when the door opened and Emma walked in, rubbing her face. She was carrying a bundle of clothes and squinting against the light, even though in her half-asleep state she still slapped her hand at the wall switch—and almost walked into him before she noticed his presence.

"Oh." She stopped and blinked at him. "I thought you were still in bed."

He spit out the toothpaste and grabbed the hand towel to wipe his mouth. "I usually make a bigger lump."

"I don't look, because you throw the covers off

and—" She broke off as her eyes drifted south to the towel, where *bigger lump* took on a whole new meaning. He'd thrown miles of punishment at his body for no reason. "Oh."

Rather than dwell on deciphering the tone of that *oh,* he took her by the shoulders and guided her far enough to the left so he could get by her. Once he was free, he closed the door behind him and swore under his breath.

The only way that could have been more awkward was if his towel had slipped off in front of her.

After getting dressed in record time, he flopped back onto the bed and stared at the ceiling. This was the kind of story a woman would share with her best friend. And her best friend was married to his cousin. His cousin had a big mouth. The story would be embellished. It was only a matter of time before one of his brothers called, asking why he was naked with the woman he wasn't supposed to be naked with.

With a sigh, he pushed himself off the bed and headed downstairs. One, he wanted coffee. And, two, he didn't want to be sprawled on the bed when Emma got around to leaving the bathroom. The only thing more awkward than being caught in a towel that didn't do much to hide an erection was talking about it.

Cat was sitting at the table, sipping tea, when he walked in. "You beat Emma down this morning."

"It doesn't happen often." He poured two mugs of

coffee and then froze. He had no clue what Emma took in her coffee. He knew she took some half-and-half, but he wasn't sure about the sugar. Putting his back between Cat and the cups, he dumped two tea-spoons in each cup.

"How do you like working with my granddaughter?"

Since he'd only worked with her for a day and a half, he couldn't really say. "It's not too bad. She works hard. Has a good head for business."

"And she has excellent control skills," Cat added.

He laughed, thinking of their trip to the grocery store. "That she does."

"I guess you know her pretty well."

She was watching him, so he concentrated on look-ing honest. Whatever that looked like. "She's a com-plicated woman. I'm not sure anybody really knows her well. Except you, of course."

She laughed as the complicated woman in question walked into the kitchen. "Morning, Gram. What's so funny?"

"Just chatting with Sean, and now that you're up, I'll start some French toast."

Sean watched Emma take the first sip of her coffee, and when she didn't shudder or make faces, he fig-ured he'd done okay. He also noticed, as Cat started hauling things out of the refrigerator, that Emma wasn't making eye contact with him.

He shouldn't have walked out, because now the awkwardness was going to fester until she felt a need to talk about the incident in the bathroom. He could have laughed it off as morning wood, making it clear the pronounced lump had nothing to do with her. That would have been a lie, of course. He'd been up for several hours and it most definitely had something to do with her. But she might have bought the story and not had to talk about it.

The kitchen felt claustrophobic all of a sudden, what with the two women he barely knew and the elephant in the room, so he took his coffee and muttered about catching the morning news. He turned on the TV in the living room and sank onto the couch with a sigh of relief. It would take a few minutes to make the French toast, so he had a few minutes of normal.

"Can I talk to you for a second?" It was Emma, of course, and there went his normal.

He sighed and moved over on the couch. "Knock yourself out."

She sat down, far enough away so none of their body parts touched. "I get the whole guy thing. Morning…you know, and I don't want this to be weird."

"It's no big deal."

"Okay." She took a sip of her coffee, then wrapped both hands around the mug. "We'll probably have more moments like this if we're going to live together for a month. Probably best to just laugh them off."

He raised an eyebrow at her. "Actually, when a guy's standing in front of you, fully hard and wearing nothing but a towel, laughing might not be the *best* way to handle it."

"True." Her cheeks turned a pretty shade of pink and she laughed softly. "If we were in a movie, the towel would have fallen off. Could've been worse."

"With my luck, I'm surprised it didn't."

"Breakfast," Cat called from the kitchen. They both stood and Sean hoped this would be the last time they had to discuss his erections.

"Make sure you fill up," Emma told him as they went toward the kitchen. "We'll be planting trees today and that'll take the piss out of you."

Physical exhaustion? He was looking forward to it. Desperately.

CHAPTER EIGHT

EMMA DIDN'T WANT her grandmother to ever leave. Gram had cut some chicken breasts into pieces and rolled them in a bowl of some kind of spices, then skewered them with sticks. A few minutes on the grill and Emma was in heaven.

It couldn't be too hard, she thought. Of course, the last time she'd tried to cook something as simple as burgers on the grill, flames had started shooting out the side and she'd ended up with blackened lumps with raw meat in the middle even her grandfather couldn't choke down. But this was chicken on a stick. How hard could it be?

"This is delicious, Cat," Sean said, licking juices off his fingers in a way that made Emma's spine tingle. "Aunt Mary makes something like it, but the spices don't pack quite as much of a punch."

"I can't wait to meet her on Saturday. From all that you've said, she's quite a woman."

Emma's spine stopped tingling and she picked up another skewer of chicken. She didn't even want to think about how stressful Saturday was going to be, what with everybody having to be careful and watch every single word they said. And, regardless of what Sean had told her, she wasn't sure Mrs. Kowalski would back them up when the time finally came.

"She's looking forward to meeting you, too," he said. "And Emma's been so busy they haven't seen her in a while."

No, she wasn't looking forward to seeing them Saturday. Lisa, yes. But it was going to be hard to look Mrs. Kowalski in the eye, no matter how many times Sean told her it would be okay.

"I rented a movie while I was in town today," Gram said. "Some action movie the girl said was very good."

Emma was all for a relaxing movie. Something mindless that she could lose herself in and stop obsessing about her body language and every word she said. A mental break was just what she needed.

She felt differently about the movie plan an hour later when Gram sat in the armchair and set her knitting basket at her feet, leaving the couch for her and Sean.

Crap. They couldn't very well sit at opposite ends of the damn thing. A happy couple would snuggle, maybe sneaking a quick kiss here and there when they thought Gram wasn't looking. Two hours of up close and personal with Sean Kowalski was about as far from relaxing as she could get.

He got there first, sitting in one corner and propping his feet on the coffee table. Putting in the DVD and getting it ready to play bought Emma a couple of minutes, but then she had to walk to the couch. He seemed to realize at the last second she wasn't going to sit on the far end, and after glancing at Gram, he lifted his arm and rested it on the back of the couch.

Since her back was momentarily to the armchair, she gave Sean an apologetic "whaddya-gonna-do" smile and sat down in the curve of his arm. He dropped his hand onto her shoulder as she hit Play on the remote control.

She tried to pay attention to the movie. She watched as a woman dropped a cookie sheet of burned cookies in the sink, and then a man walked into her kitchen. He had a gun and he told her he'd kidnapped her son. Emma followed along at first.

But Sean's body was putting off enough heat to melt marshmallows, and a whole lot of his body was touching her body. His arm around her shoulders. His thigh pressed to hers. Their feet sometimes brushing. It was distracting.

"You watch," Gram said. "The man she has to deliver to the kidnappers is going to end up being the father of her son and I bet he doesn't know."

Emma managed to keep enough focus on the television to see that she was right, but Sean was relaxing, which meant even more of his body was touching hers. And minute by minute she was becoming a marshmallow, melting against him. He smelled good and felt good and…she was in so much trouble. This wasn't her man to lust after. Well, technically, she could. She just couldn't act on it.

Sean was temporary. There was no sense in getting used to having a man to snuggle on the couch with or to open stubborn jars or to do her heavy lifting, because as soon as Gram was gone, so was he. And that's the way she wanted it. It would probably be another five years before Landscaping by Emma was ready for her to do the husband-and-babies thing.

And when she did go husband shopping, she wasn't going to settle for a guy whose entire life revolved around football, steak, beer and women. Or a guy who thought only Bob or Fred could mow lawns. Sean wouldn't even let her drive her own truck.

Halfway through a scene in which the mom and dad were rappelling out of a helicopter with guns blazing to rescue their kidnapped son, Sean's hand shifted and his fingertips started tracing circles against her shoulder. His attention was on the screen, as was Gram's, so Emma wasn't sure he was even aware he was doing it.

She was aware of it, though, that was for damn sure. Aware of the warmth of his touch through her T-shirt and very, very aware of the way her body reacted as if he were stroking parts of her a lot farther south than her shoulder.

When his fingers worked their way down to the end of her short sleeve and touched bare skin, she totally lost track of the plot unfolding on the television screen. Temporary or not, it sure was nice being touched by a man. It had been…a long time.

"Can you pause it for a minute?" Gram asked. "Intermission."

When Emma leaned forward for the remote, Sean withdrew his arm and let his feet fall to the floor. "Sounds like a plan."

Gram left in the direction of the kitchen and Emma stood, intending to get out of Sean's way, but when he stood, he grabbed her elbow and spun her around.

His mouth met hers, hot and hungry, and she wrapped her arms around his neck as she responded in kind. So what if he was temporary? She'd enjoy it while it lasted. His hands were on her hips and he pulled her closer—close enough so she could feel he wasn't pretending to want her.

The kiss was incredible and she stood on tiptoe, reaching for more. Her fingertips found the back of his neck and she stroked him from the knot at the top of his spine and up into his hair and back.

Sean pulled away from her so fast she almost fell over. "Shit."

"Flattering." Her senses were still so overwhelmed by him she didn't trust herself to say more.

He ran his hand over his hair, shaking his head. "That was…"

Wonderful, Emma thought. Amazing. Toe-curling. "That was what?"

"A mistake." He pushed by her and a few seconds later she heard his footsteps climbing the stairs.

"Jerk," she muttered, but the word didn't have a lot of oomph behind it. She was still too breathless from being kissed so thoroughly by a man who knew what kissing was all about.

No doubt about it—she was in trouble.

SEAN HAD TO GET OUT of the house or he was totally going to lose it. He wasn't sure if that meant punching a hole in the wall or tossing Emma over his shoulder and carrying her off to bed caveman-style, but either was a bad idea.

Time to go for a ride and get some space, but first he stuck another sticky note to the mirror and uncapped the Sharpie.

You can hold my hand or pat my head or scratch my belly, but don't rub the back of my neck again unless you want to get naked.

He went back downstairs and grabbed the keys to his truck off the hook by the door. Cat was back in her chair when he popped his head into the living room.

"I have to bail, ladies. Kevin called while I was upstairs and needs a hand with something."

"But the movie," Cat said.

"You'll have to tell me how it ends." He forced himself to look at Emma, who was doing a pretty poor job of hiding her annoyance. "I might be late, so don't wait up."

"Have fun" was all she said.

He jumped on the highway and drove a little too fast with the music a little too loud, hoping to leave no room in his thoughts for remembering the taste of Emma's lips.

Even before he'd spun her around, he'd known kissing her was a big mistake. He hadn't realized the mistake was actually colossal, though, until she started stroking the back of his neck and his body reacted with an urgency that led nowhere but to bed. Together. Hot and sweaty and breathing hard between the sheets.

He got lucky and found a parking spot near Jasper's Bar & Grille and breathed a sigh of relief as he walked through the door. Men drinking beer. Pretty waitresses. Sports on the big screens. Sanity.

It was a little slow, which wasn't surprising for a Wednesday night, so there were plenty of open seats at the bar, where Kevin appeared to be holding down the fort.

"Didn't think I'd see you here tonight," he said as his cousin set a beer in front of him.

Kevin shrugged. "Terry's having one of those parties where the women all get together and one of them sells the others a bunch of shit they don't need so she can earn a free salad bowl or whatever. Paulie wanted to go and I sure as hell didn't, so here I am. How's fake almost-married life treating you?"

"I kissed her." He chugged down a quarter of the mug.

"Yeah, so? Engaged people do that sometimes."

"I kissed her *after* Cat left the room. I didn't kiss her because we were pretending. I kissed her because... Hell, I don't need to draw you a map."

"When did that happen?"

Sean looked at his watch. "About a half hour ago."

Kevin gave a low whistle. "She still sleeping on the couch?"

"Yes. And she's staying there, too, goddammit."

"Did she punch you in the face? Knee you in the balls?"

"No."

Kevin grinned. "So what's the problem? You want her. She can at least tolerate you. Get it out of your system."

He was afraid sleeping with Emma wouldn't get her out of his system, but get her a little further under his skin, instead. "Bad idea."

"Call it a fringe benefit."

"She's already pretending she's in love with me. Throwing real sex on top of that could get it all mixed up in her head."

"You worried about her mixing it up...or you?"

That was ridiculous, so he snorted and swallowed some more beer. He had no interest in settling down—signing his life over to somebody else so soon after getting it back from Uncle Sam—and he sure as hell wasn't planting flowers until retirement age. Assuming he didn't lose his mind and suffocate himself in a mound of mulch before then.

"You ready for Saturday?" Kevin asked.

"Hell, no." He didn't even want to think about that.

Kevin had to move on down the bar, so Sean sipped his beer and stared at the television without really seeing what was on.

Emma had felt way too good tucked up against his body on the couch. She was warm and her body fit perfectly against his, and the viewing angle had let him appreciate all too much how long and perfectly shaped her legs were. And the heat of her thigh pressed against his...

Sean knocked back the rest of his beer and set the mug out on the far edge, looking for a refill.

Kevin came back and refilled it. "Nurse this one if you're driving home. If you have another, you're staying upstairs."

"I'll nurse it. Why don't you throw in an order of chili-cheese fries for me, too."

He watched the game and ate his fries, making the beer last. Emma would probably be asleep by the time he got back, those amazing legs peeking out from the worn flannel shorts that wouldn't have been sexy on anybody else.

Hopefully, the long, icy-cold shower he was going to need wouldn't wake her up.

EMMA RIPPED THE STICKY NOTE off the bathroom mirror and tossed it in the trash.

Sean didn't have to worry about her rubbing the back of his neck again anytime soon. And he certainly didn't have to worry about her wanting to get naked. Not with him.

If they were a real couple, she'd throw his pillow onto the couch and let *his* feet dangle over the edge for a change. It was pathetic how fast he'd come up with a lame excuse to run away just because he'd kissed her.

It was just a kiss. A great kiss, yes, but still just a kiss. She hadn't asked him to marry her—to *really* marry her, of course—or told him she wanted to have his baby. A hot, steamy, toe-curling, bone-melting kiss between two single adults was nothing to run from.

But now he'd made a big deal out of it and everything was going to be even more awkward than it had been for the past few days.

She'd been curled up on the couch, fuming, for almost an hour when she heard Sean's truck pull in to the driveway. It was another ten minutes before he crept into the bedroom and closed the door behind him. Since she was facing the back of the couch, she didn't have to make much of an effort to ignore him.

He was in the shower so long she must have fallen asleep to the drone of running water, because the next thing Emma knew, her alarm was going off and it was time to face another day in the hell she'd created.

But first she had to face Sean. She got first crack at the bathroom, and when she came out, he was sitting on the side of the bed, fully clothed. Thank goodness.

He scrubbed his hands over his face. "We should talk about last night."

"How's Kevin?"

"He's good. And I meant before that."

"You should have stayed for the end of the movie. It was good."

"Dammit, Emma, you know that's not what I'm talking about."

"Oh, you mean the practice kiss?" She clipped her cell phone onto her front pocket. "We're getting better at it. That was almost convincing."

"Practice kiss?" He stood, probably so he could

look down at her, but she was tall enough it didn't make much of an impact. "Almost convincing?"

"Yeah," she said, though she turned her back on him, heading toward the door to avoid eye contact, because that was no practice kiss and it could have convinced even the CIA's finest.

He was muttering when she left the room, but she shut the door on him and went downstairs. She didn't want to talk about it. And she didn't want to think about the fact he wasn't happy she called it a practice kiss.

That meant he considered it a real kiss. And not only a real kiss, but one that had shaken him up. The only reason kissing a woman should bother a man like him was if he was trying to fight being attracted to her.

Hopefully, he'd win, she thought as she headed toward the kitchen, because she was waging that battle herself and didn't appear to be headed for a victory. Maybe he had enough willpower and self-control for both of them.

Other than a little morning chitchat with Gram, neither of them spoke as they ate breakfast and headed off to work—with him driving her truck again. But after ten minutes on the road with fifteen more to go, she couldn't take it anymore. "Why are you mad at me?"

He didn't look at her. "I'm not mad."

"You're not happy."

His fingers tightened on the steering wheel. "That was no practice kiss."

"I know it wasn't. I was trying to give us a reason not to talk about it."

"Oh. So you don't think we should talk about it?"

"I thought guys hated talking things out."

He drummed his fingers on the wheel. "I just don't want you getting any ideas, that's all."

Getting any ideas? Emma was speechless for a moment, unable to believe he'd actually said that. "Since I was walking away from you when you spun me around and kissed me, I'd say *you're* the one getting ideas."

"Of course I'm getting ideas. You're hot and I'm not dead. But I know enough not to confuse lust with anything else."

She snorted and looked out her window. "Oh, yes, Sean Kowalski. Your amazing kisses have made all rational thought fly out of my besotted brain. If only you could fill me with your magic penis, I know we'd fall madly in love and live happily ever after."

The truck jerked and she glanced over to find him glaring at her. "Don't ever say that again."

"What? The 'madly in love' or the 'happily ever after'?"

"My penis isn't magic." His tone was grumpy,

but then he smiled at the windshield. "It does tricks, though."

"The only trick your penis needs to know for the next three and a half weeks is *down boy.*" How the hell had she gotten herself into this conversation? "To get back to the point, if you think I have any interest in a real relationship with a guy who thinks he's a better driver than me just because I have breasts, you're insane."

"It's not because you have breasts. Women don't drive as well because they lack a magic penis."

She turned toward the passenger door, letting him know with her body language she had no interest in talking to him anymore. "Why didn't I tell Gram I was dating Bob from the post office?"

He laughed at her. "You've met the Kowalskis. You were doomed the minute you said the name out loud."

Doomed, she thought, glaring at the passing scenery. That was a good word for it.

CHAPTER NINE

"OH, WHAT A LOVELY HOME!"

Sean pulled into his aunt and uncle's driveway and killed the engine. "Thanks, Cat. My cousin Joe bought it for them after his horror novels started landing on the *New York Times* bestseller list on a regular basis."

"It's big, which must come in handy with all those grandchildren."

All those grandchildren she was about to meet, Sean thought, resisting the urge to beat his head against the steering wheel. He wasn't too worried about Steph, Joey and Danny, but Brian and Bobby were loose cannons. To say nothing of Aunt Mary.

The introductions didn't go too badly. His uncle's gruff humor put Cat at ease, and his aunt was warm and welcoming, even though Sean knew she had serious reservations about the whole thing.

"I'm Bobby," a young voice piped up, and it seemed as if everybody but Cat sucked in a breath at the same time. "Guess what?"

"What?" Cat said, seemingly oblivious to the frantic hand gestures being waved in Bobby's direction.

"Sean's my cousin. He got out of the army a long time ago and he lives with Emma and he's going to marry her."

Joey, Mike's oldest boy, laughed and put his arm around his little brother to not so subtly start dragging him away. "They have telephones in Florida, dummy. Mrs. Shaw already knows that."

Lisa stepped forward before Bobby could argue. "Now that you kids have all said hello to Mrs. Shaw, you can go to the basement and play your game."

Bobby jumped up and down. "Sean bought us 'Rock Band' for the Wii and all the instruments, so we're going to have a 'Rock Band' Tournament of Doom."

Sean hadn't known he'd bought the kids a bunch of video-game crap, but he couldn't very well argue the point. No doubt Mike and the rest would just put it on his tab.

Luckily, Cat and Aunt Mary seemed to hit it off pretty easily and—since Cat didn't seem in imminent danger of asking Mary outright if his and Emma's engagement was real—Sean started to relax.

They all went out to the backyard, where the women took over the chairs on the deck and the men gathered around the grill. It wasn't time to start cooking yet, but gathering around the cold grill was better than sitting with the women.

"Mary's been a wreck about this for days," Leo said, for once managing to lower his voice so the whole neighborhood wouldn't hear him.

"I know she didn't want to do this." Sean watched the women laugh at something Cat said. Or, more specifically, he watched Emma laugh. "I'll make it up to her somehow."

They talked about the usual stuff. The Red Sox. How deep into summer vacation they'd get before Lisa's grip on her sanity started slipping. Evan's new truck, which he'd bought in white because Terry said not to buy a white one because they were impossible to keep clean. How Evan and Terry's marriage counseling was going.

Joe nudged Sean's arm. "I swear, I could tell time by how often Emma looks at you just by counting off the seconds."

Sean resisted the urge to turn and look. "She's nervous, that's all."

"That's not nerves."

"I think I know her better than you do."

Joe laughed. "You've known her a week."

"Ten days."

"Hate to burst your bubble, but I've known her longer than ten days. Not well, but I've run into her at Mike and Lisa's. Not that it matters. That look on a woman's face is pretty universal."

"There's no look."

"Oh, there's a look," Kevin said.

"There might be a look," Leo added.

"Mike and I can't see," Evan added. "We're facing the wrong way. We could turn around, but she might wonder why we're all staring at her."

Even though he figured his cousins were pulling his leg, Sean angled his body a little so he could see her in his peripheral vision.

Okay, so she was looking at him. A lot. But Joe and Kevin were still full of crap because there was no *look*. The glances were too quick to read anything into, never mind the kind of message they were implying she was sending.

He watched her watching him for a while, and then Aunt Mary told them to get the meat ready so they could fire the grill. Since his cousins made for more than enough chefs stirring the soup and he needed a break from the visual game of tag he and Emma were playing, he grabbed a beer and made his way to the big toolshed. It was the unofficial Kowalski man cave, where females feared to tread. Even Aunt Mary would just stand outside and bellow rather than cross the threshold.

It smelled of the old motor oil that had dripped onto and soaked into the wooden floor, and the stack of wood next to the old woodstove meant to ensure that even in the cold months, there was a place a man could go for a few minutes of peace and quiet. The walls were lined with shelves of old mason jars containing nuts and bolts and screws and washers and all the other debris a good toolshed collected over time.

Sean cracked open his beer, flipped on the ancient radio and perched on one of the bar stools somebody had probably lifted from Jasper's. He was too wound up to sit still, though, so he set down his beer and got up to investigate the current project, which appeared to be rebuilding the snowblower's engine.

He was in the process of using gasoline and a wire brush to clean some gunked-up bolts when the door opened and his uncle walked in. "Hey, Uncle Leo."

"Thought I might find you out here." He inspected Sean's work and nodded in approval. "I've been teaching the boys to turn a wrench here and there. Steph used to help me out sometimes, too, but now her thumbs are too busy with that texting crap to twist a bolt."

"I should ask her how to run this damn phone I bought. I can do phone calls with it, but that's about it."

Leo grabbed another brush and pulled up a milk crate next to Sean. "So how you doing?"

"Not bad, I guess, considering what I let myself get dragged into."

"No, son. How are you *really* doing?"

Sean shrugged and grabbed a rag to wipe off some diluted gunk. "I'm doing okay. Lot of guys—and women—had it worse than me over there. I was lucky and now I'm out, no worse for wear."

"Thought about what you're going to do when this charade of yours is over?"

"Probably the same thing I planned to do before this charade started. Get a job pounding nails somewhere until I figure out where I want to land."

"Your aunt's got it in her head you and Emma have chemistry."

Sean snorted and stood to stretch his legs and reach his beer. "Between deployment and being sucked in by Typhoon Emma, I haven't had a chance to sow my wild oats in a good long time. Trust me, right now I've got chemistry with a telephone pole."

The last thing he wanted was chemistry with Emma Shaw—especially chemistry strong enough for other people to notice.

"Leo?" Aunt Mary yelled from outside. "Are you in that damn shed again? Is Sean in there with you? It's time to eat."

"Oops." Sean wiped his hands the best he could on a semiclean rag. "Busted."

"Listen, if you need to talk about…anything, you know where to find me."

"Thanks, Uncle Leo." He put out his hand, but instead of shaking it, Leo used it to pull him in for an awkward hug and a slap on the back.

"I'm proud you served, but I'm damn glad to have you home."

Sean would have said something, but his throat had tightened up on him, so he just gave the old man's shoulders a squeeze and nodded.

"Sean Michael Kowalski!"

"You better go," his uncle said, releasing him, "before she gets her wooden spoon and storms my castle."

IT WAS ALMOST THE END of the evening before Cat managed to get Mary alone in the kitchen. If she didn't know better, she'd almost think Sean's aunt was avoiding her.

"Wonderful meal, Mary."

The other woman spun around, clutching a box of aluminum foil. "Oh! You startled me. And thank you, though the boys did most of it."

"I'll have to beg that marinade recipe from you." Cat leaned against the counter and crossed her arms. "So, why are my granddaughter and your nephew pretending to be engaged?"

Clearly caught off guard, Mary was silent for a few seconds. Then her expression cleared. "They're not pretending. He asked her to marry him and she said yes. That's engaged."

Mary went back to dividing up leftovers and Cat narrowed her eyes at the woman's back. The question hadn't surprised Mary at all. She hadn't wanted to know why Cat would think that or what would possess her to ask such a thing. Obviously there was a conspiracy afoot.

"Okay," she said after a moment's thought. "Why are they pretending they've been in love and living together for over a year?"

Mary practically flinched and Cat watched the tips of her ears turn a darkish pink. "Sean's been a part of your granddaughter's life for a long time."

Though it was artfully done, Cat could tell Mary was skirting the truth. "How long ago did Sean get out of the army?"

"Oh, he's been out awhile. Would you care for more cobbler? I swear I made enough to feed the entire neighborhood."

"No, thank you. Have Sean and Emma been living together for a year and a half?"

"It's been…oh, I don't know. I can barely keep track of my own four kids and all the grandkids."

She was good. Very good. "We hadn't even left the airport yet and I knew they weren't a couple. Or if they were, they hadn't even been dating long enough to get to second base. What I haven't been able to figure out is…why?"

Mary turned to face her and leaned back against

the counter with a sigh, her arms crossed. "If Emma felt a need to invent a relationship with Sean—and I'm not saying she did—maybe she thought *you* couldn't be happy until *she* was happy."

"That doesn't make any sense." Or maybe it did.

Thinking back on their many telephone conversations, Cat realized she may not have done a very good job of hiding how much she worried about Emma. She was always asking her about the house and if she'd had the furnace checked, and admonishing her not to clean the gutters alone or climb a ladder or...a hundred other things. And she'd probably said the big old house was too much for Emma more than once.

And, looking back, maybe she *had* relaxed a little when Emma told her she was dating a really nice guy. Once Sean had supposedly moved in, she'd probably stopped using their time on the phone to fret and had talked about herself and how much she was enjoying Florida instead.

Cat sighed and shook her head. "You must all think I'm a pathetic, doddering old woman for my granddaughter to feel a need to put everybody through this."

"No, we don't think that at all." She looked sincere. "Emma loves you and she didn't want you worrying about her. Obviously it got out of hand. But for what it's worth, I think Sean's very attracted to her."

Cat thought about that for a minute. "Emma's definitely attracted to him."

"They make a lovely couple, and I wouldn't mind seeing Sean settle down. I'm tired of worrying about that boy."

"If I tell them I know they're lying, Sean will leave and go back to whatever he was doing before."

"He hadn't had a chance to do anything yet. He hasn't been out of the army very long and he was going to stay over Kevin's bar until he figured out what to do with his life." Mary paused and then smiled. "I think it's a very good idea not to let on you know."

"This could be fun."

Mary Kowalski's smile spread into a grin that rivaled her sons'. "Oh, it will be."

"HAVE YOU TWO set a date yet?"

Mrs. Kowalski's question sent Emma's iced tea rushing down the wrong pipe and she coughed until Sean pounded her on the back—maybe a little more enthusiastically than was required.

"No, we haven't," Sean answered while she attempted to clear her throat. "Nothing wrong with a long engagement."

"But not too long," Gram said. "I'm ready for some great-grandchildren."

"I wouldn't mind a grandnephew or -niece, either," Mrs. Kowalski added.

Emma wasn't sure, but she thought Sean might have stopped breathing. "We'll think about it."

"Hey," Mike interjected, "you could get married while Mrs. Shaw's home from Florida! A justice of the peace and a big, rented canopy. Couple of barbecue grills."

Emma was afraid Sean was going to chuck his glass at his cousin—who was obviously enjoying himself—so she laid her hand on his arm. It twitched under her fingers, but she turned her attention to Mike. "I don't really want a burgers-in-the-backyard kind of wedding."

"What kind of wedding do you want?" Mary asked.

"A big one," Emma said. "They take a long time to plan."

"And to save up for," Sean added.

"I bet Stephanie would love to be a bridesmaid," Terry said with an angelic smile.

Emma squirmed on the inside, though she did her best to hide it. Sean's family was brutal. They were doing their part in the deception, but they were having way too much fun with it, too.

They were all on the back deck, watching the kids play a very unstructured, rules-free game of badminton. It should have been a relaxing end to a fabulous meal, but all Emma could think about was getting the hell out before she had a total nervous breakdown.

"I still have a stack of bridal magazines and catalogs," Keri said. "We'll have to get together and have a wedding-planning party."

They were diabolical, every last one of them. "Maybe. This is my busy season at work, but... maybe."

"Of course she'll make time," Gram assured Joe's wife, while reaching over to pat Emma's knee. "Weddings are so exciting!"

"You know what's exciting? The Red Sox bull pen," Leo said in that loud voice of his, and Emma wanted to jump up and kiss him for changing the subject as the women rolled their eyes and the men started talking over each other.

Twenty minutes later, Gram yawned and Emma jumped on it like a starving woman jumping on a cheeseburger. "It's been a long day. We should probably get going."

Cat chattered about Sean's family all the way home, while Emma slumped in her seat, thankful the ordeal was over. They'd survived and now she was exhausted.

When they finally parked in front of the house, Gram went in while Emma and Sean took their time gathering the army's worth of leftovers Mary had sent home with them.

"That went pretty well," he said.

She laughed. "Your family has a twisted sense of humor."

"That they do, and they're going to give us both shit whenever they can. But nobody spilled the beans."

As they crossed the porch, Emma shifted her leftovers so she could touch his arm. He turned and looked at her in the fading sun. "Thank you, Sean. For doing this even though your aunt's not very happy about it and your family's never going to let you live it down."

"Don't worry about it. And that was the biggest hurdle, so it'll only get easier from here."

Somehow, she doubted that.

CHAPTER TEN

A KNOCK ON THE DOOR jerked Emma awake and she blinked at the clock across the room, next to the bed where Sean was now sitting up straight. Six twenty-five.

"Are you both decent? I can't wait to show you what I found!"

Oh, crap. Gram wanted in. She scrambled off the couch. "Just a second!"

After draping the blanket in a half-assed way over the back of the couch, she grabbed her pillow and crossed to the bed in a tiptoe jog, dodging the squeaky spot in the floor. Sean pushed his pillow back to one side and lifted the covers for her, and even though she tried not to look, she caught a glimpse of a gray boxer-brief-clad bulge as she slid between the sheets. She wouldn't mind waking up to that every morning.

Instead, she was waking up to an impromptu visit from her grandmother. She gave Sean an apologetic glance and he flopped backward onto his pillow, throwing his forearm over his eyes. "Come on in."

Gram opened the door and stepped in, carrying

an old shoe box decorated with bits of lace and pink hearts cut out of construction paper. She smiled at them and held it up. "Your wedding box!"

Emma's stomach dropped. She'd forgotten about the wedding box. For years she'd been obsessed with weddings—maybe because the only pictures she had of her parents together in the same shot were wedding photos. She'd cut pictures out of magazines and drawn primitive sketches of whatever she couldn't find in the colorful pages. She'd written notes about her future wedding in a crayon scrawl and then penciled block letters. She'd even done a few in cursive with a hot-pink pen before she finally outgrew the box. She hadn't thought about it in years, and she certainly hadn't expected to see it at the crack of dawn on a Monday morning.

"It was in the back of my armoire, way down at the bottom," Gram said. "I was going to start breakfast, but I remembered it Saturday night while we were talking about what kind of wedding you want. I finally found it this morning and I just couldn't wait to show you and I knew you'd be getting up for work."

Emma rubbed her face, wishing the friction could jump-start her brain. "You don't have to make breakfast."

"For the last time, I'm not a fan of instant oatmeal and I don't mind doing it." She walked over to set the wedding box on Emma's lap and headed for the door. "I'll see you downstairs in a few minutes."

She was almost to the door when Emma's alarm went off. The alarm from her cell phone, which was across the room and plugged in next to the couch where she had been sleeping only a few minutes before. Emma watched Gram stop and look at it, frowning.

"I keep it over there because it's too easy to hit Snooze when it's next to the bed. If I get up to shut it off, I stay up."

"Makes sense." Gram smiled and left, closing the door behind her.

Emma groaned and climbed out of her bed—her wonderful, comfortable bed that she missed very much—and crossed the room to shut off the alarm and unplug her phone. When she turned around, Sean was sitting up, rummaging through the box.

He held up a small piece of paper she recognized with a pang as being from the pink stationery set her grandfather had bought her for her tenth birthday.

"'I want to marry a man who will wear pink shirts because it's my favorite color,'" he read aloud, and then he looked up at her. "Really? That's your criteria?"

"It seemed important when I was *ten*."

"'Bouquet—pink gladioli tied with white ribbon,'"

he read from a torn piece of school notebook paper. "What the hell is gladioli? Sounds like pasta."

"Glads are my favorite flower." She grabbed her clothes and went into the bathroom, closing the door none too softly behind her.

When she emerged, he was still in bed and still rummaging through her childish dreams for her future. She watched him frown at a hand-drawn picture of a wedding cake decorated with pink flowers before he set it aside and pulled out another piece of pink stationery.

"'If the man who wants to marry me doesn't get down on one knee to propose,'" he read in a high-pitched, mock-feminine voice, "'I'll tell him no.'"

"My younger self had very high standards," she snapped. "Obviously *that's* changed."

He just laughed at her. "Were you going to put all this into spreadsheet form? Maybe give the poor schmuck a checklist?"

"Are you going to get up and go to work today or are you going to stay in bed and mock a little girl's dreams?"

"I can probably do both."

When he put the lid back on her wedding box and set it aside, she bolted before he could throw back the covers to get up. One glimpse of his boxer-brief-clad body was all she could take in a day.

Gram was making blueberry pancakes, which

improved Emma's mood drastically. She fixed two coffees and set Sean's army mug in his spot before sipping her own.

"Thanks for finding my box, Gram."

"You used to work on that box for hours. You were so little when you started, your grandfather had to help you cut the pictures out of the magazines because you cried if you cut into the pretty dresses."

She'd had such big dreams. Prince Charming was going to charge into her life with his white horse and his pink shirt and sweep her off her feet. There would be romance and roses and champagne every day, and he'd write poems about his love for her.

Things had definitely changed since then. If and when she finally reached a point when settling down and starting a family was an option, she'd settle for love, reliability and respect over romance and roses.

She was on her second pancake by the time Sean finally appeared, his hair damp from his shower, and he dug in with relish after making a fuss over Gram.

"I'm going to cry when you go back to Florida and I'm back to instant oatmeal and fast-food drive-through windows," he said.

"Kiss ass," Emma muttered against the rim of her coffee mug, but he just grinned at her.

Gram plopped another pancake on Sean's plate. "Mary invited us all to their big Fourth of July bash on Saturday. They have a party and then go watch the fireworks over the lake. I told her we'd be there, of course. She said your family sometimes comes, too, Sean."

And there went Emma's appetite. "You didn't tell me that."

He shrugged. "Mitch said he'd be there. I haven't heard from the others yet."

Banging her head against the table wasn't an option, so Emma shoved another bite of blueberry pancake into her mouth and chewed slowly to buy herself time to stop screaming on the inside.

Not only were more people getting dragged into the mess she'd made, but his brothers and sister would be even worse because she'd have to pretend they weren't total strangers. Just thinking about it gave her a headache.

She shoved back from the table and rinsed her plate. "I've got a few phone calls to make before we leave. And we'll be working in the sun all day, Sean, so you might want to take it easy on the breakfast."

"Are you okay, honey?" Gram asked, her eyes full of concern. "You looked fine before, but now you're a little pale."

She forced herself to smile. "Just trying to sort my schedule in my head, Gram. I'm not sure about Saturday. I might need to work."

"Don't be silly. Nobody's backyard is more important than your family. If Sean's family can make the time, so can you."

"Okay, Gram. I'll make it work." She kissed her grandmother's cheek and escaped to her office for a few minutes of peace.

Sean hadn't mentioned the upcoming family bash or the fact his aunt would expect them to be there. Or the fact some of his siblings might show up.

Emma rested her forehead on the cool surface of her desk and sighed. Just what she needed. More Kowalskis.

SEAN STILL DIDN'T HAVE MUCH of a plan for what he'd do when the month was over, but he was pretty sure of one thing he *wouldn't* be doing—landscape design for finicky people with too much damn money.

They were spending the day on the shores of Lake Winnipesaukee again, at one of those little summer cottages that were really mansions, adding to landscaping Emma had previously done.

"Is she going to make you take these all out after?" he asked, making sure the mulch he was spreading was level enough to satisfy his boss's insane control freakishness when it came to her work.

"She might. But she'll pay for it, so I'll do it. But these are mostly annuals, anyway, so she can leave them for the rest of the summer without ruining the overall landscaping plan."

Mrs. Somebody-or-other was hosting a baby shower for her spoiled princess at the cottage the following week and the much-heralded first grandchild was reportedly a girl. Emma's job—and therefore Sean's, as well—was to turn the beachfront property into an explosion of pink.

There were tall, skinny pink flowers and short, bushy pink flowers and all different kinds of pink flowers he knew nothing about. There were even some of those gladioli things she'd been talking about that morning. But he wasn't likely to learn anything about them since she didn't trust him to do more than carry over whichever pot she pointed to and then spread mulch when and where she told him to.

Being surrounded by so much pink made it impossible to put the morning out of his mind because every flower made him think of a ten-year-old Emma wanting to marry a guy wearing a pink shirt.

That thought invariably led to thoughts of a very grown-up Emma sliding between the sheets, her long leg brushing against his thigh and making him think all kinds of naughty things. Luckily, the steamy thoughts of pulling her body, still warm from sleep, up against his had fled when her grandmother walked into the room. Residual desire had remained, though, even while they went on about that stupid box, so it was a damn good thing Emma had jumped out of bed to shut off her alarm.

The whole thing seemed wrong to him somehow, though, the more he thought about it. Cat didn't seem like the kind of woman to work herself into such a tizzy over finding a box that she had to burst in on them before they were out of bed. Excitement at the breakfast table, sure, but she'd been too respectful of their fake need for privacy for her actions to make any sense.

"I think Cat's onto us."

Emma sat back on her heels and brushed dirt off her gloves. "What makes you think that?"

"Just a feeling." He couldn't really explain it. "The way she watches us sometimes. And coming into our room at twenty after six? That didn't seem suspicious to you?"

"She was excited." But that excuse was weak and she knew it. "Gram would say something if she thought I was lying to her."

"Maybe not. Maybe she wants to figure out what we're up to."

She seemed to consider his comment for a moment, then she shook her head. "I don't think she could keep quiet about it. But, just in case she's suspicious, we'll have to step it up."

Step it up? If they stepped it up any more, his balls were going to explode. "What do you mean by that, exactly?"

"I don't know. Maybe…more touching or something?"

"No." He hadn't meant to say that out loud, but he meant it. He couldn't take any more touching. "I mean, I don't think that's the problem."

Actually, touching was exactly the problem, but not in the way she was thinking. He was horny, plain and simple, and the constant touching and looking and pretending was killing him. Slowly and seemingly without end.

The nights were the worst. Emma was a restless sleeper and he was a light sleeper and the combination made for a constant state of low-grade sleep deprivation. The sight of her dark curls spread across her pillow and her long legs kicked free of the blanket made for a constant state of high-grade lust.

"What do you think *is* the problem, then?"

He shook his head. "Forget it. Probably just my imagination."

When she pushed herself to her feet and stretched, he tried not to watch, but he couldn't look away. He knew being bent over the garden was hell on the muscles, but the way she put her hands to the back of her waist and arched her back—which pushed out her breasts—was hell on his self-control.

"How come you didn't tell me about your aunt and uncle's big holiday bash?"

"Because you'd just worry about it and stress, and

it's only Monday. I thought I'd wait until Friday to bring it up."

"Gee, thanks."

"Have you talked to Cat about the house yet?"

She shook her head. "I keep hoping she'll bring it up, but she hasn't. And it never seems like the right time."

"If you let her go back to Florida without selling you the house, this was all for nothing, you know."

"Yes, I know," she snapped. "I know it doesn't seem that way, but I don't *like* lying to my grand-mother this way, and now that the time has come, I'm finding it hard to bring up the house."

His phone rang and he pulled it out of his pocket to look at the caller-ID window. "Shit."

"Who is it?"

"My sister. Sorry, I have to take it or she'll keep calling back." He flipped open the phone as he put a little space between him and Emma. "Hi, Liz."

"You're an idiot."

"I miss you, too."

"Tell me Mitch is full of shit."

"He usually is."

Her sigh practically vibrated his phone. "Are you living with some woman you just met and pretending to be her fiancé?"

"Yup."

"Does that seem normal to you?"

"I never claimed it was normal. It's pretty crazy, actually, but we're making it work." More or less. Other than an unexpected case of blue balls, it was going better than he would have guessed it would.

"And Aunt Mary's going along with this?"

"Reluctantly, but yes."

"I can't make it, but Mitch is going to be there for the Fourth. If he tells me he thinks this woman's up to no good, I'm going to sic Rosie on you."

"Nobody's up to no good, Liz, and we're not hurting anybody. I promise."

"We'll see what Mitch has to say." He heard a voice in the background and what sounded like a door slamming. "I have to run. I'll call you next week, after I talk to Mitch."

"Thanks for the warning," he said, but she'd already hung up.

He shoved his phone back in his pocket and smiled at Emma. "She sends her regards."

"I bet. She's not coming here, is she?"

"Not for the party. If Mitch reports back that I've fallen into the clutches of an evil, scheming temptress, she'll be here. Otherwise, she doesn't come home much."

Emma knelt in front of the garden bed and went back to planting pink flowers. "You said she lives in New Mexico. What does she do?"

"She waits tables at a truck stop to support the

deadbeat artist wannabe who swept her off her feet and talked her into dropping out of college when she was nineteen."

"Oh. I guess that's not a happy story."

"No. But she's as stubborn as all four of us boys put together and I think she stays with him just so she won't have to admit our old man was right."

"Even though he passed away almost a decade ago? That's…stubborn."

"That's Liz." He scowled at the mulch she pushed in his direction. "We've all tried to talk some sense into her and we've had a few chats with him, too, but she won't leave him."

"Are they married?"

He snorted. "No. Asshole's too much of a free spirit to embrace government regulation of their relation-ship."

"One of those, huh?"

"Yeah. She'll get tired of his shit eventually. I hope."

"So none of you are married?"

"Nope. Liz has been wasting her time with her deadbeat for thirteen years. Ryan's divorced. And Mitch, Josh and I are too hard to pin down."

"You mean you haven't found women willing to put up with *your* shit yet."

He laughed. "Pretty much."

Of course, he hadn't been looking too hard, either.

But he imagined when it was time to look—way down the road—he'd probably fall for somebody like Emma. She was smart and funny and loyal to her family. And, unlike a lot of women, she didn't take any of his crap.

Sure, she had some annoying habits. Like those little moaning sounds she made in her sleep. And she could be a bit of a smart-ass. The cleaning thing, of course. She'd taken a toothbrush to his sneakers the other night and they weren't even really broken in yet.

But, overall, if the urge to settle down ever struck him, he wouldn't mind a woman like Emma.

"It's all a sham?" Russell leaned against his counter, shaking his head. "The living together? The engagement? All a lie?"

"Yes." Cat sighed. It was a little embarrassing to admit Emma would resort to such an elaborate scheme to protect her peace of mind. But she'd told him the whole thing, anyway, including her conversation with Mary Kowalski, while he chuckled.

"She must really love you to go to all that trouble," he said when she was through, and Cat smiled.

"I guess you're right. She's a good girl, even if she did think I'd fall for this." But she hadn't worked up her courage and come into town to talk about Emma. "You owe me a dance, Russell Walker."

He gave her a sheepish smile. "I'm keeping my

eye out for a nice place to take you. Heard there's a chem-free graduation fundraiser dance Saturday after next at the high school for the older crowd. It won't be fancy, but it's close and for a good cause."

"That might be nice."

"So it's a date, then?"

A date? What the heck was she doing dating at her age? "It's a date."

"Good. Are you and the kids doing anything for the Fourth?"

"We're going to spend the day with the Kowalskis and then all go over and watch the fireworks go off over the big lake."

He nodded. "Dani and her husband, Roger, always do that, too."

Cat picked up the bag of clearance gardening tools she'd bought just to have an excuse to stop at the hardware store. "If you go with them, maybe I'll see you there."

"Maybe you will. Where are you off to now?"

"I'm driving down to Concord to meet Mary Kowalski for lunch."

"Those poor kids don't stand a chance, do they?"

She laughed. "Nope."

Mary was already waiting at the fancy café they'd chosen because it was unlikely to attract any of the other family members and they could have a friendly lunch. Cat was older than her, of course, but not by much. She'd had Johnny young, and Johnny and his wife had been young when they had Emma.

Mary had gotten them a pitcher of water, but they both asked for tea to go with the salads they reluctantly ordered. With all the barbecuing going on, they had to be good when they had the chance. Cat still had guilt over the hash-and-cheese omelet and it had been almost a week.

They chatted about family and the weather until the salads arrived, and then Mary broached the subject of Sean and Emma. "How are things going between them?"

"I found out she sleeps on the couch in the bedroom. When I knocked on the door, I could hear her crossing the room to get into the bed before she called me to come in. And her phone, which she uses as an alarm clock, was plugged in next to the couch, too."

"I'm surprised they've managed to resist each other this long."

Cat nodded and drizzled a low-calorie dressing over her salad. "Me, too. I'm not sure why they're trying so hard, actually. Did you tell anybody I've figured out their little scheme?"

"No. I can't be sure none of them will tell Sean. Or that Lisa won't tell Emma. I haven't even told Leo, so it's just between us."

"It's going to be fun watching my granddaughter pretend Mitch isn't a total stranger to her."

"Having him here this weekend will help push Sean over the edge."

"You think so?"

Mary smiled. "Mitch is quite the ladies' man. There's also a betting pool they think I don't know anything about, and they don't want Sean to win. Once Mitch starts flirting with Emma, we'll find out in a hurry how Sean really feels about her."

"I hope you're right. They definitely need a nudge."

"Trust me. I know my boys."

CHAPTER ELEVEN

SATURDAY ROLLED AROUND and Emma knew she was in trouble when a slightly taller and older version of Sean spotted her across the Kowalskis' big backyard.

He grinned and started toward her. "Emma!"

When he picked her up off her feet—which was no easy feat considering how tall she was—and spun her around, she clutched his shoulders. "Mitch...hi."

Thank goodness only one of his brothers could come. Not only because there were fewer people to keep track of, but because there was a much better chance this actually *was* Mitch.

"Laying it on a little thick?" she heard Sean mutter.

"Can't help it," Mitch said, setting her back on her feet. "My future sister-in-law's quite the looker, you lucky bastard."

Sean made a snorting sound, but she couldn't tell if it was directed at the fact he'd called her his future sister-in-law, that she was a looker or that he was a lucky bastard, so she ignored him.

She'd noticed right off Mitch was a little taller and older than Sean, but his eyes were a little darker shade of blue and his hair was longer and scruffier. And he was leaner, too, though still pretty well built.

She jumped when Sean slid his arm around her waist and put his face close to hers. "Stop ogling my brother."

"He's taller than you."

"Older, too."

"Maybe, but what's a few years?" When he made a growling sound, she laughed and elbowed him in the side. "You're not jealous, are you?"

"Of Mitch? Please."

"I could totally take you, little brother," Mitch said. "Now, introduce me to your future grandmother-in-law so I can go back to my beer."

Emma mingled and laughed and ate too much and laughed some more as the day went on. Everybody was relaxed and nobody seemed particularly interested in watching her and Sean—or in pushing his buttons with wedding talk—so she relaxed, too.

She was licking a Fudgsicle stick clean when her grandmother dragged a chair close to hers and sat down. "Hi, Gram. Having fun?"

"I'm having a blast. Sean has a very nice family. And they really like you."

"I like them, too," she said, and it wasn't a lie. It was hard not to like them, even when they were giving her and Sean a hard time.

"I've been thinking about it and I'm going to give you the house as a wedding present."

All the food and the cookies and the chips and the ice cream she'd eaten turned over in Emma's stomach. "No, Gram."

"Yes. It's pretty clear you've made it your home, and I want you to have it. Your grandfather wanted you to have it, too. We'd talked about it before he passed away."

"I want it, too, Gram, but I want to *buy* it. It's worth too much for you to just give it to me."

Gram scoffed at her words. "That monster's been paid off forever. There's no sense in putting another mortgage on it now. I've got enough money to keep me happy, and you've got a business to keep going."

Emma struggled not to cry. She wanted the house. And she'd been willing to buy it under iffy circumstances. But she couldn't let Gram give it to her as a wedding present when there wasn't going to be a wedding.

She took a deep breath. "Gram, I—"

Bobby ran up on the deck and skidded to a stop in front of them. "It's time for the Kowalski Fourth of July Football Game of Doom!"

Cat laughed and pushed herself out of her seat. "We'll talk about this some other time, Emma. Go have fun."

"I'm not sure I want to play football. Especially if

there's doom involved," she said, but Bobby grabbed her hand and dragged her off the deck.

They were divvied up into teams roughly by size, each with an assortment of men, women and children. Emma was on Sean's team, which was good. She'd just hide behind him, because the only thing she knew about football was that it involved a lot of hitting.

It only took a few plays to see that the Kowalskis played by their own rules and the few they had were fluid. Mostly they served to ensure the smaller kids didn't get plowed over, victims of the adults' competitive streak.

Five minutes into the game, Emma somehow ended up with the ball. She squealed and looked around for somebody—anybody—to hand it off to, but there was nobody. Well, there was Danny, but he was doubled over in laughter.

"Run, Emma," Lisa yelled.

She ran in the direction her friend was frantically waving her hand, but she only went a few feet before two very strong arms wrapped around her waist and then she was falling. Luckily, she landed on a body instead of the ground.

"I love football," Mitch said, grinning up at her.

Emma grimaced and managed to get one of her knees on solid ground so she could push herself to her feet. He was quicker and freed himself to stand and help her up.

"They should give you the ball more often," he said, his blue eyes sparkling and the grin so like Sean's—but not quite as naughty—in full force.

"Hands off my girl," Sean told him, pulling on Emma's elbow.

"You should do a better job of blocking for her."

"Let's go," Brian shouted.

The very next play, Mitch intercepted Mike's pass to Evan and turned to run toward the other end zone. He was halfway there when Sean took him down hard. They hit the ground with a bone-jarring thud that made Emma wince, and came up pushing and shoving.

When Sean drew back his arm to throw the first punch, Mary blew her whistle from the sidelines. "Boys! Enough!"

Instead of heading straight for the huddle, Sean walked to Emma and pulled her into his arms for a hard, almost punishing caveman kiss that made her skin sizzle and her knees go wobbly. Then he glared at his brother for a few long seconds and went back to his team, leaving Emma standing there breathless and discombobulated.

Lisa was staring at her. So were Terry and Beth and Keri. All with raised-eyebrow speculation that made her want to bolt for a hiding place. So what if Sean had gone all Neanderthal on her? It didn't mean anything. It wasn't as if he'd staked a claim. It was probably just an instinctual reaction to his older brother flirting with the woman he'd brought to the party. That had to be it.

A few plays later, Emma ended up with the ball again. There seemed to be some kind of unspoken rule that everybody got a chance to make a play, even if they sucked. She was going to run, but then she saw Stephanie bearing down on her with that killer Kowalski spirit in her eyes and tossed the ball up in the air.

Mitch—who hadn't touched her since his first misguided tackle—snatched it out of the air and ran it back for a touchdown, much to the vocal dismay of her teammates.

"You play football even worse than you drive," Sean muttered.

"Clearly, it's my lack of—"

He yanked her back against his body and wrapped his arms around her so he could whisper in her ear. "Don't you dare say it."

She laughed and leaned back against his chest. "Don't say what?"

"If you mention the magic penis in front of these guys, I'll never hear the end of it. Never. Hell, fifty years from now when our dicks are shriveled up and useless, they'll still be cracking magic-penis jokes."

"What's it worth to you?"

He tightened his arms around her and nuzzled her hair. "What are you looking to get?"

She turned her head so her lips were almost touching his cheek and dropped her voice down into the sexy bedroom range. "I want…to drive home."

He snorted. "Figures."

"Just imagine Mike all old and decrepit and toothless and leaning on his walker cackling and shouting, 'Hey, Sean, how's the magic penis hanging?'"

"Okay, you win. You can drive."

"You gonna play or what?" Leo shouted at them.

Sean let go of her and headed back toward the ball, but as Emma looked over at the sidelines and debated making a break for it, she saw Mary watching her with what looked like a rather smug smile curving her lips.

Emma wasn't sure exactly what that could mean, but she wasn't sure she wanted to know, either, so she forced herself to rejoin her team. They were in a huddle, discussing a play that, thankfully, didn't seem to include her, but she listened, anyway. And jumped when the huddle broke up and Sean slapped her on the ass.

His brother flirting with her had really brought out the touchy-feely in him, she mused as Terry ran past her with the ball.

"Emma, take her down," Terry's husband shouted,

but it was too late. And she wasn't stupid. Tackling Terry would hurt.

The score was either twenty-one to forty-two or tied at thirty-five, depending on who you asked, when Mary blew the whistle. "Time to clean up and get ready for the fireworks. Kids, make sure you go to the bathroom *before* we leave this year."

Maybe it was only because Mitch was nearby and Mary had her eye on them, but Emma didn't pull away when Sean took her hand in his for the walk into the house.

IT WAS ALMOST DUSK before the horde of Kowalskis got themselves settled on a patchwork island of old quilts. Cat staked her claim on one corner by setting down her bag and the straw hat she'd worn earlier to keep the sun off her face. Then she wandered away to see who she could run into.

She stopped here and there, saying hello to a few friends, but when she saw Russell Walker sitting on one of the park benches, she was forced to admit to herself she'd been looking for him. He was alone, so she took a deep breath to steady her ridiculous school-girl nerves and walked over.

"Is this seat taken?"

His face brightened when he saw her and he patted the empty bench next to him. "I was sitting on a blanket with Dani and her husband, but I'm a little old for that."

"Emma and I are with Sean's family, but I thought I'd go for a walk and put off sitting on the ground for as long as possible."

"Would they be upset at all if you stayed here with me?"

With the number of people on the Kowalskis' acre of blankets, they probably wouldn't even notice she was gone. "Probably not."

"Do you care if they are?"

She smiled and shook her head. "Not really, no."

And speaking of Emma, there she came, obviously looking for her. She waved her hand to get her attention and didn't miss the surprise that crossed Emma's face.

"Hi, Mr. Walker. We were starting to think Gram got lost."

"I think I'm going to watch the fireworks with Russell."

"Oh." Cat watched Emma try to wrap her mind around that. "Okay."

"You look lovely tonight," Russell said. "Clearly, love agrees with you."

Because she was looking for it, Cat saw the flash of guilt in Emma's eyes before she smiled and couldn't resist poking at her. "Russell tells me he hasn't met Sean yet."

"No. He...uh...Sean's not much of a shopper. And he goes down to the stores in the city when he needs stuff so he can visit his aunt and uncle at the same time."

At least the girl was consistent. Cat wondered if she'd made up cue cards. "You'll have to bring him over after the fireworks."

"Yeah. Maybe. So...have fun."

She walked away, but Cat caught her looking back with a frown, as if trying to puzzle out why her Gram was choosing to watch the fireworks with the guy who owned the hardware store instead of with her family.

Then they fired a test shot, and Cat put Emma out of her mind as the burst lit up the darkening sky.

They oohed and aahed along with the rest of the crowd, and as the show built toward the grand finale, Russell's hand bumped hers. It rested there for a moment and then he threaded his fingers through hers.

"WHERE'S CAT?"

Emma sighed and looked toward where she'd found Gram and Russell Walker, even though it was too dark to see them. "She ran into a friend. She's sitting on the bench with him, over by the trees."

"Him?"

"Yeah. Russell Walker, who owns the hardware store."

Sean shrugged. "Probably beats sitting on the ground."

With her grandmother watching the fireworks with Russell, Emma was free to put a little space between her and Sean on their part of an old, gaily colored quilt. Not too much space, of course, because there were a lot of Kowalskis and they had to keep the kids spread farther apart than jabbing elbows could reach.

"Need a Valium?" Sean leaned over to ask in a low voice.

"No. Why?"

"You spin that engagement ring around on your finger when you're stressed, and right now, it looks like you're trying to generate electricity with it."

Emma locked her fingers together and hooked her clasped hands over her drawn-up knees. Stressed? Why would she be stressed? Her body was still humming from that caveman kiss during the football game, her grandmother had ditched her for Mr. Walker from the hardware store, and she couldn't make sense of either event.

It wasn't for lack of trying. Her mind raced, trying to sort it all out, as colors burst above her in the dark sky. Maybe Sean was right and Gram had simply taken a seat on the bench next to Mr. Walker because she didn't want to sit on the ground. And maybe Sean had only kissed her because he thought that's what a man in love would do when his older brother was flirting with his fiancée. All very innocent.

But she'd been watching Sean pretend to be in love with her for two weeks, and while he didn't do too badly, she didn't think he had the acting chops to fake the primal, possessive gleam in his eye right before he'd claimed her mouth.

Sean scooted a little closer, probably so his mouth could be near her ear. The discretion, she appreciated. His warm breath against her skin, not so much. "You're not even trying to enjoy this, are you?"

"I am, too." She enjoyed the feel of his shoulder pressing against hers. And the way he smelled. And the way the fireworks kept lighting up his face.

He didn't seem inclined to say any more, but he didn't move away, either, so they watched the fireworks and laughed at the kids, who were oohing and aahing with exaggerated exuberance. They were all decked out in glowing neon bracelets and necklaces, and they were as lively and vivid as a Vegas show.

After a while, Emma shifted her weight, trying to find a reasonably comfortable position on the hard ground. It wasn't easy, until Sean pulled her close and she rested against his chest. It was very comfy… physically. Played hell on her senses, though, and she was surprised—and not in a good way—to find herself wishing Gram was with them on the blanket so

Sean would have an excuse to wrap his arms around her and kiss the back of her neck.

She was starting to wish Sean had excuses to do a *lot* of things to her. Especially things he couldn't do in front of Gram.

They were only halfway through the month, and she'd spent so much time wondering what sex with Sean would be like, she was afraid someday soon he was going to touch her and she'd burst into spontaneous orgasm. The trip from the bathroom to the couch every night was the worst, requiring her full concentration. She didn't trust her body not to hang a right and climb into bed with him.

"What are you thinking about now?" Sean whispered against her ear, and she cursed under her breath. She really had to stop thinking about sex near him.

"I'm thinking about all those cakes and pies waiting at your aunt's house," she lied.

He chuckled, the sound almost masked by the fireworks. "I had no idea desserts had that effect on you. I'll have to remember that."

Rather than deal with the implied promise in those words and the husky bedroom voice it was implied in, she turned her face away and ignored him. But she couldn't ignore the aching need he'd brought back to the surface. *I'll have to remember that.*

When the last loud and colorful bursts of the grand finale lit up the sky over the lake, the Kowalski family clapped and cheered, then started gathering their things. In just the short time they'd been on the quilts, it looked as if the family had taken up residence, with drink bottles and snack wrappers and toys spread all over the place. Sean pushed himself to his feet and then held out his hands to her.

She hesitated to touch him, which was dumb. He was a gentleman, so of course he'd help her up. The fact she was still all shivery and freaked out on the inside from the kiss earlier was her problem, not his.

Once on her feet, she withdrew her hands as quickly as she could, then looked down at her grandmother's hat and bag. "Gram wanted me to bring you over after the fireworks. To introduce you to Mr. Walker, I guess."

"Does it bother you?"

"Introducing you?"

He shook his head and pulled her off the quilt because Terry was trying to fold them up. "That she watched the fireworks with him."

The mature thing to do would be to scoff at the suggestion she was bothered by her grandmother having a friend, but she couldn't quite pull it off. Not with him watching her so intently. "I don't know. I didn't see it coming, that's for sure. Where did Mitch go?"

"Blonde. Over by the grandstand."

She turned to look and saw Mitch talking to a

pretty blonde woman in a skimpy yellow sundress. She had the kind of primped and polished look that implied she'd shown up alone solely for the purpose of finding a man to take her home. "He doesn't waste any time."

Sean snorted, and she couldn't tell if the look he gave his brother was annoyance with the ladies'-man routine or annoyance he wasn't free to find his own sure thing in a skimpy sundress.

Before she could figure it out, Gram showed up with Russell Walker in tow and behind him a couple who looked younger than what her parents would have been, but not by much.

"Emma," Gram said, "this is Russell's daughter, Dani, and her husband, Roger. This is my grand-daughter, Emma, and her fiancé, Sean."

Emma smiled and shook hands, and then kept smiling as the introductions continued around her. Inside, though, her brain was going numb. Performance exhaustion, she told herself. It was tiring, all this pretending, and she wanted to go home and make Sean crash on the couch so she could curl up in her bed and sleep. But at least this night was almost over.

"If you're not doing anything," Mary said to Russell and the others, "you should come back with us and have dessert."

Or maybe not.

CHAPTER TWELVE

SEAN WAS GOING TO KILL his cousins. Slowly. Painfully. And he'd kick the crap out of both of them first.

They'd all gone back to his aunt and uncle's after the fireworks, as expected. What wasn't expected was Cat introducing Russell and his daughter, Dani, and her husband, Roger, to the Kowalskis, who then invited them along for post-fireworks decaf and dessert.

After the pies and cakes were demolished, Mike and Lisa had taken their boys home and the two babies, Lily and Brianna, were asleep, so the older generation decided on some card game nobody under forty knew how to play. So the under-forty crowd had retreated to the rec room in the basement, except Mitch, who'd said his goodbyes before he left the fireworks with the gorgeous blonde in the barely there sundress.

Joe had a perfect game to pass the time, he'd said. Kevin had smirked and agreed. And there were four couples, so it was perfect. Sean should have known better.

The reason having four couples was perfect, he found out too late, was because the game was a kind of demented adult version of *The Newlywed Game*. And now Joe and Kevin were laughing their asses off on the inside because Dani and Roger's presence meant Sean and Emma had to keep up the pretense or Dani would tell her dad, who would in turn rat them out to Cat.

"'What's the first place you had sex?'" Roger read from a card.

Dani hit the timer and six of them bent over their notepads, furiously scribbling down answers. Sean looked down at his blank page and decided to keep it simple. Hopefully, Emma would do the same.

When the timer dinged, he tossed his pencil down. Joe and Keri scored the first point by both writing, *In the backseat of Joe's 1979 Ford Granada.* For Kevin and Beth it was the hotel where Joe and Keri's wedding reception was held, and Dani and Roger both wrote, *Dani's dorm room.*

Emma grimaced at Sean and then held up her notepad. "'On a quilt, under the flowering dogwood.'"

The other women made sweet *awww* noises, but Joe and Kevin were already snickering. That wasn't keeping it simple. Under a flowering dogwood?

"We need your answer," Roger said.

Sean held up his paper. "'In a bed.'"

His cousins' snickers became full belly laughs, while Dani and Roger just looked a little confused.

"Oh," Emma said. "You meant sex with *each other?*"

It was a nice save, but Sean had a gut feeling it was only going to go downhill from here. And since he and Emma would be lucky if they got out of there with their secret intact, never mind having a snowball's chance in hell of winning, he might as well have some fun with it.

Then came Dani's turn to read a question. "'Who's in charge in the bedroom?'"

Much to the group's amusement, none of them got a match, and Sean didn't think they would either as he held up his notepad. "'I am, since I carry the big stick.'"

Emma read hers with a remarkably straight face. "'Sean, because he has a magic penis.'"

"Wow. Um…so Sean and Emma have a point," Dani said as the men nearly pissed themselves laughing.

No way in hell was he leaving that unpunished, and he winked at Emma when Kevin read the next question. "'Where's the kinkiest place you've had sex?'"

The fact that Joe and Keri had done the dirty deed on the back of his ATV led to a few questions about the logistics of that, but then it was Emma's turn. "'In bed, because Sean has no imagination.'"

Roger threw an embarrassed wince his way, but his cousins weren't shy about laughing their asses off.

Sean just shrugged and held up his notepad. "In the car in the mall parking lot. Emma's lying because she doesn't want anybody to know being watched turns her on."

Her jaw dropped, but she recovered quickly and gave him a sweet smile that didn't jibe with the "you are so going to get it" look in her eyes.

Beth asked the next question. "'Women, where does your man secretly dream of having sex?'"

Keri knew Joe wanted to have sex in the reportedly very haunted Stanley Hotel, from King's *The Shining*. Dani claimed Roger wanted to do the deed on a Caribbean beach, but he said that was her fantasy and that his was to have sex in an igloo. No amount of heckling could get him to say why. And when it came to Kevin, even Sean knew he dreamed of getting laid on the pitcher's mound at Fenway Park.

Then, God help him, it was Emma's turn to show her answer. "'In a Burger King bathroom.'"

The room fell silent until Dani said, "Ew. Really?"

"No, not really," Sean growled.

"Really," Emma said over him. "He knows that's the only way he can slip me a whopper."

As the room erupted in laughter, Sean knew humor was the only way they'd get through the evening with their secret intact, but he didn't find that one very funny, himself.

It was the final answer that really did him in, though. The question: "If your sex had a motto, what would it be?"

Joe and Keri's was, not surprisingly, *Don't wake the baby.* Kevin and Beth both wrote, *Better than chocolate cake,* whatever that was supposed to mean. Dani wrote, *Gets better with time, like fine wine,* and Roger wrote, *Like cheese, the older you get, the better it is,* which led to a powwow about whether or not to give them a point. They probably would have gotten it if they weren't tied with Keri and Joe, who took *competitive* to a cutthroat level.

When they all looked at Sean, he groaned and turned his paper around. They'd lost any chance of winning way back, but he was already dreading what the smart-ass he wasn't really engaged to had written down. "'She's the boss.'"

The look Emma gave him as she slowly turned the notepad around gave him advance warning she was about to lay down the royal flush in this little game they'd been playing.

"'Size really *doesn't* matter,'" she said in what sounded to him like a really loud voice.

Before he could say anything—and he had no idea what was going to come out of his mouth, but he had to say *something*—Cat appeared at the top of the stairs.

"I hate to break up the party," she said, "but it's getting late, so we're calling it a night."

Maybe Cat was, but Sean was just getting started.

IF GRAM WASN'T IN THE TRUCK, Emma would have given Sean a ride home he'd never forget. As it was, she pushed it a little, enjoying his sucked-in breaths and the way his foot kept reaching for a brake pedal he didn't have.

Because it was so late, Gram went right to bed, and Sean followed her up the stairs. By the time Emma was done locking up, she heard snoring coming from her grandmother's room as she paused on her way by.

Sean wasn't snoring, but he was already in bed. He was on his back with his hands tucked under his head, scowling at the ceiling. Rather than give him time to grumble at her for driving like a girl, she went straight into the bathroom to clean up and get ready for bed.

In her hurry, though, she'd forgotten to grab her pajamas, which was a dilemma. She could either go out and get them and return to the bathroom to change, or she could go out there and put them on. If Sean didn't like it, he didn't have to watch.

After leaving the bathroom, she turned off the overhead light in the bedroom, but it didn't do much good. The night was clear, the moon was bright, and she knew she was all too visible when she undid her jeans and shimmied them down over her hips.

"What the hell are you doing?"

"Changing into my pajamas."

"You always do that in the bathroom." His voice was low and rough, but she noticed he didn't look away.

"I forgot them, and there's no point in going back in there." She kicked off the jeans and was going to pull on the shorts before changing shirts, but then she remembered his stupid answers to the stupid questions in that game and changed her mind.

"The point is that you don't do it in front of me."

"Oh, did you forget? Being watched turns me on." And she pulled her T-shirt over her head.

She had to bite down on a surprised yelp once she was free of it because suddenly Sean was standing in front of her, wearing nothing but blue boxer briefs and a scowl. "You said I had no imagination."

"And having no imagination is *so* much worse than your best friend's family thinking you're an exhibitionist."

"And we're not ever going to talk about the other thing you said. Ever."

He was crowding her personal space, so she put her hands on his chest to push him back, but he caught her wrists. Standing there with her palms pressed against his naked skin, she could feel his heart beating at a quickened pace that matched her own and she knew she had two choices. Walk away or end up in bed with him.

She leaned her body a little closer and splayed her fingers across his chest. "Which thing aren't we talking about? The fast-food-joint bathroom or—"

"Don't push me too far, Emma. It's been a long time for me."

"How long?"

"Too damn long." He lifted her hands from his chest, but didn't let go of her wrists. "And I never even got to scope out the dating situation here before you showed up at my door with this half-assed scheme."

"And since we... You haven't..."

"The last thing I need is to get caught cheating on a woman I can't tell anybody I'm not really in a relationship with." His gaze dropped from her face to her lacy white bra and he sighed. "You're killing me."

"Lying awake on the couch every night, wondering what it would be like to slide into bed with you has been killing me for two weeks."

"Yeah." He let go of her wrists and slid his hands up the back of her neck and into her hair. "I've thought about that, too. A lot. Pretty much constantly, actually."

"We're two single adults. There's no reason we have to suffer."

He was pulling her slowly closer, his fingertips still massaging the back of her skull, and she was starting to lose patience with the talking. She wanted more doing.

Sean apparently hadn't turned that page yet. "This won't change anything, Emma, so I don't want you getting any ideas. The day we drive Cat to the airport, I'm moving on. This isn't...real."

"The orgasms will be real, right?"

"Very real. And numerous."

"I'll take it."

With a deep, guttural groan, Sean pulled her face to his and claimed her mouth. It was a hard and demanding kiss, the way he'd kissed her on the makeshift football field earlier, but there was nothing quick about it. His tongue flicked across hers as one hand tightened in her hair.

With the other hand, he pulled her hips against his, and she felt hard evidence she'd been so very, very wrong to imply he wasn't blessed below the waist.

Her hands slid from his chest to his shoulders and then to his back, holding him to her because she never wanted him to stop kissing her. Then she squeezed him, holding tight as he reached down the backs of her thighs and lifted her so she could wrap her legs around his waist.

A moment later he had her on the bed, his body covering hers and his erection nestled between her legs. She lifted her hips, urging him to get on with it, but he didn't seem to be in much of a hurry for a guy who said it had been a long time.

Then he lifted his head and looked down into her face. "Before we go any further, one more thing."

She groaned. "Seriously?"

"One wisecrack about a magic penis," he warned, "and I don't care if I have to dump ice cubes down my pants, I'll walk away. Bowlegged, probably, but I'll walk."

She laughed and slid her hands under her back to undo her bra. "I'll try to contain myself."

Sean slid the straps free of her arms and flung the bra aside before lowering his mouth to her breasts. When he drew her nipple into his mouth and sucked gently, she moaned and ground her hips against his.

He gave the same attention to her other breast, then lifted his head so he could see her face. He was panting a little—they both were—and he gave her a sheepish grin.

"As much as I'd love to wow you with my stamina and imagination, maybe we could do that tomorrow night."

She wrapped her legs around his calves, running her foot up his leg. "Tomorrow night? You're not getting any ideas, are you?"

"I have ideas about what I'd like to do to you tomorrow night. Right now there's a little…urgency, if you know what I mean."

"I know exactly what you mean." She tugged down on her panties, and Sean moved so he could pull them all the way off before reaching into her nightstand drawer and pulling out a condom.

"Hey. You put condoms in my nightstand?"

"I'm an optimist." Then he stood and dropped his boxer briefs and Emma got optimistic, too.

When he lowered himself over her again, Emma wrapped her legs around his hips, urging him forward. He resisted, lowering his head to give her another blistering kiss before settling between her thighs.

And, holy hell, he was everything she'd thought he'd be during the last two weeks' worth of restless nights. He filled her with excruciatingly slow strokes until her nails dug into his back and she was whimpering, begging for more in barely coherent, fractured sentences.

When he hooked his arm under her right knee and then drove even more deeply into her, she sucked in a hard breath and moaned his name.

"Shh," he whispered, and then he did it again.

There was no way she could be quiet. Not when she wanted to yell at him to do it faster and harder, so she twisted her body around and he caught the hint pretty quickly. Then she was on her knees, her weight resting on her forearms as she buried her face in his pillow.

Sean's fingers bit into her hips as he drove into her, each stroke a little harder than the one before. She moaned into the pillow, clutching the pillowcase in her fists as the very real orgasm shook her body.

Sean groaned, his hand squeezing her hips as he shuddered and drove into her a few final times. Then he collapsed on top of her, stretching her body out flat against the mattress.

Turning her head so she wouldn't suffocate in the pillow, Emma sucked in air and basked in the heat of his heavy, trembling body. He kissed the back of her neck and started to lift himself, but then he collapsed again.

"Just another minute," he murmured into her hair.

"Mmm." She didn't have words yet, but if she did she'd tell him she didn't want him to move. She was content just the way they were.

He got up after a minute to go into the bathroom, and on his way back, he grabbed her pillow off the couch and tossed it onto the bed. "Get over. You're on my side of the bed."

"It's my bed," she muttered, already half-asleep. "You don't have a side."

"Get over."

She got over, but only because she didn't want to ruin the glow with bickering. And once he'd gotten in on *his* side of her bed and pulled her close again, she didn't really care.

"That was amazing," he whispered.

"Magic."

She yelped when he slapped her ass, but he was chuckling when he wrapped his arm around her and nuzzled his face in her hair. She was still smiling as she fell asleep.

SEAN WOKE TO THE SOUND of a phone going off. For a few seconds he was confused because it was Sunday, so Emma's alarm shouldn't go off. Then he realized his cell phone was ringing on the nightstand.

At the same time he also realized Emma had rolled to face him during the night and the blankets had slipped down, and, damn, she had nice breasts. But she was stirring, probably because his phone was ringing, so he stopped staring and answered it.

"What?"

"I'd say I hope I didn't wake you, but I'm guessing I did." It was Mitch and he didn't sound too sorry about it.

"It's seven o'clock on a Sunday, asshole. Of course you woke me up."

And he'd also woken Emma up, and Sean sighed in disappointment when she slid out of bed, grabbed her clothes and went into the bathroom. Not the way he'd envisioned their waking up when he'd been drifting off to sleep last night.

"I need a favor," Mitch said.

"Call Triple-A."

"You're my brother."

Sean swung his feet to the floor and scrubbed at his face. "What's up?"

"My rental car has a dead battery and they can't do anything about it until midafternoon. And April doesn't have a car."

"April. Oh, wait…is that the blonde's name?"

"Yeah. I need you to come get me and drive me to the airport."

"Call a cab."

"I tried. This ain't Boston, dude. The soonest I can get a taxi here that'll take me to Manchester is ten minutes after I have to *be* in Manchester. I just need a ride. The rental company's going to come get their shitbox."

"Fine. How do I get to April's house?"

By the time he'd scrawled directions on a sticky note and promised his brother he was as good as on his way, Emma was on her way out of the bedroom, leaving flower-scented shower steam in her wake. He thought about calling her back, but he didn't have a clue what he'd say, so he went into the bathroom to see if she'd left him any hot water.

Before he went downstairs, he pulled out his

Sharpie and stuck a fresh sticky note on the mirror. *Btw, THAT was my favorite sexual position.* He almost added a happy face to it, but decided just in time that would be lame. It was a slippery slope that led nowhere but to dotting his *i*'s with hearts.

When he went into the kitchen and found a plate of scrambled eggs and bacon at his seat, he looked at the clock and decided Mitch could cool his heels for a few more minutes.

Emma was an unusual flurry of activity, all of it seeming to require she not look at him. She buttered toast and put the juice away and spent a few minutes wiping up an invisible coffee spill, from what he could tell. Maybe it was the fact her grandmother was in the room, but she seemed a little embarrassed that they'd had sex last night.

Great sex. Sex he wasn't embarrassed about at all and hoped to do again as soon as bedtime rolled around. Only, an extended version this time, like a director's cut. He could add back in all the parts of his performance he'd had to cut to fit the time slot his long-neglected sex drive had given him.

For now, he had to deal with Mitch. After shoveling down his breakfast in record time, he rinsed his plate and kissed Cat's cheek. "I hate to eat and run, but my brother needs a ride to the airport."

When he went to kiss Emma goodbye, as he always did because that's what a fiancé would do, he half expected her to shy away. Instead, when his mouth met hers, she flicked her tongue over his bottom lip and gave him a look that promised they'd be putting his imagination to good use later.

He found April's house with no problem and sat in his truck while Mitch kissed her goodbye in the doorway. And then kissed her goodbye again, and so thoroughly Sean finally tapped on the horn to break up the party.

The blonde was smiling and waving as they pulled out of sight, and Sean shook his head. Not only would she never see Mitch Kowalski again, but she knew she wouldn't. His oldest brother had an amazing ability to love and leave women without them bearing him any ill will at all.

It didn't take long for Mitch's good mood to get on his nerves. "If you keep whistling, you're going to walk."

"Hey, it's not my fault you hooked up with a woman who's only pretending to like you."

Sean's fingers tightened on the steering wheel. It was tempting to tell Mitch Emma hadn't been pretending last night, but he kept his mouth shut until the urge passed.

For one, there was money on the line. If he confided in Mitch, he'd tell Ryan and Josh before he even got on the plane so they could determine who'd won the pool. But that wasn't a big deal. There were always betting pools, and sometimes he won and sometimes he lost.

What *was* a big deal was the possibility—no, probability—that Mitch would also tell one of their cousins, who would tell the other cousins, who would then tell their spouses and…it was only a matter of time before the news reached Aunt Mary. And if Aunt Mary got it in her head he and Emma were becoming a *real* couple, she'd jump on him in a second, pushing him into settling down.

Better to keep his mouth shut because, no matter how much Emma had rocked his world last night, settling down was the last thing on his mind.

CHAPTER THIRTEEN

As soon as Emma and Sean left in separate trucks—Emma having been called not five minutes after Sean left by an upset customer whose new garden had been ravaged by some nocturnal creature—Cat did a victory dance in the kitchen. It couldn't have been more obvious they'd had sex if they'd had T-shirts made to mark the occasion.

They'd barely said two words to each other and they'd avoided eye contact at all costs, but they weren't fighting. Anger wasn't the vibe filling the kitchen with tension. No, it was morning-after awkwardness and she couldn't be happier about it.

By the time she was done puttering around the kitchen, it was a decent enough hour to call Mary. She brewed herself some tea and took it into the living room to get comfortable.

"You were right about Mitch making a difference," she said after they'd exchanged hellos.

"Sean didn't like him touching her. I swear, that kiss almost set the grass under their feet on fire."

"Guess who *didn't* sleep on the couch last night?"

"And the plot thickens," Mary said, and they laughed.

"Speaking of thickening plots, I told Emma I want to give her the house as a wedding gift, and I thought she was going to throw up in my lap."

"That's interesting."

Cat took a sip of her tea. "I think, besides worrying about me, she was also afraid I'd sell the house."

"So making up a relationship with Sean put your mind at ease, but also made you stop telling her the house was too much for a woman alone."

"Exactly."

"What did she say?"

"She kept insisting she wanted to buy it from me, not have it given to her. I know my granddaughter. I don't think she'll accept the house as a gift under false pretenses."

"I'd like to think you're right. What are you going to do?"

Cat sighed. "I'm going to leave it alone for now. If I push, she might decide to tell me the truth. Since they've only just…discovered each other, so to speak, I'd rather leave things as they are for a bit longer."

"Good point." Mary dropped her voice a little. "Speaking of discovering each other, what's going on between you and Russell Walker?"

"We're friends," she said, but her friend only

laughed. "Okay, *friends* might not be a strong enough word."

"What *would* be a strong enough word?"

"I don't know. It's so silly. When I'm away from him I tell myself I'm too old to be flirting with a man. But when I'm with him, I don't feel old at all."

"He's smitten with you. Anybody can see that."

"Smitten." Cat chuckled. "I like that word. But I'm going home in less than two weeks and his whole life is here."

"You said his store was going out of business."

"Yes, but he's still a part of the community and his daughter's here."

"Like your granddaughter's here?" She heard Mary's *tsk* clearly across the line. "That's not an obstacle."

"Maybe not, but I'm also set in my ways. He's charming and I enjoy his company, but I'm not sure I want to spend my remaining years unballing another man's socks. It's been a long time since I've had to do that."

"I unball Leo's socks. Leo rubs my feet. It works for me."

Cat sipped more of her tea, then sighed, wondering if Russell would rub her feet. "It's ridiculous."

"I bet that's what Sean and Emma said, too."

And the conversation circled back to the kids, which was just fine with Cat. She hadn't yet sorted out how she felt about Russell, so she didn't want to talk about it.

Maybe it was infatuation. They'd both been alone a long time. But that didn't mean either of them wanted to pack up and start a new life together. That was a big commitment and she wasn't sure she had the energy or the desire for that at this point.

It was much easier to meddle in Sean's and Emma's lives than dwell on her own.

ONCE HE'D DUMPED his brother off at the airport, Sean had nothing to do but kill time until it was time to get Emma back in his bed. Or *her* bed, actually. He tried out the sound of *their* bed, but his mind shied away from it. Made them sound too much like a real couple.

As long as Emma was naked in it, he didn't really care whose bed it was. He'd been quick on the trigger last night, and while he didn't have anything to prove, he intended to take his time with her tonight. If tonight ever came. The only time he'd ever seen clocks move so slowly was during his flight back to the States.

Emma's truck wasn't in the driveway when he pulled in, and at first, he thought the house was empty. But then he heard laughter and looked out the window to find Cat in the backyard swing, the cordless house phone pressed to her ear. Since he wasn't about to interrupt her conversation to ask her where

Emma had taken off to, he grabbed his book and stretched out on the couch to read.

He must have dozed off because the next thing he knew, the sun had shifted and he could hear Emma's voice coming from the direction of the kitchen. He stretched and sat up to set his book on the coffee table. That wasn't a bad way to kill some time. After a detour upstairs to take a leak and kill the nap breath, he went looking for the women. They were on the deck, but they had the windows and the back door open to let in the light breeze, so he could hear them clearly as he opened the fridge to grab a beer.

"So Lisa as your matron of honor and Stephanie as bridesmaid," Cat was saying. "Do you know who Sean wants as best man?"

"No. We haven't gotten that far yet." He didn't hear any tension in Emma's voice, but he guessed she was feeling it. Planning a wedding that wasn't going to happen was weird, to say the least.

"Maybe he could ask Mike's oldest son—Joey, right?—to be a groomsman so he can escort Stephanie."

"I don't know," Emma said. "I don't think it's very fair to ask one of the boys and not the others."

"True. Maybe they could be ushers and then join their parents once everybody's seated."

Sean had just decided to beat a fast retreat back to the living room, when he heard a chair scrape back.

"We can talk about that later, Gram. Right now I should go wake Sean so he's not still groggy when we ask him to fire up the grill."

He didn't have time to escape, so he leaned against the counter and twisted the top of his beer. Emma paused when she saw him, and then grabbed his hand and dragged him down the hall to the living room.

"Where did you disappear to?" he asked.

"What? Oh, a client had an emergency. But—"

"There are gardening emergencies?"

She blew out an exasperated breath. "Yes. When you're rich, everything's an emergency. But did you hear what Gram was saying?"

"Yeah. How the hell are guys supposed to pick a best man, anyway? I've got three brothers and I like them all. And what about Mikey? Or Kevin or Joe? It seems easier to pick a stranger off the street so you don't have to play favorites. I guess maybe I'd ask Mitch. He's the oldest, so most of what the rest of us know about catching a woman we learned from him."

"In case you've forgotten, you haven't actually caught a woman yet. And it doesn't really matter who you choose, because there *is* no wedding."

She was wound up like an eight-day clock, so he didn't dare laugh at her. Her cheeks were bright and she kept spinning her ring around and around on her finger. Since there was nothing he could say to make her feel better about Cat wanting to plan their fake wedding, he slid the hand not holding his beer around her waist and hauled her close.

"You worry too much," he told her.

"And you—"

He kissed her to shut her up. And because all he'd been able to think about since the last time he'd had his hands on her was getting his hands on her again. And, most of all, because he liked kissing her. A lot. Maybe too much, if he thought about it.

So he didn't think about it. Instead, he lost himself in the taste of her mouth and the softness of her lips and the way her hands slid over his lower back, holding him close.

"Oh," Cat said from behind him. "I didn't mean to interrupt."

"No," Emma said. "We were just…talking."

"I can see that."

Since it was going to be at least a couple of minutes before he was fit to turn around and face anybody, never mind her grandmother, Sean sidestepped around Emma and grabbed the television remote. "I'm going to see if I can catch tomorrow's weather and then I'll start the grill."

Fortunately, they made it through the evening without any more talk of bridesmaids and ushers thanks to Emma and him steering the conversation toward Florida and television and anything else they could think of that didn't involve weddings. But if he'd thought the minutes were slow to tick away before, the seemingly endless time between dinner and bedtime was excruciating.

Finally the time came for him to crawl naked between the sheets and wait for Emma to come out of the bathroom. He didn't really care if she was naked or not. It would only take a few seconds to get her out of what she wore to bed.

When she finally came out, wearing her usual sleepwear, he grinned and flipped back the covers for her.

She arched an eyebrow at him, then went over to shut off the light. "Pretty cocky, don't you think? Just assuming I'll sleep with you again?"

"Last night was a little quick. I think we can do better."

By the time Emma reached the bed, she was naked, leaving behind her a trail of clothes. "Are you saying you can do better? Because you set the bar pretty high, you know."

He didn't waste any more time with words. Once she was in the bed, he rolled onto his side and cupped her face in his hand. Her eyes were dark pools he wanted to drown in, so he moved his gaze to her mouth. She was worrying at her bottom lip with her teeth and he kissed her to make her stop. And then he kept kissing her because even the promise of the good feelings to come didn't intrigue him more than her mouth.

"You're very good at that," she said a little breathlessly when he reluctantly broke it off.

"I'm very good at many things."

"Oh, really? And you can back that up?" When he nodded, she stretched her body like a cat's, offering herself to him. "Take your time."

Even though his blood was practically boiling, he flicked his tongue over her lip and smiled. "I intend to."

He explored every inch of her, definitely taking his time as he learned where and how to touch her to make her crazy. He kept touching her, with his hands and with his mouth, until she was panting and squirming under him. Then he slid his finger into her wet heat and rubbed her clit with his thumb until her hips bucked and she pounded his shoulder with her fist because she couldn't scream.

And then he did it all again.

He lost track of time. Lost track of everything but Emma and the way he wanted to make her feel, until she grabbed him by the hair and dragged him up her body.

"Whatever you were trying to prove, you proved," she said between panted breaths. "I want you inside me. Now."

He slipped on a condom in record time and settled

between her legs. She lifted her head, kissing him fiercely as he entered her, and then dropped her head to the pillow. He watched her eyes, letting them drag him under as he thrust into her. They were both too far gone for finesse, and it wasn't nearly long enough before the pleasure hit him and knocked him for a loop as Emma bit her knuckle, trying to be quiet as the orgasm racked her body.

Oh, yeah, that was better. When he'd finally caught his breath, Sean disposed of the condom and then pulled the covers up over them. He tried to nudge her over a little, but she was as limp as overcooked spaghetti, and when he told her to move over, she mumbled something he couldn't hear into the pillow.

Curling up around her, Sean grinned as he closed his eyes. Maybe tomorrow night he'd make her do all the work.

"Do you think if you stare at those trees long enough, they'll shrivel up and disappear?"

Emma struggled to refocus her attention on Sean and away from the problem at hand. "What?"

"You've been staring at that spot for half an hour now."

She was sitting on the summer cottage's back steps, looking over a piece of property she'd been invited to bid on. "I'm not looking at the trees. It's the exposed roots that are the problem. And the overall drainage."

He was leaning against a tree, one hand holding a soda and the other hooked in his pocket. "And staring helps?"

"Yes, it does." She stood and brushed off the seat of her jeans. "See those places where the dead leaves are thick and decomposing? That means the water was collecting there during the snowmelt and spring rains. The drainage sucks, party because of these exposed tree roots, and standing water's a problem I need to deal with *before* I get hands-on with the landscaping."

"Does the home owner want the shade or can you rip the trees out?"

She shook her head and slid her phone out of her pocket. She'd already taken a dozen photos of the property, but she snapped a couple more from that angle. "Can't take the trees out. This shoreline's more regulated than nuclear waste."

"Even the tree roots?"

"Huge erosion factor. I have to work around them." But there was nothing else she could do on-site. She had the photos and the measurements to plug into her software, so she'd be spending several hours with her computer to generate prints and estimates for the home owner to consider. "We're done here."

"Okay, boss," he said, winking at her as he pushed away from the tree.

"Oh, sure. Now I'm the boss. How come I'm never the boss when I want to drive my truck?"

He didn't answer her, but she could see the smirk flirting with his lips as he disappeared around the corner of the cottage. After tucking her phone and memo book back into her pockets, she followed him and wasn't surprised at all to find him already in the driver's seat.

"Where to now?" he asked once she was in and buckled up.

"Take a right and then a left when we hit the main road. The Johnsons think they've got some tree limbs about to come down and they want me to look. They don't want to pay a tree service if they don't have to."

"I thought your clients didn't mind throwing their money around."

"If they have it. The Johnsons were one of my first clients. Their kids all moved away and they were moving into a smaller house. Mrs. Johnson didn't want to leave her peonies behind, so I transplanted them for her. They're far from rich."

"We can take care of the tree limbs." She gave him a doubtful look, but he was serious. "I grew up in a lodge in the middle of the woods. I've limbed a few trees in my time."

They reached the main road and she pointed left as a reminder even as he turned his blinker on. "How come you came to New Hampshire when you left the army instead of going home?"

"Wanted to see Uncle Leo and Aunt Mary. Hang out with my cousins."

After a few moments passed, she realized he wasn't going to say anything else. And that made her think about how most of what she knew about him, she'd actually learned from Lisa before she'd even met him. "What was it like, growing up in a snowmobile lodge?"

"It was...okay. The Northern Star's a big place and has a lot of land, so we had room to run. Our bedrooms were separate from the guest rooms, and we had our own family room and bathroom. But it's weird having strangers in your house every weekend and I never got used to it."

"So you don't want to go back there, then?"

He turned his head to look at her, an unreadable expression on his face. "Not really, no."

"Take your next left," she said after a few miles of silence. "After Gram leaves, are you going to go back to the apartment over Jasper's?"

He didn't say anything for a few seconds, but he was drumming his fingers on the steering wheel. "Don't know."

"Okay." She directed him through a few more turns. "It's the last house on the right. Beige, with cranberry shutters."

He pulled into the driveway and killed the engine, but didn't make a move toward getting out. "What's with the questions? We have sex and all of a sudden you're interested in my childhood?"

Too stunned to respond, Emma stared at him for a minute. Then she laughed. "You are *so* paranoid. It's called making conversation."

"So you're not getting ideas now that we're sleeping together?"

Still laughing, she opened her door and slid out of the truck. "No, I'm not getting any ideas about you and me."

She had a few ideas an hour later, though, when Sean was sweaty and all sexy and in charge. Ideas about him getting sweaty with her. Ideas about him naked and soapy in the shower. She even had a few ideas about finding someplace secluded to park the truck and not waiting until they got home.

After giving the Johnsons' tree limbs a good looking over, Sean had grabbed some rope and the chain saw out of toolboxes in the back of her truck and gone to work. He was about halfway through the job now, and so far, she hadn't had to do anything but guide a few of the smaller limbs away from the house with the rope after he tied them off.

Once he dropped a main limb, he made quick work of cutting off the smaller branches before cutting it into chunks of wood Emma, along with the home owners, could set off to one side. It would be a while before it would be any good in a woodstove, but Mr. Johnson was going to stack it and let it dry out. She didn't normally let her clients work alongside her, but it made her feel better about the fact she was going to charge them next to nothing. But after a while, Mrs. Johnson brought out lemonade for Emma and Sean, then fussed at her husband to get in out of the sun for a few minutes.

"I was out of line before," Sean said when they were alone.

"When before? Not letting me drive? The sticky note on the bathroom asking me to never make pasta salad again?"

"Before, when I assumed you were picking out white picket fences just because you asked me about my childhood."

"I already have a white fence. Which I installed all by myself, by the way." She took a sip of her lemonade. "I'm not sure what kind of women you've dated before, but I don't hear wedding bells during sex."

"I guess I've dated some women who do, then. Just wanted to make sure things aren't getting messy." He drained his glass, then he pulled up the hem of his T-shirt and mopped the sweat off his face, baring the abs she loved running her hands over. And, of course, he caught her looking. "Speaking of sex, maybe you should—"

That thought was cut off by the reappearance of Mrs. Johnson, and Sean flashed Emma a naughty grin. "I'll tell you later."

She'd look forward to it.

CHAPTER FOURTEEN

ON WEDNESDAY they only worked half a day, leaving Sean free to pay a visit to his aunt and uncle while Emma caught up on some paperwork. Emma's truck wasn't in the driveway when he got home, but he could hear music, so he knew somebody was home.

Sean found Emma in the kitchen and he almost turned around to go anywhere else. She had the refrigerator pulled away from the wall and was cleaning the baseboard trim behind it with a toothbrush. While the view of her ass was sweet since she was on her hands and knees, it didn't bode well for his frame of mind.

But when he got closer and saw the coils on the back of the fridge had not only been vacuumed, but were actually gleaming, he got a little worried. A person whose refrigerator coils could pass a military inspection couldn't be right in the head.

"You okay?" he asked.

She didn't stop scrubbing. "Sure."

"Liar."

"Whatever."

"Emma, stop for a sec."

Much to his surprise, she listened. Tossing the toothbrush into a bucket, she sat back on her heels and turned her head to look at him. "What's up?"

"Where's Cat?"

"Said she had some errands to do, so she took my truck and went into town. She's probably just sneaking off to see Russell."

Clue number one. "She's sixty-five years old. I doubt she needs to sneak off if she wants to see a man."

Her jaw tightened. "Then why didn't she tell me that's where she was going?"

"Maybe she's not. Maybe she has errands to do." When she rolled her eyes, he had to bite the inside of his cheek to keep from laughing at her. "Why don't you let me push the fridge back and I'll take you out to lunch."

"Why?"

"Because you clean when you're upset and taking a toothbrush to the back of the fridge means you're on the ragged edge. I'll take you down to Concord for a Jasper burger. They can fix anything."

She laughed, but it was on the bitter side. "Yeah, 'cause I need more Kowalskis in my day."

"Hey, whatever it is, I didn't do it."

"I'm just not in a good mood today."

He grinned and rocked back on his heels. "This is

because of my magic penis, isn't it? Four nights of it too much for you?"

"Ha. Don't flatter yourself, Kowalski. I'm only having sex with you so I can sleep in my own bed again."

The renewed color in her cheeks let him know she was full of crap. "So if I offered to do you right here on the kitchen floor, you'd say no?"

"I'd have to say no just to prove my point now."

"Damn."

Emma sighed and pushed herself to her feet. "You know what? A Jasper burger sounds really good, actually. It seems like it's been forever since I had one."

After she wiped down the baseboard and retrieved the bucket, he pushed the fridge back into place for her, then waited for her in the truck.

She was distracted on the drive down, staring out her window and sighing a lot. Figuring she'd feel better after a burger and a beer, he let her stew in silence.

Kevin's bar was quiet and he was nowhere to be seen, much to Sean's relief. He didn't really want to get any crap for taking his fake fiancée out to lunch, though he hadn't thought of that until *after* he suggested Jasper burgers.

Paulie, the stacked redhead, was behind the bar, but other than a casual wave, she didn't show much of an interest in them. Sean found a table in a dimly lit back corner and ordered a couple of beers and Jasper burgers for each of them.

Once their waitress set their glasses down and went to place their food order, Emma seemed to relax a little, but her mouth was tight and she was tapping the toe of her sneaker against the table leg.

"So what are you upset about today?" he asked when he got tired of the silence.

"Nothing."

"You afraid Cat's going to fall madly in love with Russell Walker and want her house back?"

With the way her head jerked back and the expression on her face, he was afraid for a second the other patrons would think he'd slapped her. "You're an asshole."

He shrugged. "I've been called worse."

"No doubt."

"If you just tell me what's bugging you today, I won't have to guess."

She looked for a second as if she was going to lash out with something bitchy, but then her body slumped in the chair and she sighed. "I want Gram to be happy. I want that more than anything. But seeing her with Mr. Walker was…weird. And I always miss Gramps, but it just hit me especially hard, I guess, seeing her with somebody else."

Tears shimmered in her eyes and he reached

across the table to hold her hand. "I think that's pretty normal, Emma."

"And they've known each other forever. Just because she watched the fireworks with him doesn't mean she's going to run off and marry him. They're friends."

"Have you asked her?"

"No."

"You should talk to her."

She sighed and he knew there was more. "At the Fourth of July party, she told me she wants to give me the house as a wedding present."

"Isn't that what you want?"

"No," she snapped, pulling her hand away. "I want her to *sell* it to me. I told you that."

"Okay." He took a second to think about what to say next. In his experience, talking to a woman in this kind of mood was like sitting on a keg of gunpowder to smoke a cigarette. It was only a matter of time before your ass got burned. "Did you tell her that?"

"Of course I did. But she said it doesn't make any sense to put another mortgage on the house when it's been free and clear so long. And she doesn't need the money."

He was going to ask her what the problem was, then, because getting a house free wouldn't bother most people. But he already knew. If at any time over the past two years Cat had offered to give her the house, she probably would have taken it. But the fact it was being offered as a gift for a nonexistent wedding was going to keep Emma up at night.

"Can you tie it in to the business somehow? You have your equipment and your office and shit there. Maybe tell her the bank thinks you should build credit by having a loan for a business location or something?" He didn't know jack about such things.

She shook her head. "Maybe if I was buying a nursery or something, but that's pretty shaky."

That left him fresh out of ideas. "You've got a couple more weeks. Maybe you can talk her into selling it."

"And how am I supposed to convince her that going two hundred thousand dollars or so into debt makes more sense than accepting as a gift the house that's been more or less mine now for two years, anyway?"

"I...don't know." He saw the waitress approaching with two plates. "But here come our burgers. That'll help."

"Jasper burgers are good, but even they can't help me out of this."

He grinned. "No, but they'll make you feel better about being in it."

JASPER BURGERS WERE BETTER than sex, Emma thought as the first bite made her taste buds stand up and happy dance. She had the same thought every time she ate at Jasper's, but the past few times she hadn't had sex recently enough to call it a fair comparison.

Technically, *nothing* was better than sex with Sean, but the burger had the edge right now because it wasn't complicated. It tasted amazing and it didn't screw up her life beyond her having to make a half-assed promise to herself to eat more salads to make up for it.

Sex with Sean was screwing up her life. As promised, the orgasms were very real and very numerous, but there should have been fine print. By accepting the orgasms, she'd also agreed to accept a level of intense intimacy she didn't think either of them had expected.

With mind-blowing sex came the tender touches. The way he'd capture her gaze with his and she couldn't look away. And he was a talker, always murmuring to her about how good she felt and how he never wanted to stop. And there was the life-screwing-up part—she never wanted him to stop, either.

"You're thinking about my magic penis again, aren't you?"

She almost choked on a fry. "No, I am not. And stop saying that."

"You started it." He leaned across the table. "And, yes, you were. I see that flush at the hollow of your throat and the way you're looking at me. You're all hot and bothered, right here in the bar. I was right about you."

"I am *not* an exhibitionist," she hissed.

"Oh, shit." She followed his gaze and saw that Kevin and Beth had just walked in and Kevin had spotted them. "Just be cool."

"Be cool?" She laughed. "We're having lunch, not planning a bank robbery."

"I just mean… Forget it."

"You don't want your cousins to know we're having sex," she said flatly.

"It complicates things."

He had that right. She was saved from further comment, however, by Kevin and Beth approaching the table. Kevin had Lily in his arms, but she clearly wanted down and they looked like a walking wrestling match.

"Hey, guys," Beth said, giving Emma a warm smile. "Couldn't resist the siren call of the Jasper burgers? I ate so many of those while I was pregnant, Kevin said Lily's first word would be *moo*. Thankfully, he was wrong."

"It was *da-da*," Kevin informed them in an exaggerated stage whisper that made Beth roll her eyes. "I was going to call you later. Me and Joe and Evan and Terry are going four-wheeling Saturday. You guys want in?"

"Hell, yeah," Sean said, but then he seemed to remember Emma was sitting across the table. "Maybe. If I can."

"I should ask Gram if she minds. But if she doesn't, I'd love to go if Lisa will let me steal her machine again. I haven't ridden since last summer."

"We'll hook you up." Lily was squirming like a fish out of water and Kevin was losing the battle. "She wants to see her aunt Paulie. Call me and let me know. By Thursday night would be good so we can figure out which trailers we need to load up."

After they left, Emma returned to her Jasperburger consumption with gusto. She'd asked Lisa once to find out the recipe for their seasoning mix, but Kevin wouldn't give it up. Plus, as Lisa had pointed out, it wouldn't do Emma any good to have it since she couldn't cook worth a damn, anyway.

"So about what I said before," Sean said after he'd wolfed down his food, "about not wanting them to know we've had sex. It's not that I'm trying to hide it, I just…"

"Don't want them to know."

"Yeah."

"That makes sense."

His face brightened. "Really?"

"No."

"Damn." He'd finished his beer, so he took a swig off the glass of water she'd requested with her meal.

"Under normal circumstances, I'd want everybody to know we're sleeping together. Trust me. I'd put a sign on my front lawn."

"But these aren't normal circumstances."

"Not even in the ballpark. I have this bet with my brothers I'd last the whole month and I don't want to listen to them gloat." Of course he had a bet with his brothers. Such a guy thing to do. "But it's more about the women."

"The women?"

"In my family, I mean. Aunt Mary, especially. They might start thinking it's more than it is. Getting ideas about us, if you know what I mean."

Emma ate her last French fry and pushed her plate away. "So we have to pretend we're madly in love and engaged...while pretending we're not having sex."

"Told you it complicates things."

"I'm going to need a color-coded chart to keep track of who thinks what."

He grinned and pulled his Sharpie out of his pocket. "I could make sticky notes."

The man loved sticky notes. He stuck them on everything. A note on the front of the microwave complaining about the disappearance of the last bag of salt-and-vinegar chips. (Emma had discovered during a particularly rough self-pity party that any chips will do, even if they burn your tongue.) A note on the back of the toilet lid telling her she used girlie toilet paper, whatever that meant.

He liked leaving them on the bathroom mirror, too. *Stop cleaning my sneakers. I'm trying to break them in.* Her personal favorite was *If you buy that cheap beer because it's on sale again, I'll piss in your mulch pile.* But sometimes they were sweet. *Thank you for doing my laundry.* And…*You make really good grilled cheese sandwiches.* That one had almost made her cry.

"Not to change the subject," she said, intending to do just that, "but I'm going to bid on a landscaping job tomorrow. The home owner wants to extend the deck out and add some built-in seating. It's a rush job because they're spending the last week of July there and want it done. I thought maybe you could do up a bid for that and we could submit it as a package. You know, if you're interested and think you can get the work done in time."

"Are you going to stand over my shoulder and double-check all my measurements and cuts?"

She felt her face blush and rolled her eyes. "No. Pounding nails is your thing, not mine."

"Then I'm interested. We could make a good team, you and I."

The words pierced some part of her heart she didn't want to think about, but she laughed. "Yeah. Just don't tell anybody."

Watching Sean flip ham steaks on the grill through the window, Emma tore up lettuce for salad. Her grandmother was cutting the tomatoes, which was probably good since she shouldn't use a knife and watch Sean cook at the same time.

"Hey, Gram, would you mind if Sean and I disappeared for a few hours on Saturday?"

"Of course not."

"A few of the Kowalskis are going four-wheeling and Kevin invited us to go. But if you want to spend the day with us, I can go—*we* can go—another time."

"I had plans of my own, actually."

Something in Gram's voice drew her attention away from admiring the way Sean wielded a meat fork. "Oh, really?"

"Russell's going to take me out for an early dinner and then we're going dancing at the high school. They're having a fundraiser for chem-free graduation."

"Oh." Emma realized she was tearing the lettuce into confetti and dropped it into the bowl. "That sounds fun."

"Do I need to have the talk with you about how going on a date with Russell doesn't change the fact I still love your grandfather very much and miss him every day?"

"No." She shook more lettuce out of the bag, just to give her hands something to do. "Maybe."

"It's the truth. Nobody will ever replace John Shaw in my heart. But I'm lonely and it's been a long time since I've had a warm body to rub my cold feet on under the covers."

Emma didn't want to think about Gram under the covers with anybody, never mind Russell Walker. "Fourteen years."

It occurred to her *after* she said the words that just because it had been fourteen years since her grandfather died didn't mean it had been fourteen years since her grandmother had rubbed her cold feet on a warm body under the covers. She propped her elbows on the counter and rested her chin on her hands, hoping she looked attentive, but mostly wanting to hide the heat she could feel in her cheeks.

"But it's more than that," Gram continued. "When I read something interesting in the paper, I don't have anybody to share it with. And when I'm watching a murder mystery, I don't have anybody to tell who I think dunnit."

It was on the tip of Emma's tongue to tell Gram she should move back home and they could figure out the plot twists together, but she bit it back. Not only because Gram was happy in Florida, but because she knew it wouldn't be the same. Gram didn't just want somebody else to make conversation with. She wanted a companion to share her life with.

"He seems like a nice man," Emma said, which

sounded lame, but she couldn't think of anything else to say.

"He is, and I enjoy his company."

"That's good, Gram." She meant it and she hoped Gram could see that she did.

Sean walked in with a plate of ham steaks and then stopped, as if his man radar had just pinged on the level of feminine drama in the room. "Everything okay?"

"Of course." Gram dumped the diced tomatoes into the salad bowl. "Emma was just telling me you're going four-wheeling Saturday."

"Only if you don't mind," he said, setting the plate on the table.

"Of course not."

"Gram's going dancing with Russell."

"Oh." He searched Emma's face for a moment, then turned to Gram. "He seems like a nice guy. Hope you have a good time."

"I haven't been dancing in ages, but I'm sure I will. Let's eat before the ham gets cold."

"Sean and I have to give an estimate on a job tomorrow, but then we can drive down to Concord and find you a dress, if you want."

Gram beamed. "I'd love that. I think the last time I bought a new dress, shoulder pads were still all the rage."

They all laughed, putting an end to any lingering

tension in the room. And later, when Sean slipped between the sheets and asked her if she was really okay with her grandmother dating, she could honestly say she was.

"I want her to be happy. If dancing with Russell makes her happy, she should go for it."

He stretched out against her body. "I agree. Know what would make *me* happy?"

"If I buy a more manly brand of toilet paper?"

"No. Well, yes. But we can talk about that when we're not naked."

She draped her arm over his shoulders and ran her fingertips over the sweet spot at the back of his neck. "What should we talk about while we're naked?"

He groaned and rolled onto his back, but he took her with him so she was straddling his hips. "Let's talk about how you look working in the sun, with your skin all shiny and a smear of dirt on your nose."

"Does me being all grubby and sweaty turn you on?"

"Watching you work turns me on. You work hard and you're not afraid to get your hands dirty. I like that in a woman."

"Flattery will get you—" she swiveled her hips, brushing over his erection and making him suck in a sharp breath "—everywhere."

He reached up and cupped her breasts, rubbing his

thumbs over her nipples. "Don't wanna be anywhere but here."

The man knew all the right words. He definitely had all the right moves. And he was a quick learner, so he already knew all the right ways to touch her to drive her out of her mind. He had a way of looking at her with those intense blue eyes that made her feel as though he'd been waiting his entire life just to make love to her.

And, as long as she wasn't stupid enough to imagine she could see forever in those eyes, she'd take it.

He ran one fingertip down her forehead to the bridge of her nose. "You're frowning. What are you thinking about?"

She shoved the word *forever* out of her mind and ran her hands over his rippled abdomen. "I was wondering why you're not inside me yet."

"Because you're frowning at me. Gives me confidence issues."

Reaching between their bodies, she stroked the hard length of him. "Confidence is never an issue for you."

He grinned and flipped her onto her back. "I'm confident I can have you whimpering my name into your pillow in five minutes or less."

"I don't know," she said as his hand brushed over

her stomach and kept going south. "I'm not an easy woman to please."

His mouth followed the trail his hand had marked against her skin. "I never could resist a challenge."

CHAPTER FIFTEEN

SATURDAY TURNED INTO an awesome day for riding. Warm enough for T-shirts, Emma thought, but not too hot under the helmet and goggles.

At the last minute Joe had bailed. Brianna had been fussy with a low-grade fever all night and he knew better than to abandon Keri, so it was Emma and Sean, along with Kevin, Evan and Terry.

She started up the ATV Kevin had borrowed from Lisa for her and backed it off the trailer, leaving it to warm up while she put on her helmet and adjusted her goggles. Sean was riding Mike's four-wheeler and he parked beside her to do the same.

"You think you can keep up?" she asked, tightening the strap under her helmet.

He snorted. "You drive like a girl and sleep in a girlie bed. I bet you ride like a girl, too."

"You know, saying that's going to make it so much more embarrassing when I leave you in the dust."

"We'll see about that."

She started to step closer to him—to maybe press up against him and ask what kind of wager he'd like to bet on that—but she remembered the others just in time.

With this group, they were just friends. Nothing more. And definitely not friends with benefits, since Sean didn't want them to know she wasn't sleeping on the couch anymore.

Instead, she turned her back on him and yanked on her riding gloves. It was ridiculous, trying to keep all these stories straight, and she was tired of it. She just wanted to relax and be herself, but she couldn't really complain since she was the one who'd gotten them into the mess to begin with.

When it was time to hit the trail, she took her frustration out on the throttle. Throwing her weight backward, she hit the gas hard and wheelied out of the parking area. When the front wheels dropped, she laughed and settled back on her seat. Let Sean chew on *that* dust for a while.

They were all experienced riders and keeping a fast pace, so she stopped dwelling on her current situation and gave all her attention to the trail ahead. Kevin was leading, with Evan and then Terry behind him, and Sean was pulling up the rear behind Emma, so there was a lot of dust. Dust meant poorer visibility, which meant paying attention and not stewing about the fact Sean was so adamant nobody in his family guess they were sleeping together.

But she couldn't help it. Why was it such a big deal

to him? There was the betting pool with his brothers, but that wasn't it. It wasn't as if the guys had all put a hundred grand on when they'd sleep together. It was simply that he didn't want them to know.

He'd said he was worried about his aunt getting ideas, but so what? Didn't mothers—and mother figures—always get ideas when a guy in his thirties started dating a new woman? Sometimes it worked out and sometimes it didn't, but you didn't hide a new girlfriend in your closet unless the maternal figure in question was a psycho. Mary Kowalski definitely wasn't a psycho.

To Emma it could only mean one thing. Sean was only in it—*it* being in her bed *with* her—for the sex. If nobody knew they were sleeping together, there wouldn't be any questions from his family after he walked away from her. No disappointment on his aunt's part. He wouldn't have to deal with Lisa's torn loyalties. Nobody would know.

She could live with that. It was what she'd agreed to—just sex without getting any ideas it might be more. And she was okay with it, too…mostly. A couple of weeks of the best sex of her life was better than no sex at all. She just wished it didn't feel so much like a dirty secret.

They ate up some miles before Kevin pulled off on the side of a grassy area bordering a pond and they all pulled in behind him. Sometimes, in the early dawn hours or around sunset, there were moose around the pond, but in the middle of the day it was abandoned.

She killed her engine and took off her helmet and goggles, trying to wipe the worst of the trail dust from her face with the back of her arm. It was a lost cause, helmet hair and a dirty face being one of the side effects of four-wheeling, but she made the effort.

Sean walked up beside her, looking as grubby as she knew she looked, but, being a guy, he didn't have the helmet hair. "I guess the next time somebody tells me I ride like a girl, maybe I should thank them for the compliment."

She grinned and leaned forward to set her helmet on the front rack. "At least you're keeping up."

"It's obvious you're not a rookie. How come you don't have your own?"

"I did. Blew the engine summer before last. I've been so busy with work I don't get out enough to justify buying a new one. If I go out with Mike and Lisa, they usually borrow somebody's for me. I'd planned to buy one for work, but then word of mouth got around and I spend most of my time in neighborhoods that frown on ATVs."

Terry was walking toward them with a couple of water bottles, no doubt on a mission to mother-hen them into staying hydrated. Sean took one and then walked away to talk to the guys.

"Thanks," Emma said, cracking the top and taking a long drink. "Dusty today."

"It'll be better once we get more into the woods. Still, it must be nice for you to get away for a few hours. You know, not having to pretend you and Sean are a couple and all that."

Emma forced herself to nod when in reality, it was just as hard pretending they weren't together as pretending they were. "Yeah, it's a little stressful at times."

"I bet the family having a little fun with it doesn't help."

"I'm so grateful everybody went along with it, I don't mind a few laughs at our expense."

Terry laughed. "It's too good not to, really. But Sean's always been a solid, levelheaded guy, so we figure it must all be for a good cause."

"My grandmother's going to go back to Florida without any worries about me, so it's definitely for a good cause." Assuming it didn't blow up in their faces before her plane left, of course.

Kevin gave the signal, and it was time to put the water away and put the gear back on. Sean winked as he walked past her to his machine, but she just smiled and put her helmet on.

After a half mile or so of dirt road they hit the woods, but Kevin didn't slow down. They crashed and banged along the rough trail, dodging the bigger rocks and low-hanging branches. And when Sean started playing—tapping the back of her machine with the front of his—Emma laughed and gave it a little more gas.

The corner came up fast, but she didn't panic. No brakes. Just goosed it a little to bring the rear end around so it would slide through the corner and she could throttle out.

Then she saw the chipmunk.

All it took was a second's hesitation and the inside wheels lifted and the ass end came up off the ground. *Oh, shit, this is gonna hurt.*

SEAN SAW EMMA'S MACHINE start to roll and there wasn't a damn thing he could do about it.

He skidded to a stop, his ATV sliding sideways, and watched as she managed to push herself off, diving for the dirt. She hit the ground, bouncing and skidding until—thank God—she was clear of the four-wheeler as it rolled twice before coming to rest against a tree.

He was off his machine and at her side before the dust even settled. Emma rolled to her back as he dropped to his knees.

"Ow" was all she said.

"Jesus, Emma. Are you hurt?"

"That would be why I said *ow.*"

He resisted the urge to grab her by the shoulders

and shake the smart-ass out of her, but just barely. "Answer the damn question. Are you hurt bad?"

"I don't think anything's broken. Just gimme a minute."

She didn't look too bad. She'd gotten lucky and plowed through a mostly rock-free patch of trail. Her arm was scuffed up a bit and she was winded and filthy, but as long as nothing was broken, she'd made out pretty good.

"Has it been a minute yet?" He wanted her on her feet so he could look her over.

"No." She took a deep breath, exhaling slowly. He watched her closely, but she didn't wince and her breath didn't hitch in her chest at all. "How bad did I muck up Lisa's machine?"

"Don't care. Are you ready to get up yet?"

"I think so."

He moved to kneel behind her head and slid his hands under her back to help her sit up. "Just sit for a couple minutes. Make sure you're not dizzy."

Riding as hard as they were didn't lend itself to looking over one's shoulder, so the group in front had kept going. Sean knew it wouldn't be long before they reached an intersection. Kevin would stop to make sure he had everybody before choosing a direction, and when he and Emma didn't show, they'd come back.

"I think I'm okay," Emma told him.

He slid his hands under her arms, gently hoisting her to her feet. "Take it nice and easy."

"I'm okay, Sean. Really." She pulled off her goggles and then undid her chin strap and lifted her helmet off.

"I shouldn't have been pushing you." She gave him a *look*. It was the kind of look he saw his cousins' wives give them and it made him bristle. "Don't give me that look."

"What, the 'you're being an ass' look? Don't be an ass and I won't give you the look."

"How am I being an ass? Because I'm sorry I was pushing you and almost got you killed?"

"No, you're an ass because you think you were pushing a *girl* to go too fast."

He crossed his arms and scowled at her. "So?"

She scowled right back at him. "So, *you* had nothing to do with it. Believe it or not, I've rolled an ATV before. Today, I was riding the way I always ride when we're dumb enough to let Kevin lead, and I got ambushed by a chipmunk. It could have been any one of us."

He couldn't help it. He stepped close and threaded his fingers through hers. "I wish it hadn't been you."

"Because I'm a girl?"

No, because being helpless to get to her when he thought she was about to be crushed by six hundred and fifty pounds of rolling four-wheeler made him feel…something. Something not good. "Because I don't want to be the one who has to tell Cat we broke you."

That made her laugh. "I'm going to feel like I got hit by a Mack truck later, but I'm not broken."

"I'll run you a hot bubble bath when we get home. That'll help with the aches and pains."

When she smiled and her face relaxed, Sean moved in for a kiss. Not because he was thinking about Emma all naked and soapy with her nipples peeking through the bubbles, but because he was so damn relieved she wasn't hurt.

His lips had barely met hers when she jerked away. First he thought he'd hurt her, and then he thought she was mad. But he realized she'd already heard the sound he was just now registering—an ATV racing toward them.

"Wouldn't want to make you lose your bet," she muttered with a faint thread of bitterness that made him feel guilty, even though he wasn't sure why.

He had no reason to feel guilty. He hadn't done anything wrong. Besides, she knew he didn't take that stupid betting pool seriously and that he didn't want his aunt disappointed when he and Emma parted ways. But he didn't get a chance to explain it.

Kevin came into view, riding fast. He braked when he saw them, and his machine had barely stopped when he jumped off. "What happened? Emma, are you okay?"

She nodded. "Chipmunk. I hesitated and blew the corner."

"You hurt?"

She showed him her scuffed arm. "I'll live. Hoping I can say the same for Lisa's four-wheeler."

Evan and Terry pulled up, and Sean stepped off to the side while they fussed over her. Kevin fired up Lisa's machine and maneuvered it back onto the trail.

"Doesn't look too bad," he said. "Cracked some plastic and scuffed the end of the grip. Pretty sure her front rack was already bent a little. Small tear in the seat. We'll slap some duct tape on it and call it good."

Emma groaned. "Duct tape. That's classy."

Terry laughed. "They have four boys. Half the stuff they own's held together by duct tape."

Sean picked Emma's helmet up off the ground and turned it over in his hands, brushing it off and looking for damage. The way she'd looked hitting the ground still had him feeling a little wobbly inside, he realized as he ran his thumb over a gouge that may or may not have been from this incident.

She could have been seriously injured, and he was having trouble processing just how much that scared him. He didn't want to see anybody get hurt, but the thought of how close they might have come to waiting for a helicopter to come airlift Emma out of the woods had his gut churning.

The feeling didn't lessen when Terry got her first-aid kit out of her cargo box and started cleaning the scrapes on Emma's arm. She was leaning against the front of Terry's machine, smiling at something Kevin and Evan were talking about, but his stomach seemed to clench up even more instead of relaxing.

She was one hell of a woman. Emma was smart and fun and tough and she worked hard, and she turned his world upside down between the sheets. And maybe that was the problem. His world was starting to feel a little upside down when they were fully clothed, too.

"You okay?" Kevin asked him, and Sean swore under his breath. He hadn't even noticed him coming.

"Yeah. Just checking out her helmet."

"You look a little peaked."

Pretty natural look for a guy whose world wasn't right-side up anymore. "Wasn't a fun thing to watch."

"I've been teaching Beth to ride when Ma can watch Lily and I swear I have a heart attack every time she so much as hits a bump."

"But she's your wife." Sean looked at Emma, who was looking back at him. "That's different."

"Is it?"

"Yes." He said it firmly, wondering which of them he was trying to convince. "Emma's a nice girl and

I don't want to see her get hurt, but it's not the same thing at all."

When she raised an eyebrow at him from across the distance, he wondered if she was a better lip-reader than he'd thought. And when she mouthed *nice girl,* with a questioning look, he knew he was busted. She wouldn't like being called that at all.

"You keep telling yourself that and I'll leave you two to make googly eyes at each other while I go check the air in my tires. Think I've got one going soft on me." Kevin slapped his shoulder. "And I don't think that's all that's going soft around here."

His cousin walked away before Sean could tell him he wasn't going soft. The fact he didn't want to see the woman he was and wasn't pretending to have sex with wrapped around a tree didn't mean he was going soft. It just meant...

It just meant he might be *starting* to get a little soft and he needed to get the hell out of there the second Cat's departing flight started its taxi down the runway.

THE FRUIT PUNCH WAS HORRIBLE, the fake disco light looked more like a police light bar and the folding metal chairs were hell on old hips, but Cat was having one of the best nights of her life in the high school gymnasium.

Frank Sinatra crooned from the speakers, her

head rested on Russell's chest and his arms wrapped around her as they swayed to the music. Neither of them were particularly snazzy dancers, but they didn't care. It was nice just to dance again.

As the song came to an end, Cat leaned back so she could smile and thank him and suggest they sit for a few minutes, but she could tell he was thinking about kissing her. His gaze flicked to her mouth several times and the butterflies in her stomach panicked.

She hadn't kissed any man but John in…for goodness' sake, it had been forty-six years. That didn't seem right to her, but she'd been nineteen when she fell in love with John Shaw and married him six months later. She hadn't been kissed by another man in almost half a century.

And she could see the hesitation in Russell's eyes, too. He was thinking of his wife, and Cat thought maybe he hadn't kissed anybody but Flo in a long, long time.

"Do you want some more punch?" she asked, hoping to take the pressure off the moment.

He laughed. "I don't ever want more of that punch. I could use a little fresh air, though."

He didn't take her hand as they went through the propped-open gymnasium doors into the cool summer night, but Cat tried not to be bothered by it. While it had been fourteen years since she'd lost her husband, for Russell it had only been six. Maybe when push came to shove, he just wasn't ready to face a new relationship.

They walked across the grass to the small copse of trees in the high school's courtyard, where granite benches sat honoring the graduates who'd lost their lives serving in the military over the decades. Surprisingly, the benches were unoccupied, and Russell finally took her hand as he pulled her down to sit beside him on one.

"I enjoy your company so much, Cat," he said quietly, and she heard the *but* coming from a mile away. "I just…I'm not sure what we're doing here."

"Enjoying each other's company?"

"That we are." He turned his head to smile at her and his gaze fixed on her mouth again. "I'm afraid if I kiss you, I might cry."

She squeezed his hand, though not as hard as his words squeezed her heart. "I might cry, too, but I'd rather cry because I feel something and not just because I'm lonely and feeling sorry for myself."

"Maybe I should do it, then, and stop trying to count how many years it's been since I kissed a woman besides my wife."

Cat tilted her face up and closed her eyes as Russell cupped the back of her head in his hand and kissed her.

She tried not to compare his mouth to John's—Russell's lips were softer and yet more aggressive—

but eventually everything and everybody except the man touching her fell away. And, as his tongue brushed hers, the dormant feelings of desire and anticipation fluttered to life.

When he reluctantly broke away—or so it seemed to Cat—there were no tears. Maybe deep down there might have been a few bittersweet pangs of sorrow, but the avalanche of renewed and wonderful feelings had buried them *way* down deep.

He looked her straight in the eye, his face softening as he smiled. "It's been about half a minute since I kissed anybody but you, Catherine Shaw."

And for the second time in her life, Cat thought maybe she'd found a man worth keeping.

CHAPTER SIXTEEN

SEAN WATCHED EMMA fumbling with her keys in the darkness. Having left earlier in the day, nobody had thought to turn the outside light on. "I can't believe Gram's out this late."

"We've got the house all to ourselves. Maybe after I run that hot bubble bath for you, I'll help you wash your back."

"As filthy as I am, I'm going to have to make do with the shower or I'll leave two inches of mud in the bottom of the tub."

"We should conserve water and shower together," he said as he followed her into the house.

"Gee, I couldn't do that. I'm a *nice girl,* remember?"

He groaned and bent forward to untie his filthy boots. "There was nothing in your owner's manual warning about your unnaturally good lip-reading ability."

"But then I wouldn't know you think I'm a nice girl, *but...*"

He wasn't even sure what he was in trouble for. "I

was trying to make him see the difference between him and his wife, and you and me. I didn't mean anything by it."

"Relax," she said with an impish gleam in her eyes. "I swear, it's so easy to push your buttons."

"You have a really twisted sense of humor."

But he forgave her when she unzipped her jeans and wriggled out of them right there in the hall. She probably didn't want to track trail dust all through the house, so he'd do the same. But he'd watch her first, since he wasn't one to pass up a striptease by a beautiful woman.

She turned and walked toward the kitchen with her T-shirt still on, though, so he sighed and resigned himself to just admiring her legs. Her bruised legs, he noticed. She had an egg-size bruise on the outside of one thigh, along with a few smaller ones. He kicked off his jeans and yanked his T-shirt over his head so he could follow her.

"You took a good whack to the thigh," he pointed out while she filled a couple of frosted mugs with water.

She twisted around so she could see the bruises. "Yeah. It's a little tender to the touch, but nothing major."

"You should let me check the rest of you over." She gave him a cold glass of water and an arched eyebrow.

"For bruises, I mean, though you do look sexy as hell with a dirty face, wearing nothing but a T-shirt."

Putting a hand on her hip, which drew the hem of her T-shirt up a tantalizing half inch, she scowled at him. "When I made you my fake fiancé, I had no idea you had this weird dirty-face fetish."

"I didn't have it before I became your fake fiancé." He took a long drink of water. "And it's not a fetish. I told you, it turns me on that you work hard and you play hard. The dirt's just a visual representation of that, I guess."

"That's very deep of you."

"Plus, it means you'll be showering soon and I like you all soaped up and slippery, too."

A slow flush burned up her neck. "Dirty. Clean. Doesn't matter to you, does it?"

He was going to tell her no, it didn't matter—that he'd take her any way he could get her—but he kept his mouth shut. It was true, of course, but nothing good would come of her knowing that. She didn't need to know that sometimes when they were curled up on the couch watching television or arguing about white versus wheat bread at the store, he would sometimes forget they were pretending to be a couple.

And she *really* didn't need to know it sometimes bummed him out when he remembered.

That was bad. Sure, he enjoyed her company—and he sure as hell enjoyed the sex—but in just a week, he'd be leaving. He'd be free to explore the wheres and whats of the rest of his life, as he'd planned to do before being waylaid by Emma's crazy scheme. He hadn't had his freedom back long enough to give it up again, especially to a woman who drove him nuts. He wasn't going to spend the rest of his life deadheading daisies and reading flowcharts on the proper order of household chores.

Emma walked past him, stripping off her T-shirt and giving him a come-hither look over her shoulder.

On the other hand…

Two of them in the shower made for a tight fit, but Sean didn't mind. The more of her skin touching his, the better. They did a quick lather and rinse to get the trail grime off and then Sean took his time, soaping her body inch by inch. He found a few more smatterings of bruises, especially near her right shoulder blade, though none as pronounced as the one on her thigh.

He kissed the ones he could reach standing up and noted the others for later. She winced a little when he carefully cleaned around the scrape on her arm and he kissed her mouth until that little gasp of pain became a moan of pleasure.

When the water started running cold, they dried off and brushed their teeth. She nudged him out of the way so she could spit and the moment hit him like a sucker punch to the gut.

It was so…domestic. They were acting like a married couple. Or like a couple who'd been living together and would be getting married in the near future. And didn't that just confuse the hell out of him, because that's what they were supposed to be. But not really.

He followed her to bed, his mind reeling as she tucked herself against him like she did every night. As if she belonged there. And he pulled her even a little closer because he did every night.

"Penny for your thoughts," she whispered.

"I'm beat. Haven't ridden in a long time, especially like that."

Her hand stroked his chest. "Starting things in the shower you can't follow through on, soldier?"

"The last thing your body needs right now is more action."

She sighed, still stroking his chest. "I don't know if I'll be able to sleep."

He rolled toward her a little so he could cup her breast. "I know a great cure for that."

"I thought you were beat."

"I am." And he wasn't so sure about being *fully* involved with her while still processing the domestic moment in the bathroom. "And you don't need any more roughhousing, but I know a little trick to take care of that."

As he spoke, he slid his hand down her stomach

and between her legs. His own body heated up along with hers, but he willed his libido into submission. She had bruises in enough places, so he wasn't going to go groping at her.

Instead, he stroked, watching as her eyelids fluttered closed and her teeth bit into her bottom lip. Her breath quickened as her hips moved against his hand and she whispered his name. Then she opened her eyes and stared into his with such intensity he kissed her just so she'd close them again. He wasn't sure what she'd see.

She moaned into his mouth as she found release and then he wrapped her in his embrace and she sighed in happy contentment.

He shouldn't hold her, he told himself. He should pat her on the ass, roll over and go to sleep. Instead, he nuzzled her hair and closed his eyes. Maybe tomorrow night he'd work on putting some distance between them.

EMMA PULLED THE COVERS over her face, mentally bargaining with her subconscious. If she could have another hour of sleep, she wouldn't hit Snooze for a whole workweek. Or at least not on Monday.

When Sean climbed onto the bed and stretched out next to her, though, she gave up and rolled over. And...*ouch.* There was that hit-by-a-Mack-truck feeling she'd been waiting for.

She opened her eyes and then frowned. "Why are you dressed?"

"Because I got up and got dressed so I could find some coffee, but I changed my mind and I'm coming back to bed."

"Fully dressed?"

"Yes. No shoes, though."

It was too early to follow along with his crazy bouncing ball of logic. "Did Gram put a pot of coffee on yet?"

He groaned and threw his arm over his eyes. "Not exactly."

"What is *wrong* with you this morning?"

"I just ran into your grandmother. She was sneaking into the house…in the same dress she wore last night."

"What?" Emma sat up, aches and pains forgotten. "You caught Gram doing the walk of shame?"

"Yes, and it was awkward and now I'm going back to bed."

She pushed his arm off his face. "What did she say?"

"She said good-morning and told me she was going to take a quick shower and then start breakfast."

"And what did you say?"

"I muttered something about taking her time and then ran like a girl."

Emma flopped back onto her pillow and stared at the ceiling. "Wow."

"I probably should have broken it to you better, but I'm not sure how I could have."

She didn't know what to say. *Go, Gram,* a part of her was thinking, but another part wanted to hide under the covers with Sean and not deal with the fact her grandmother was currently taking a shower after doing the walk of shame. That was obviously the same side of himself Sean was currently listening to.

"We have to go down eventually," she said. "I need coffee. And food."

"I'll wait here. Bring some back."

She laughed and slapped his thigh. "If I can face her, so can you. She's not *your* grandmother."

"It was awkward."

"I'm sure it's awkward for her, knowing we're having sex, but she's an adult about it."

That just made him cover his face with his arm again. "That's different."

"Why? Because she's sixty-five?"

"No. Because, as you just said, she's a grand-mother. *Your* grandmother."

"Come on. We'll go down together." She slid out of bed and walked toward the bathroom. "Stop making it such a big deal."

Gram was still in the shower when they went past the bathroom on their way down the hall. They could tell because she was whistling a very cheery tune that made Sean wince.

Emma grabbed his arm and tugged him toward the stairs. "Coffee."

They got a pot going and sat at the table in silence until enough had brewed to sneak two cups from it. Emma put the kettle on and dropped a tea bag into Gram's mug.

The woman of the hour appeared just as it whistled, looking refreshed and cheerful. "Good morning."

"Morning," they both mumbled.

"Thank you for making my— What happened to your arm?"

Emma looked down at the angry-looking scrape and then tucked her arm behind her back. "I took a little spill yesterday, that's all."

"I told you to be careful."

"I was. There was a chipmunk."

Gram cast an accusing glare at Sean and he held up his hands. "Hey, don't look at me. You've been in the truck with her. You know how she drives."

"Yes, my husband taught her to drive, unfortunately." Emma saw the fleeting shadow cross her face. "I was thinking omelets today. Maybe broccoli and cheese?"

Sean's head slumped over his coffee cup and Emma knew she had to say something...without telling her grandmother she'd fed her own fiancé a food he hated her first night home. "Um...how about mushrooms instead?"

Gram rummaged in the fridge. "I don't see any mushrooms. We still have broccoli, though."

"Sean only eats broccoli once in a while, like for special occasions," Emma said in a rush. "He loves it, but it...it makes him gassy."

Since Gram still had her head over the crisper drawer, Sean was free to give her a what-the-hell look and she gave him an apologetic smile. After three weeks of living a lie—or two different lies— she should have been better at thinking on her feet.

"We can't have that," Gram said. "We still have some leftover ham. How do ham-and-cheese omelets sound?"

"That sounds wonderful," Sean said, still glaring at Emma.

She set the table while Gram cooked, and then refilled the coffee cups. At this rate, they'd need the caffeine.

"So, Sean," Gram said, dropping diced ham into the pan, "how do you like this old house?"

He looked startled by the question. "It's a nice house. Big and homey."

"Lots of room for children."

Emma barely managed to swallow her coffee before it went down the wrong pipe. "Gram. We're not ready to have kids yet."

"No, but you will soon, I'm sure. We'll have to get the calendar out after breakfast and start looking at possible wedding dates."

Sean shifted in his seat and Emma put her hand on his knee so he wouldn't be tempted to go back to bed again. "We haven't even figured out if we want summer or winter. There's no rush."

"Don't you want to get married in the garden? You always did."

Emma shot a desperately pleading look at Sean and he cleared his throat. "If we get married in the winter, we can honeymoon at my family's lodge and…snowmobile and stuff."

"You can do that any winter," Gram insisted. "But it's up to you two, of course."

She used the spatula to cut the omelet and slid pieces onto their waiting plates. Emma wasn't surprised when Sean wolfed his down and then excused himself before disappearing like a superhero blur.

Since the women were eating at a normal pace, Emma was left with her grandmother. "Did you have a nice time? At the dance, I mean?"

Gram smiled at her plate. "I had a lovely time at the dance. And after the dance, as well."

"Oh. I'm happy for you. Really."

"Don't go making more of it than it is. We're just enjoying each other's company for a little while. I'll be going home at the end of the week, so...like I said, we're just enjoying each other's company."

That sounded familiar, Emma thought, moving egg and cheese and ham bits around on her plate. Just temporarily keeping each other's feet warm, as the case may be.

They talked about inane things while they cleaned up, and then Emma went in search of Sean. When she didn't find him downstairs, she went up to their room, but he wasn't there, either. There was, however, a sticky note on the mirror.

Gassy? Payback's a bitch, honey.

She laughed and dropped the note into the bottom drawer with the others she'd collected. They amused her too much to throw away and sometimes she'd pull one out and reread it. But that made her feel like some kind of lovesick teenager, so she closed the drawer and continued the search.

When she looked out the living room window, she finally found him. He was sitting in one of the rockers, his head back and eyes closed. Probably looking for a short reprieve from the craziness she'd dragged him into, so she dropped the curtain and left him alone.

She had a wedding date to pick out, anyway.

And, a half hour later, with her head next to her grandmother's looking at the calendar, she tried not to think about the phone call she'd eventually have to place to Florida, telling Gram she and Sean had gone their separate ways.

WHEN SEAN'S PHONE RANG, he pulled it out and read the caller-ID screen: Northern Star Lodge. It would be either Josh or Rosie, so he flipped it open and said hello.

"Hey." It was Josh. "Did I win yet?"

He shook his head even though his dumbass youngest brother couldn't see him, and left the rocking chair to move farther away from the house. "Nobody's won a damn thing."

That technically wasn't a lie since he hadn't officially ceded yet and he wasn't sure who'd put money on two weeks. Speaking of which, he had to remember to pick up another box or two or three of condoms. He didn't think he should add them to Emma's list on the refrigerator.

"You're almost done with the whole thing, aren't you?"

"A week," Sean said, not that he was counting. "Cat's flying out Sunday."

"Then what are you going to do?"

He wasn't going to go back to the lodge, if that's what Josh was after. "Not sure yet. Thinking about taking the scenic route to New Mexico and visiting Liz."

There were a few seconds' silence on the line.

"She'd probably be glad to see you. She talked to Mitch after the Fourth, by the way. He seems to think you and this Emma woman are serious."

"That's the point." Sean didn't want to talk to his brother about Emma. "People are *supposed* to think we're serious."

"We grew up with you, stupid. Ain't nobody standing in line to give your ass an Oscar."

Sean leaned against the front fender of his truck and tilted his head back to look up at the sky. "I'm not looking for serious, Josh. Not looking for anything right now."

"Just because you're not looking for something doesn't mean you won't find it."

"Well, aren't you quite the fucking fortune cookie."

His brother laughed. "That's me. So, hey, why don't you come home for a few days before you head west?"

Because if he went home for a few days, he might get sucked into staying and he wasn't ready to do that. "I don't know what I'm going to do yet. We'll see."

They talked about the lodge for a few minutes, and then Josh had to run. Sean slid his phone back into his pocket and sighed. Time to go back in the house and see what the women were up to. Probably picking a wedding date.

And knowing Cat, probably making a list of baby names. He supposed it was natural for people to assume that after the wedding bells came the stork, but it had still given him the cold sweats to hear her talking about children. Not that he didn't like kids. Mike and Terry's kids were cool, but first you had to get through the phase Kevin's and Joe's kids were stuck in, and he wasn't ready for that yet.

He paused in the doorway to the kitchen, watching Cat and Emma flip through the pages of the calendar. The wedding box was on the table, too, which meant good old Grams was stepping it up. Emma was smiling and nodding, but he could tell she wanted to be anywhere but there.

He could see the tension in her face and the way she held her shoulders. She was fidgeting with the ring he'd given her, spinning it around on her finger. He could see how uncomfortable she was, because he knew her.

How could he not know her? He lived with her. They worked together and played together and brushed their damn teeth together. He understood her. He loved... *Shit.*

No, he didn't love her. He *pretend* loved her and he was sick of his mind getting that mixed up.

Emma looked up and saw him then, and she frowned. "Is everything okay?"

"What? Yeah." He shook it off and walked to the counter to steal the last dark dregs of coffee. "Josh called and he always annoys the crap out of me."

Emma was watching him, and he guessed his expression had been more horrified than annoyed. And she'd know that because she knew him. Just like he knew her.

"Before you run off again," Gram said, "I don't want to be all mopey and sad Saturday night, so I invited everybody over for a bon voyage party."

"Sounds like fun," he said. "Who's everybody?"

"Your family, of course. And Russell and Dani and Roger. I'm thinking burgers and dogs, and Mary already said she'd bring a dump-truck load of that amazing coleslaw of hers."

"We'll take care of the cooking, Gram, so you can relax." When he and Cat both looked at her, Emma blushed. "Okay, fine. Sean will take care of the grilling so you can relax."

"I was counting on it. And, Sean, why don't you sit down and help us settle on a wedding date."

"I told Emma to tell me when to be there and I'd be there."

"Nonsense. Sit down."

He'd rather be dipped in barbecue sauce and dropped in the desert, but he sat. One more week and it would be over.

Then he wouldn't have to think about Emma anymore. Not think about marrying her or having babies with her or holding her in his arms at night. He'd be gone and she'd be some funny story his brothers brought up sitting around the fire knocking back beer.

"Really, Sean, are you okay?" Cat asked him, putting her hand on his arm.

He realized he'd been rubbing his chest, and he forced himself to lean forward and prop his arms on the table so he wouldn't do it again. "I'm fine. Let's pick a date."

CHAPTER SEVENTEEN

IF ANYBODY HAD ASKED HER, Cat would have said she was at least a couple of decades past having butterflies of nervous anticipation fluttering around inside. But as she put her hand on the door of Walker Hardware and prepared to push it open, a winged *Nutcracker* ballet was being performed in her stomach.

She'd spent a little time talking to Russell on the telephone over the past couple of days, but this would be the first time she actually saw him since kissing him goodbye the previous morning.

Maybe she shouldn't have come. Sure, they'd talked on the phone, but he hadn't asked her out again. Maybe it had been too much, too fast, and rather than tell her he didn't want to see her again, he thought he'd just play along until she went back to Florida.

She pulled her hand back and took a deep breath. She was being silly. It wasn't some grand romance they were embarking on, anyway. They were good friends, that's all. Friends with occasional benefits, as the younger generation would say. With no pressure, there was no reason not to casually drop in and say hello.

There was a tapping on the glass and she looked up to see Russell standing on the other side of the door, watching her. The amusement on his face made her laugh at herself as he pulled open the door and made the bell ring.

"That must have been quite the dilemma you were sorting through," he said as she walked by him. "Maybe I shouldn't have interrupted you."

"I was being ridiculous. I'm glad you did or who knows how long I would have stood out there arguing with myself."

"Were you winning?" The laugh lines around his eyes danced as he smiled at her.

"I was, actually." She looked around at the shelves, which didn't look much more empty than they had the first time she'd been in. "I had to come into town for sugar and I thought I'd stop in and say hello."

"I left a message at the house. Wish I'd caught you before you drove over here."

"The phone started ringing right after I locked the door behind me and it's usually for Emma's business, so I didn't go back."

"I was wondering if you'd want to take a ride down to Concord with me tonight. Get some dinner and see a movie maybe?"

He looked as nervous as she'd felt standing on his front step, she realized, and she smiled back at him. "I'd love to."

"Should I pick you up at your house around five or..."

"That would be lovely. I'm not sure if the kids will be home by then. They had a couple of things to take care of before they could head to the big job for this week. Sean has to get that deck done, so they might work late."

"How's that going?"

"Honestly, if I was just meeting Sean for the first time now, I'd never guess they aren't a real couple."

"So your plan is working, then?"

"It seems to be, which is good because the clock's ticking." She sighed and glanced at the door. "Speaking of ticking clocks, I should move along if I'm going to get everything done before five. I'll probably make up some dinner for the kids before I go. If left to her own devices, Emma would work that poor man into the ground and then give him a grilled cheese sandwich for supper."

"I'll see you at five, then," he said.

She nodded and moved to open the door, but he caught her hand and stopped her. One long, lingering kiss later, the butterflies were dancing again. "I'll be looking forward to it."

"YOU'RE NOT VERY GOOD at this," Emma said, laughing at the frustration on Sean's face.

He pulled his hand out from under the back of her T-shirt. "You're distracting me."

"How am I distracting you?" She shook the bag at Sean, reminding him to pull two letter tiles to replace the *C* and the *T* he'd used to make *CAT.*

"You look totally hot. And you did it on purpose so I wouldn't be able to concentrate and you'd win."

Emma laughed. Sure, she'd thrown on baggy flannel boxers and an old Red Sox T-shirt after her shower just to seduce him out of triple-word scores. "You not having a shirt on is distracting. And you keep pretending you want to rub my back so you can peek at my tile rack."

"Nothing wrong with checking out your rack." He craned his neck to see better and she shoved him away. It wasn't easy playing Scrabble sitting side by side on the couch, but after a long workday, neither was willing to take the floor.

They'd found a note from Gram on the counter when they got home. She was going to dinner and a movie with Russell and they shouldn't wait up. She'd also left a small casserole in the fridge with *very* specific instructions on how to warm it up. Cleaned up, well fed and facing a long, rainy evening together, they'd hit the game cupboard. And, ironically, Scrabble had been Sean's choice.

"Did you call your brother back?" she asked while looking over the board. Ryan had called while they were intent on obliterating a nasty patch of poison oak for a family with several kids and Sean had sent the message to voice mail.

"Not yet. I'll give him a shout back tomorrow."

"Are you avoiding him?" She dropped an *O* and *T* on the end of *BALL* and noted her points.

"Yup." He rearranged some tiles on his rack, frowning. "They're taking turns calling me to see if anybody's won the bet yet."

And he wouldn't tell them because somebody might tell the women and he didn't want them getting ideas. She was about to tell him it was lame to avoid his siblings over a stupid bet, when he laid down his tiles, adding a *Q, U, A* and an *R* on a triple-word-score space before the *T* she'd put down, and then a *Z* on the end. "You did *not* just use a *Q* and a *Z* on a triple-word score."

"I think that puts me in the lead." He grinned and picked up the pencil and paper. "Never count a Kowalski out. We don't like to lose."

"Obviously I'm not hot enough. Maybe I should have put on some mascara."

He grabbed her arm and pulled her close. "You don't need shit on your face to be hot."

"Just a dirt smudge here and there?"

He laughed and leaned forward to kiss her. She

wanted more and threw her leg over his so she was straddling his lap. He moaned against her mouth, his hands going to her hips as she put her hands on his bare chest and pushed him back against the couch.

"Now I know you're trying to distract me," he muttered against her lips.

"I don't like to lose, either."

It was her turn to moan when he lightly caught her nipple between his teeth, the thin T-shirt doing nothing to dampen the delicious sensation. He slid his hands under the fabric, pushing it up until her breasts were bared to his mouth.

She reached down to undo his fly, but his arm blocked hers. He worked his hand into the wide leg opening of her boxers and found...only her. Groaning, he slid his fingers over her slick flesh and her fingers dug into his shoulders.

"Please tell me we don't have to go all the way upstairs for a condom," she said.

"Back pocket." She leaned with him as he fished it out, then tried to help him get his jeans down over his hips. Her foot hit the coffee table, which snagged on the throw rug and sent the Scrabble tiles sliding all over the board.

She laughed as he tore open the condom packet. "Now nobody wins."

"I was ahead." He put one hand on her hip, using the other to guide himself into her. "So I win."

Emma moaned as he filled her, bracing herself against the couch with a hand on either side of his head. "The game wasn't over. It's a draw."

He pulled down on her hips as he drove up into her, making her gasp. "Ties are for pussies. Admit I won."

She looked down into his blue eyes, crinkled with amusement as he grinned at her. God, she loved… having sex with this man. "One good word isn't a victory."

"That's not what the score sheet said." He stopped moving, and when she tried to rock against him, he held down on her hips so she couldn't move, either. Then he had the nerve to chuckle at her growl of sexual frustration. "Admit it. I can sit here all night."

"Oh, really?" She went straight for a known weak spot—nipping at his earlobe before sucking it into her mouth.

He let go of her hips with one hand, intending to push her mouth away, but she rocked her hips. He groaned and put his hand back. She breathed softly against his ear and then ran her tongue along the outside.

"Admit I was going to win," she whispered, "because I can do this all night."

With one leg, he kicked at the table, sending it over and the letter tiles flying. Before Emma could react, she was on her back on the throw rug with Sean between her legs and her hands held over her head.

"I don't lose." He crossed her wrists so he could hold them with one hand, then used the other to pull her leg up over his hip so he was totally buried in her. "Give up?"

She shook her head, but couldn't hold back the sigh as he oh, so slowly withdrew almost completely and then just as slowly filled her again. "You're cheating."

He did it again and again, the slow friction delicious and frustrating, until they were both trembling and on the edge.

Then, as he was pulling out of her once again with a self-control that made her want to scream, it became a matter of life or death, because she was going to die if she didn't get what her body was looking for. "Okay, fine. You win."

He drove into her hard, his fingers biting into her wrists before he released them so he could lift her legs to her shoulder. She cried his name as his fingers dug into her hips and he gave them what they both wanted.

When he collapsed on top of her, breathing hard against her neck, she wrapped her legs and arms around him, holding him close.

"Another one for the win column," he said once they'd caught their breath.

"It has an asterisk, though, because you totally cheated."

"All's fair in sex and Scrabble, baby." He propped

his head on his hand and smiled down at her. "What should we play next?"

"I've still got clothes on. You've still got clothes on. Maybe we should break out a deck of cards."

"You're my kinda girl, Emma Shaw," he said, and thankfully, he was in the process of getting up off the floor, because she didn't think she did a good job of hiding how happy those words made her.

SEAN EYEBALLED THE BUBBLE, making sure it was exact dead center in the level, and then drove the last screw home. The stairs were done. Tomorrow he'd lay the seats for the built-in bench seating and the deck would be done.

Just in time, too, since tomorrow was his last day of work. He and Emma were taking Thursday and Friday off to spend with Cat since she was leaving on Sunday.

Which meant he'd be leaving on Sunday, too.

"Nice work," Emma said, startling him because he'd been so lost in thought he hadn't heard her approach.

"I told you it'd be good. If it's treated properly, this deck will outlast the house." And he wouldn't be the one treating it. Either Emma would have to see to the weatherproofing or hire somebody else to do it. He wouldn't be around anymore.

"Are you going to be able to finish the benches to-morrow?"

"Yup." He turned around and looked out at the property Emma had transformed while he built the deck. "They're going to love this place."

She took off her gloves and tossed them down next to his toolbox. "I think so, too. It all came together even better than I thought."

They made a good pair, just as he'd thought they would, but he didn't say it out loud. It was something he'd had to do a lot lately—watching what he said. He'd gone with her the previous afternoon to look at a lakefront property and he'd almost pointed out they really needed to rebuild the owners' boat dock. And when they'd stopped at the grocery store to pick up some steaks, he'd noticed the pot roasts were on sale and almost asked her if she could use a Crock-Pot, because nothing beat slow-cooked pot roast on a chilly autumn day.

Luckily he'd remembered he wouldn't be there for any chilly autumn days before he'd opened his mouth. And, even if he did get a job pounding nails after he left, he shouldn't bid on pounding any nails with her. She'd managed to get under his skin so completely, the only way he was going to get out of there was to walk away and not look back.

"Are you okay?"

He shook off his thoughts and looked at Emma. She was frowning at him. "Yeah, why?"

"You just looked really unhappy for a minute."

"Just hungry. Thinking about those steaks we bought and how good they're going to taste tonight."

She gave him an uncertain look, but didn't argue. "We should start picking up. I didn't realize how late it was, and Gram likes to eat on the early side."

He started gathering his tools, wondering if Emma had moments like that. Moments when she was making plans or thinking about something they were going to do before remembering he wouldn't be there come Monday morning. And if she did, if she cared.

After carrying his tool bucket to the truck, he helped Emma clean her tools and carried them around for her.

"I'm going to miss having you around," she said lightly, carrying nothing but her gloves. "I'll have to do my own heavy lifting again."

Was that the only reason? "You should hire somebody. You can afford to pay me, so you can afford to pay somebody else."

She only shrugged, as if she might think about it, and he let it go. Wasn't his business what she did with her company. Once he had her tools stowed in the diamond-plate lockboxes in the back of her truck, he brushed off his hands and opened her door for her since she was just standing there looking at him.

"What's bothering you?" she asked again. "And don't tell me you're hungry."

What was he supposed to say? He wasn't going to tell her he was moping because she didn't seem too broken up over the fact he'd be leaving soon and wouldn't be coming back. Except for the fact she wouldn't have him around to carry her tools anymore.

Instead, he backed her up against the inside of the open truck door and kissed her. It was a good kiss, too, but apparently not good enough, because she pushed him back. "Don't put me off like that. We've already had the discussion about your kisses not making my brain empty of any intelligent thought."

"Fine. Building a deck alone is hard work and I'm tired. I've also been thinking a lot about what I'm going to be doing next week because being a lazy, unemployed bum isn't really my style."

And there was the opening. If she had any interest at all in keeping whatever was between them going, she'd at least offer to keep him on with her. Not that he wanted to be a landscaper by trade, but she could ask.

"Okay." She sighed. "You'll be back where you started before I knocked on your door, so I'm sure you'll figure it out. And if you let me drive home, I'll give you a massage later."

Back to sex, which was a pretty solid way of reminding him exactly where their non-relationship
stood. He could live with sex. Shaking off the mushy-
feelings stuff, he smiled and hooked his fingers in
her front pockets. "How about I drive and I give you
a massage later?"

"You're not going to let me drive, are you?"

"I have the magic penis, so I get the keys, remember?"

She laughed and tried to shove him away. "You're
a penis, all right. A big walking, talking penis."

He kissed her again, this time until she surrendered
and wrapped her arms around his neck. There were
only a few more days of kissing her in his future, so
he intended to make it a priority.

"Okay," she whispered when he was done. "You
can drive. But I get to pick exactly what part of me
you're massaging."

"I can live with that." He slapped her on the butt
when she climbed into the truck, and then laughed as
he walked around to the driver's side and caught her
flipping him off through the window.

He'd make her pay for that later.

CHAPTER EIGHTEEN

"I NEEDED TO GRAB ANOTHER BOX of screws, but, when I got to the truck, I realized I'd left my wallet in my tool bucket. When I went back around the house to get it, she had my plans open and was double-checking all my measurements."

Emma's cheeks burned when Gram laughed at Sean's story, but, since she couldn't deny it, she stuck her last bite of the fabulous steak he'd grilled into her mouth.

"That's my Emma," Gram said. "I think her first words were 'If you want something done right, do it yourself.'"

"In my defense," she said when she'd swallowed, pointing her fork at Sean for emphasis, "my name is on the truck, and being able to pound nails doesn't make you a builder. I have a responsibility to my clients to make sure they get quality work."

"I do quality work."

"I know you build a quality deck, but stairs are tricky." She smiled sweetly at him. "I had to double-check."

"It's all done but the seating now and it's good work, even though I practically had to duct tape you to a tree in order to work in peace."

She might have taken offense at his words if not for the fact he was playing footsie with her under the table. And when he nudged her foot to get her to look at him, he winked in that way that—along with the grin—made it almost impossible for her to be mad at him.

"It's Sean's turn to wash tonight. Emma, you dry and I'll put away."

"I'll wash, Gram. Sean can dry."

"I can wash," Sean told her. "The world won't come to an end if I wash the silverware before the cups."

"It makes me twitch."

"I know it does. That's why I do it." He leaned over and kissed her before she could protest.

"That new undercover-cop show I like is on to-night," Gram said as they cleared the table. "Maybe Sean won't snort his way through this episode."

He laughed and started filling the sink with hot, soapy water. "I'm sorry, but if he keeps shoving his gun in his waistband like that, he's going to shoot his...he's going to shoot himself in a place men don't want to be shot."

Emma watched him dump the plates and silverware into the water—while three coffee mugs sat on the counter waiting to be washed—but forced herself to ignore it. "Can't be worse than the movie the other night."

"That was just stupid," Sean said while Gram laughed.

They'd tried to watch a military-action movie and by the time they were fifteen minutes in, she thought they were going to have to medicate Sean if they wanted to see the end. After a particularly heated lecture about what helicopters could and couldn't do, Emma had hushed him, but he'd still snorted so often in derision she was surprised he hadn't done permanent damage to his sinuses.

"I don't want you to think that's real life," he told them.

"I promise," Gram said, "if I ever want to use a tank to break somebody out of a federal prison, I'll ask you how to do it correctly first."

He kissed the top of her head. "Thanks, Cat. At least you appreciate me, unlike Emma, who just tells me to shut up."

"I'd appreciate you more if there wasn't salad dressing floating in the dishwater you're about to wash my coffee cup in."

"According to the official guy's handbook, if I

keep doing it wrong, you're supposed to let me watch *SportsCenter* while you do it yourself."

"Did the official guy's handbook also tell you that if that happens, you'll also be free to watch the late-night sports shows while I do *other* things myself?"

The tips of his ears turned pink as he cast a sideways glance at her grandmother, but Gram just laughed.

Emma couldn't put her finger on exactly when it happened, but at some point the time she spent with just Sean and Gram had become her new normal. And she liked her new normal.

Laughter over the dinner table. Banter during the cleaning up. Then Gram in her chair, knitting while they watched television. Sean stretched out on the couch with his head in her lap. She could stroke his hair or give him a kiss in the kitchen and not feel like a fraud. And without the Kowalskis stirring up trouble, they'd fallen into a comfortable evening routine that felt a little more *real* every day.

It was a tourism commercial for Florida that popped her bubble. It was a too-cheerful reminder that in less than a week, Gram would be flying back to North Fort Meyers. And that meant Sean would be leaving, too.

She'd be alone again. She hadn't minded it before—had enjoyed having the big house all to herself—but now she couldn't imagine sitting alone and watching TV. Or heating up a microwave meal. Not having anybody to talk to or to laugh with.

It wasn't only Gram she couldn't imagine her life without. It was Sean, and that scared her so badly she nudged him and told him she wanted to get up.

"You okay?" He touched her face, clearly concerned.

"Fine. I just need to… I'll be back in a few minutes."

She went upstairs to their bedroom—*her* bedroom—and then locked herself in the little bathroom. Once there, she discovered a possible culprit for her emotional state, but she knew it was far worse than hormones on their monthly roller-coaster ride.

Despite his warnings, she'd gone and gotten ideas about Sean. She was afraid she'd fallen in love with him and there was nothing she could do to talk herself out of it now.

Just great, she thought, pressing the heels of her hands against her eyes in an effort to stem the tears. Now she had to pretend not to the love the man she was pretending to love while pretending she wasn't sleeping with him.

SEAN GAVE EMMA TWENTY MINUTES before he decided to go after her. Something had obviously upset her, and he suspected it was the Florida commercial. Now that she was in her last week with Gram, it had probably hit her Cat would be going home soon.

"Do you want to pause this?" Cat asked him when he got up off the couch.

"No, go ahead and watch it. I'm going to check on Emma. I think…I think maybe she doesn't feel good, so I'm not sure if we'll be back down or not."

She gave him a warm smile and went back to her knitting, so he went up the stairs and into their room. Emma was curled up on the couch, wrapped in the blanket, and she'd brought her pillow.

"What happened?" he asked, crouching next to her and pushing her hair back from her face. She wasn't crying, but she had been recently.

"Nothing."

"Was it the commercial? The one about Florida?" She hesitated a few seconds, then nodded. "I'll miss her, too. She's a great lady."

A tear spilled onto Emma's cheek and he wiped it away. "Is that all that's bothering you?"

She lifted one shoulder in a half-assed shrug. "I'm just tired."

He tucked her hair behind her ear. "Then we'll go to bed. Why are you on the couch?"

"Because…" She sniffled and her cheeks turned pink. "It's, um…*that* time."

"Oh." Plumbing issues, as his uncle so delicately

referred to *that* time, explained a lot. "You'll be more comfortable in the bed."

She shook her head and pulled the blanket up over her face, so he stood and considered his options. He could go back downstairs and finish watching the show with Cat, but he didn't really like leaving Emma alone, not that there was anything he could do to ease her misery. And he couldn't stand next to the couch all night watching her, so he went into the bathroom and got ready for bed.

After turning off the light and punching his pillow into shape, Sean sprawled on the bed and tried to force himself to sleep. He had the whole bed to himself and he didn't have to share the covers, so it should have been all good.

But he was too aware of her across the room and he didn't want her there. He wasn't going to be able to sleep with her there. He wanted her next to him, where she was supposed to be.

His eyes flew open and he flopped onto his back, staring at the ceiling. That was wrong. She wasn't *supposed* to be sleeping next to him. She was *supposed* to be sleeping on the couch, which was exactly where she was. What they had between them wasn't real, so he should be able to do something as simple as fall asleep without her in his arms, dammit.

He'd be leaving in less than a week. He'd probably go back to the apartment over Jasper's Bar & Grille.

Or, screw it, maybe he'd go back to Maine and stay at the Northern Star until he figured out what he wanted to do. Or hop in his truck and drive to New Mexico to check on his sister.

No matter what he did or where he went, there'd be no more Emma for him.

When she sniffled and then shifted for what seemed like the tenth time in two minutes, Sean had had enough. She wasn't on the couch because she was more comfortable there. She was there because she didn't think he'd share the bed if there was no sex in it for him. He got up and walked across the bedroom. Then he threw the blanket across the back of the couch and scooped her up, pillow and all, to carry her to the bed.

The look she gave him, all sleepy and questioning, as he crawled in beside her squeezed something inside him. "I can't sleep with you tossing and turning on the couch, that's all."

Only when she'd snuggled against him and drifted off to sleep did Sean close his eyes. He still didn't sleep, though, because that *wasn't* all. There was also the fact having the rest of his life in front of him like an open road, with no obligations or strings, just made him feel empty inside.

He must have slept at some point because her alarm clock startled him awake. Emma was curled up on her side, facing him, and he smiled when she opened her eyes.

"How you feeling this morning?"

"I'd feel better if you got up and shut my alarm off." She'd plugged it in next to the couch, the way she had in the beginning of their nonrelationship.

"Now you're just taking advantage," he said, but he got up and killed the phone.

He turned back to the bed and froze. She was watching him, her eyes sleepy and her hair tumbled across the pillow. A smile curved her lips and he found himself smiling in response.

God, she was gorgeous, bedhead and ratty T-shirt and all.

"I'm starving," she said and then she stretched, which made him turn away so he didn't have to go down to breakfast walking funny.

"Do you want me to bring you up a tray of food?"

"Like room service?"

"I don't know." He shrugged. "I wasn't sure if you were up to going downstairs. Or working."

"I'm okay, and you have two days to get that deck done. You can have dibs on the bathroom and then I'll get dressed."

Cat was flipping the first batch of banana pancakes when Sean hit the kitchen. "Morning, Cat."

"Good morning. How's Emma today?"

"Better. She's, uh...it's *that* time," he said, going with Emma's terminology.

"Huh. It doesn't usually affect her much."

"I think she also realized you're not going to be here much longer." And neither would he.

Emma would probably be relieved to have him out from underfoot. She could go back to driving her truck and sleeping on her side of the bed and washing her dishes in the proper order.

"I'm going to miss her, too," Cat said. "Both of you."

"I'm going to miss your cooking, that's for sure," he said, sitting in front of the pancakes she set down for him. "You sure we can't talk you into staying?"

Then he stopped with the fork halfway to his mouth. He had to stop doing that. There was no *we*.

"I miss Emma when I'm there, but I really enjoy Florida."

He was on his second pancake when Emma came downstairs, looking a hell of a lot better than she had the night before. She kissed her grandmother's cheek and picked at a pancake before disappearing into her office to make a phone call.

"What are you going to do today, Cat?" Sean asked when the woman just stood there staring after Emma, concern in her eyes.

"Oh, I'll probably go into town and see if I can sweet-talk Russell into buying me lunch."

He wondered how that budding romance was going to turn out, since she was leaving in a few days, but it wasn't his place to ask. "I should get my boots on. If I'm not ready to leave before her, she might get the truck keys first."

She touched his shoulder for a moment as she leaned in to take his empty plate, and he felt a pang of…something. Maybe guilt. But also affection and sorrow that she'd be flying out of his life soon and she didn't know it would be for the last time.

On his way to the foyer, he paused to kiss her cheek. "Say hi to Russell for me."

"Try not to let Emma drive you crazy today."

"Fat chance of that," he said, grinning. Then he went off to get to Emma's key ring before she got off the phone.

THE BELL RANG AS CAT walked into Walker Hardware and she smiled, anticipating the way he'd look up and see her and his face would light up with a warm smile.

He didn't let her down. "Cat, I was just thinking about you."

"Good thoughts, I hope."

"Of course. I was debating calling you and asking you to lunch, but I wasn't sure if you'd have plans with Emma since…you're leaving soon."

Maybe she was imagining it, but she thought his smile might have dimmed a little when he mentioned her leaving. "They have to work today and then they're taking tomorrow and Friday off. I came to invite *you* to lunch, actually."

She met him at their usual café in town, where she ordered a salad and he told her he'd have the grilled chicken instead of the fried. "It would be a real shame if I went to hell in a handbasket now."

They talked about the store and the liquidation sale. It wasn't going as well as he'd hoped because people weren't too comfortable taking advantage of the bargain prices. "One of my regular customers said she felt as though she was picking at my carcass."

Cat laughed. "That's a horrible visual, but I think I understand what she meant by it. It's nice that people care about how you feel in all this."

"One of the many reasons I love this town." He smiled at her and sipped his water.

She smiled back, though she felt a pang of sorrow deep inside. Russell not only loved the town, but his family was here. His friends. She'd been starting to play with a foolish notion about asking him to come down to Florida. Maybe for a visit or maybe for more.

"Have you figured out what to do about Emma yet?"

Cat sighed. "No. But if I don't do something, we're going to part ways with this silliness between us and I don't want that."

"You're still planning to give her the house?"

"Definitely. John and I both wanted her to have it, and that was before she grew up and made it her home." She took a bite of her salad, at a loss as to what to do.

"You said she got upset at the Fourth of July barbecue when you mentioned giving it to her as a wedding gift. Have you mentioned it again?"

"No. That day I thought she was on the verge of confessing everything and we didn't want that. *We* meaning Mary Kowalski and I. We wanted Sean and Emma to have a little more time together."

He nodded as though it all made perfect sense to him. "But now time's running out, anyway."

"Maybe I'll push her on the subject tomorrow. I need to see a lawyer about it, anyway, so I might as well start the process before I go home."

"And you think she'll confess?"

"I don't think she'll accept the house as a wedding gift knowing it's a lie. I know she won't."

He toyed with the mashed potatoes on his plate, dragging his fork through them in a grid pattern. "And what are you hoping will happen between her and Sean when that happens?"

That was a harder question to answer. "I'm hoping that, when faced with going their separate ways, they'll both realize they don't want to do that. And maybe they'll go on as they are now, only they won't be pretending."

"They do seem like a nice couple."

"They really are good together, though I'm not sure they see it." She chuckled. "Leave it to my grand-daughter to accidentally choose her Mr. Right to be her fake fiancé."

CHAPTER NINETEEN

EVEN WITH HER ALARM turned off, Emma was up at the crack of dawn. They weren't working these last three days before Gram flew back to Florida, so she slid out of bed without waking Sean and threw on her boxers and T-shirt.

Not surprisingly, Gram was already up. There were no signs of breakfast yet, but she told Emma she'd brewed a pot of coffee along with making herself tea, so Emma poured a cup and sat down at the table.

"I can't believe we only have three days left," she said after the first bracing sip.

"I know. And I'll miss you, honey. You know I will, but I miss being there. My friends and all my activities."

Emma smiled. "I'm glad, Gram. You know I miss you, too, but it's great that you have all that in your life."

"Before I go, I'm going into town to talk to a lawyer about giving you the house."

The little bit of coffee she'd gotten into her stomach did a slow roll. "I told you I want to buy it from you, fair and square. We'll get a fair market value for it and then you can sell it to me."

"That's ridiculous. It's a gift."

"I don't feel right about that. And it'll be good for my business to build credit."

Gram snorted. "Then you buy a new truck and lease a tractor or something. You don't buy an old farmhouse. My mind's made up, Emma."

Crap. Once she said that, it was over. But there was no way she would let Gram give her the house without knowing the truth. She stared down into her coffee for a minute, and then took a deep breath. They'd almost made it, but it was time.

"It's all a lie, Gram. All of it. There's not going to be a wedding."

There. Now it was done and the entire month had been for nothing. Now her grandmother would be angry and maybe sell the house to a stranger, anyway. And Sean would have no reason to stay. She wasn't sure which hurt more.

"Maybe you should explain yourself."

"I made up a boyfriend so you'd stop being so nervous about me being alone. Sean's name just kind of popped out. He was still in the army until a month or so ago. And I met him for the first time four days before you arrived, when I knocked on his door and asked him to pretend to be my fiancé."

Gram actually chuckled. "That must have been an interesting conversation."

Emma was confused. The very last reaction she expected from her grandmother was amusement. She'd been hoping and praying her confession wouldn't fracture their relationship beyond repair. Laughter wasn't something she'd anticipated.

"You're not upset?" She looked into the older woman's eyes and reluctantly recognized the truth. "You already knew."

"Of course I knew. Couples who've lived together for a year are comfortable with each other. There's familiarity. I could tell as soon as I got off the plane you and Sean didn't have that."

She'd known the *entire* time? "Why didn't you say anything?"

"Because I wanted to figure out what you were up to. And then, later, Mary and I decided you two needed a little more time to get to know each other, so we played along."

"Oh, my God." Emma covered her face with her hands. "Mrs. Kowalski knew you knew?"

"I had to practically drag the truth out of her, but once she realized I already knew you two were lying, she gave up. I must confess, though, I was a little put out that you thought I'd fall for this."

"By the time I realized how really crazy it was, I was in too deep to back out. I know it sounds dumb, but I did it because I love you, Gram. I wanted you to let me go so you could enjoy being in Florida."

"I'll never let you go. But maybe I did give you the impression I was worrying more about you than enjoying myself. But you also wanted the house."

Emma's cheeks burned. "Of course I wanted the house. It's my home. But I wanted you to *sell* it to me. I never expected you to just give it to me. You have to believe that."

Gram reached across the table and squeezed her hand. "I knew you wouldn't take it. I told Mary and Russell both you wouldn't accept it as a wedding gift without telling me the truth, and I was right."

"If you'd said something, we wouldn't have wasted the entire month playing games."

"Oh, I don't think it was a waste," Gram said, smiling. "I see Sean's sleeping in this morning. Did you keep him up too late last night?"

When the implication behind her grandmother's words sank in, Emma shook her head. "It's not like that. We're not... It's not real."

"Well, it's certainly not pretend."

"No." Emma really didn't want to have this conversation. "It's like friends with benefits, Gram. Once he knows I told you the truth, he's going to pack up his stuff and go."

"Maybe he won't if you ask him to stay."

"Who says I want him to stay?" she asked, forcing a little attitude into her voice. Maybe if she could convince somebody else she didn't care, she'd believe it herself.

"I think we've had enough lies, Emma."

"We had a deal, Gram. Love wasn't part of it."

"I've spent the last month living with you two and I've watched your relationship change. Don't sell him short, honey."

She got up and rinsed her empty teacup, then walked over to kiss the top of Emma's head. "I'm going to go have a nice bath and get dressed. I'm still going into town and I'm still giving you the house."

"Gram, I—"

"My mind is made up, Emma," she said as she left the kitchen.

SEAN WAS WHISTLING when he hit the kitchen, hunting for coffee, but he stopped when he saw Emma sitting at the table. Her nose was a little blotchy and her eyes still damp from a cry.

"I told Gram the truth," she said. "It's over."

His lungs deflated in a rush, leaving behind an ache he hoped was a lack of oxygen and not the beginning of a heartache. That would be stupid, since it wasn't as if what they had was real. It was all pretend and he'd known the day would come he'd walk away from her without looking back.

But he thought he had three and a half more days before he had to face that.

"Are you okay?" he asked. She nodded, even though she didn't look it. "How did she take it?"

"You were right, that day we were working and you said you thought she was onto us. She knew all along."

That set him back a bit. "She knew?"

"She said she suspected as soon as she saw us together in the airport because we didn't look like a couple who'd...been intimate. And she and Mrs. Kowalski have been in cahoots since the first barbecue."

"I don't understand. Why didn't she say anything? And in cahoots with Aunt Mary to what?"

"She didn't say anything because she wanted to know what we were up to." Her cheeks flushed and she looked down at the table. "And they were in cahoots to make us a real couple."

"Oh." He really didn't know what to say to that. "They thought we'd make a good couple?"

"Crazy, huh?"

That wasn't the direction he'd been heading, but it was probably best she'd said it. It *was* crazy. They were so different. They were in different places in their lives and wanted different things.

"Where's Cat now?"

"Taking a bath. Then she's going into town and—"

She had to stop because she was tearing up again, and then she took a deep, shuddering breath. "She's going to talk to a lawyer about giving me the house."

"That's good, then."

"That's why I told her the truth. She was insisting on giving me the house as a wedding gift, so I had to tell her."

"But she already knew."

"And she knew I wouldn't accept it based on a lie. She wanted me to tell her the truth."

Sean poured himself a cup of coffee, hoping the caffeine would help restore some of his equilibrium. Even though he'd been blindsided, this turn of events was a good thing for Emma. She could stop lying to her grandmother. Cat wouldn't be selling the house out from under her. And, while Emma would still be single, maybe the shenanigans would be a wake-up call to Cat that she didn't need to worry quite so much.

"I'm happy for you," he said, and he meant it. What he wasn't sure was how he felt on his own behalf.

She nodded, but she didn't look as happy as he expected her to. With the house soon to be in her name and him soon to be out from under her feet, he was surprised she wasn't dancing across the kitchen.

He took a bracing sip of the coffee, not bothering with cream or sugar. "So...I guess that's it, then."

She nodded again, her hands folded so tightly on the table her knuckles were pale. "I guess it is."

He started for the door, but then stopped and looked back at her. "Are you sure you're okay?"

"I'm sure." She even managed a wobbly smile. "Emotional shock, I guess. So much drama for...no reason. Telling her was terrifying and such a relief at the same time, so it's probably just the letdown."

"Okay, then." He took his coffee into her office and closed the door.

It was over. He was free to go be his own man again, his life revolving around steak, football, beer and women. He could go back to his wild pluralizing ways, as she'd put it during their first dinner together.

Before it could all settle in, he pulled out his phone and hit Kevin's number on the speed dial. He answered on the second ring, sounding groggy, and Sean belatedly remembered that, due to owning a sports bar, Kevin and his family stayed up late and slept late in the morning.

"Shit. I didn't mean to wake you." Sean scrubbed a hand over his face, realizing it was too early to be calling anybody. "Quick question and then you can go back to sleep. Can I still mooch that apartment?"

"Uh-oh."

"Long story short, she told Cat the truth, so my services are no longer needed."

"You okay?"

He wasn't sure yet. "Why wouldn't I be?"

"Okay. You still got the key?"

"Yup."

"It's yours, then. Head on down for a beer later, on the house. You know, when it's not dark o'clock."

"The sun's up, dude. But thanks."

It took him a depressingly short time to pack his stuff. A few minutes to empty his drawer. Less than two to grab his stuff out of the closet. It took him a little longer in the bathroom sorting his toiletries from hers. He'd just retrieved the stash of condoms from the bedside drawer and tossed them in the duffel because he'd be damned if he'd facilitate her sleeping with some other guy in the future, when Emma walked in.

"I'll be out of your way in a few minutes," he told her. "Just have to gather up a few things downstairs."

"You don't have to run out of here, Sean."

"No sense in hanging around," he said, maybe a little more gruffly than he'd intended.

"Oh. Okay, then. Gram wants me to go to town with her and she's ready to go."

"I'll put the key in the mailbox when I leave. Don't forget to grab it later."

"Sean." He shoved a pile of socks into the bag. It was like ripping off a Band-Aid. A clean and fast exit was best for everybody. "Goddammit, Sean, it's ob-

vious you can't wait to get out of here, but she wants
to say goodbye to you before you go."

"What about her goodbye barbecue? Or am I un-
invited?"

"There's no sense in dragging your family over
here now. She'll probably have lunch with your aunt
or something."

She tossed something onto the bed and then turned
and walked away before he could apologize. He was
being a jerk and he couldn't help it. If he showed any
weakness and she gave him some indication she didn't
want him to go, he might stay, and this wasn't where
he'd wanted to end up.

Sean shifted his bag so he could see what she'd
tossed onto the bed. It was the small diamond ring
he'd put on her finger a month ago when he asked her
to marry him, and as the sun hit the stone, it winked
at him. Feeling nothing but hollow, he closed his fingers around it, squeezing it in his fist. Then he tucked
it into the front pocket of his jeans and took a deep
breath.

It was best for both of them if he shut Emma out
and walked away. But first he had to get through a
moment he'd been dreading.

Cat was waiting for him at the bottom of the stairs.
Emma was next to her, but she wouldn't even look at
him. He could tell by the way her jaw was set he'd
pissed her off.

"I'll wait in the truck," she said, and then she seemed to collect herself. She turned to face him and stuck out her hand. "Thanks, Sean."

A handshake? After all that, he was getting brushed off with a handshake? But he was the one who'd made it very clear to her none of what they had was real.

He gripped her hand in his, running his thumb over hers. "I'll see you around, Emma."

She nodded and pulled her hand back. Sean squeezed her fingers for a second, but he couldn't hold on to her. Before he could say anything else, she walked out of the house.

"You two are going to be stubborn about this, aren't you?"

Sean turned to Cat and chose to ignore her words. "I'm going to miss you. And I mean that."

"Even though Emma thinks a party isn't a good idea now because it would be awkward, I'm sure I'll see you again."

"Don't know where I'm going from here. But you never know. Maybe I'll drive down to Florida and crash one of your wild and crazy beach parties someday."

She opened her arms and he enveloped her in a hug. "You're welcome to hang out under my beach umbrella anytime."

After extricating himself from her arms, he kissed her cheek. "Take care of yourself, Cat."

"And you...don't be *too* stubborn."

She went out the door before he could ask her what that was supposed to mean. He heard the truck door close and then it was heading down the driveway.

He stood there for a few minutes and then went into the kitchen. Over the past few months, he'd actually accumulated a few things, and his belongings didn't fit in the duffel anymore. He grabbed a trash bag because what the hell did he care, then scoured the downstairs, tossing in anything that belonged to him.

Then he finished upstairs and there was nothing left but to get in his truck and drive away. But first he went into the bathroom and pulled the pad of sticky notes out of his pocket. He stuck a pink one to the mirror and pulled the cap off his Sharpie.

And...nothing. What could he say? Something flip like *Thanks for the good times* didn't feel right. Maybe *Goodbye.* Or *Why does it feel so shitty to be leaving right now?*

He stared at the blank note a long time, then put the cap back on the marker and shoved it in his pocket. There was nothing left to say, so he grabbed his bags and walked out of Emma's house.

CAT AND MARY MET at a coffee shop, the mood pessimistic. The month certainly hadn't ended the way either of them had thought—and hoped—it would.

"She was so cold to him before we left," Cat said, "but about a half hour after we got home, I heard her crying. I peeked into her room and she was sitting on the floor with a sticky note in her hand, sobbing her heart out."

"Could you read what it said?"

"That's the thing—it was blank. Just a blank sticky note."

Mary frowned. "That doesn't make any sense."

"I don't know what the deal is with the sticky note, but I know she cares about him a whole lot more than she wanted him to know."

"Sean's not answering his phone. I made Kevin go up and knock on his door. He said Sean wasn't in a really sociable mood and we should just leave him alone for a few days."

Cat shook her head and put another sugar cube in her tea just to get the kick. "They're both hardheaded. I'm afraid if they're left alone for a few days, they won't come around at all."

"When I talked to Lisa earlier, she gave me the impression you weren't going to have your goodbye party since we're not all going to be one big happy family. Maybe you should."

"I hadn't even thought about it yet. Emma's knee-jerk reaction was to cancel it but, to be honest, even if she and Sean boycott, I still want to say goodbye to everybody."

"Sean won't boycott." She said it with the certainty of a woman who'd brook no argument from the men in her life.

"Emma won't, either."

"Maybe a little more time together, without the lies, is just what they need."

Cat smiled and took a sip of her tea. The bad part of the plan was the fact she'd have to say goodbye to Sean all over again. She wouldn't look forward to that, considering how sad doing it the first time had made her. But it would be worth it if there was a chance of bringing him and Emma together, especially if it happened before she flew back to Florida.

They talked about the party for a few minutes, but then Mary finished her tea and dug a few dollars out of her purse. "I hate to run, but I promised I'd watch Brianna this afternoon. Joe has a writing deadline and Keri has an editing deadline and the baby doesn't really care about either one."

Once she was gone, Cat asked for a tea to go and walked down to the patch of grass that passed for a public park and pulled out her phone.

"Walker Hardware."

Just hearing his voice brightened her day. "Hi, Russell. Are you busy?"

"Nope. Already had my customer for the day. What's up?"

She told him the whole story, starting with Emma's

confession and ending with their intention to have the party as planned. "I hope you'll still come. And Dani and Roger, too."

"We'll be there. It sounds like you've had a big day. Do you want me to close up early?"

He was such a good man. "No, but thank you for offering. I'm going to go home and see how Emma's holding up. If I know my girl, she'll have her everything's-okay mask in place by the time I get there. And she'll be scrubbing the crisper drawer runners or reorganizing the junk drawer."

"I'll be thinking of you, Cat. And call me later if you need somebody to talk to."

"I will." She closed her cell phone and took a deep breath.

They had two days to keep the kids on an even keel, and then they'd see how things went at the party. She had her fingers crossed forty-eight hours would be long enough for Sean and Emma to realize how much they missed each other.

CHAPTER TWENTY

SEAN WAS GOING TO CRACK. Or his steering wheel was going to crack if he didn't loosen his grip on it.

He was fourth in the caravan of Kowalski vehicles heading to the house with those stupid daisies painted on the mailbox to eat cheeseburgers and say goodbye to Cat. And it was a damn good thing he was alone in the truck because he needed the time to steady himself so he didn't totally lose his shit in front of his entire family.

It would be a final goodbye to Emma, too. Now that they didn't have to pretend anymore, it should have been easy. A fun barbecue with friends and family. No deception. No trying to remember who was getting which story.

But Sean was still pretending. He was pretending it didn't bother him his fake engagement had come to an end.

The rest of his life stretched before him and the time had come to figure out what he wanted to do with it, but he couldn't see it. Every time he tried, he pictured Emma.

All too soon, they were pulling into the driveway and parking down the sides so nobody got blocked in. He could still make a break for it, he thought. Drive out across the lawn and back out onto the street.

But he wouldn't. He'd man up and see this hellish day through.

Everybody was out back, and he made his way through the crowd to say hello to Cat, and then Russell, Dani and Roger. Emma wasn't in the yard, and when he looked toward the house, he saw her in the kitchen window. She was watching him, and in the seconds before she moved away, he saw that she looked as tired as he felt.

The kids immediately went off to explore Emma's yard, but there wasn't much to hold their interest. Bobby had his Nerf football with him, though, so an impromptu game broke out.

He watched Cat say something to Russell, who went over and fired up the grill. It was a stupid thing, really, but Sean had to look away. That had been his job when he was the man of the house, and seeing Russell do it just brought it home it had all been a fraud.

He'd never been the man of Emma's house. He'd been an actor filling a role.

Mike handed him a beer and pulled up a seat next to him. "Which one of us won?"

Sean looked around, but nobody was paying any attention to them. "Whoever called two weeks."

"So what now?"

Wasn't that the twenty-five-thousand-dollar question? "What do you mean?"

"Kev said you moved back into the apartment over the bar, but are you guys going to keep seeing each other?"

He shook his head and took a long pull on his beer so he wouldn't have to say it out loud.

"Why not?"

"Leave it alone, Mikey," he growled.

Emma came out the back door with an armful of potato-chip bags, which she dumped on the patio table. She smiled at him, but it was a little shaky, and went back inside.

"You should talk to her."

"Thanks, Oprah."

"Whatever. I know sometimes you guys feel sorry for me. Poor Mikey, with the mortgage and the mini-van and no life. Well, guess what? I feel sorry for you because I've got an amazing wife and four kids that rock my world every day."

Rather than tell his cousin to pound sand, Sean drained the rest of his beer and dangled the empty bottle between his fingers. "I'm happy for you, but not everybody wants that."

"No, but you do. You're just too chickenshit to go for it."

Sean shook his head. "What the hell do you know about it? We were sharing a room. She's hot. We had sex. End of story."

"If you say so."

"I do." And when Emma came out of the house with a tray of condiments, he turned his head and watched the kids tossing the football.

After a few minutes, Mike got bored with the brooding silence and, after slapping him on the shoulder to let him know there were no hard feelings, got up and walked away. Rather than sit and draw the attention of any more amateur shrinks in the family, he followed suit, forcing himself to be sociable. It wore on him, though, and after a while he wandered around to the front of the house, looking for some peace and quiet.

He found Keri sitting in one of the porch chairs, rocking Brianna. He hadn't seen much of her in the backyard, and the baby was probably why.

Keri smiled when she saw him. "I just fed her. Hoping if I sit here and rock long enough, she'll take a nice nap."

"I'm in the mood to sit for a while and you haven't gotten to visit at all. Hand her over and I'll rock her while she naps."

"Don't offer if you don't mean it," she warned.

"I mean it."

She got up so he could sit down and then she deposited the warm lump of baby in his lap. Brianna squirmed and sniffled a little, but then he started rocking and she quieted down. Keri peeked at her daughter's face, smiled at Sean and then ran, probably afraid he'd change his mind.

The rocking motion soothed his frayed nerves after a while and he leaned his head back and closed his eyes. He was too paranoid about dropping the baby to nod off, but he relaxed and let himself enjoy the summer breeze and the smell of freshly cut grass. The sounds of a happy, boisterous family in the backyard. The squeak of the chair every time he rocked backward.

For a few minutes he could even pretend it was what he'd wanted all along.

"HAVE YOU SEEN SEAN?" Emma couldn't find the big spatula and she was hoping he knew where it was.

Joe nodded. "Keri said he's on the front porch, rocking Brianna while she naps."

"That explains why Keri's having a good time," she said, which made him laugh.

Rather than go back through the house, Emma walked around the outside, her feet silent in the grass. And when she turned the corner, her heart did a painful somersault in her chest.

Sean was in one of the rocking chairs, the baby cradled in his arms as he gently rocked. His head was tipped back and his eyes were closed, but it was his mouth that drew her attention.

He was almost smiling. Not quite, but enough to give him a peaceful and contented look that made her ache. They could have had this. They could have had a baby he would rock on the porch on midsummer evenings. She could have had a man like Sean.

Instead, she'd had a performance.

"I told you what happens when you stare at people," he said in a quiet voice without opening his eyes.

"You weren't sleeping."

"No, but same principle." He did open his eyes then, turning his head to look at her. "Were you looking for me?"

"I'm looking for the big spatula and thought maybe you might know where it is."

"Check the pantry. I was putting stuff away and I had it in my hand and my phone rang. I might have set it down in there."

"Okay." She waited a second, but he didn't say anything else. "Thanks."

Bypassing the gauntlet of loved ones, she went in through the front door and walked back to the kitchen. The spatula was on the second shelf of the pantry, and she gripped it in one shaking hand.

It was all wrong. Her Sean would have teased her about his putting something away in the wrong place just to push her buttons. There would have been warmth and humor in his eyes. This Sean was closed off, giving her nothing.

It made sense. Her Sean had never been anything but a lie. Just her luck to choose a man who lied so well she'd almost believed it herself.

"Emma?" It wasn't until she heard Lisa's voice that she realized she was standing in the pantry holding a spatula and crying. "Emma, what's wrong?"

"Nothing," she tried to say, but it got all caught up in a sob and didn't come out right.

Lisa took the spatula out of her hand and tossed it on the table before pushing her toward the stairs.

"The burgers—"

"They'll find the spatula," Lisa said firmly. She pushed Emma up the stairs and down the hall to her room.

It hurt so much to look at the bed. The tears ran freely down her face and there wasn't a damn thing she could do to stop them. "I fell in love with him."

"Oh. Oh, shit." Lisa shook her head. "Kowalski men do that. They show up in your life and drive you so insane you want to slap them upside the head and then—*bam*—all of a sudden you can't live without them."

"That's pretty much what happened."

"Did you tell him?"

She shook her head, mopping her face with a tissue Lisa pulled from the travel pack she always had in her back pocket. "I can't do that to him. He disrupted his whole life to do me a huge favor and I'm not going to repay him by dumping my emotions in his lap."

"I *really* think you should tell him, Emma. Mike told me they all think he's serious about you."

A glimmer of hope flickered to life in her chest, but it fizzled almost instantly. "When I told him it was over, he ran out of here like the house was on fire. He didn't look back. And just now... He doesn't feel anything."

Lisa blew out a breath and crossed her arms. "Sometimes they need a little help."

"It's over, Lisa." The words echoed like a mournful bell tolling in her mind. "But I'll be fine. Really."

"We know Sean almost better than anybody and he does feel something. We've all seen it."

"Hell of an actor, isn't he?"

"No, he's not. He's such a bad liar none of us really thought he could pull this off in the first place."

Emma refused to let herself feel hopeful again. She may as well have been a complete stranger for all the emotion he'd shown her today, and it hurt too much to poke and prod, looking for scraps.

"You should go downstairs," she told Lisa. "If

people start looking for us, I'll end up with your whole damn family in here."

"Do you want me to tell them you don't feel good?"

"No. I'm going to take a couple minutes and wash my face, and then I'll be down."

Her friend gave her a quick hug. "I'll save you some Doritos."

She managed to smile, but it faded as soon as Lisa left the room. Throwing herself facedown on her bed and having a good cry sounded like a good idea, but she couldn't. Having an emotional breakdown would ruin Gram's party.

Instead, she doused her face with ice-cold water and did a little makeup magic. She didn't look her best, but maybe she could get through the rest of the day without anybody guessing she was totally coming undone on the inside.

"IT'S NOT WORKING," Mary said quietly, and Cat had to reluctantly admit she was right.

Sean and Emma couldn't have had more distance between them if they were in different counties. Cat and Mary were smooshed together in front of the kitchen sink, watching the party through the window. Sean on one end of the yard, Emma on the other.

"Why are they being so stubborn?"

Mary snorted. "He's a Kowalski. I'm not sure what Emma's excuse is."

They sighed in unison. "I know there's something there. I've lived with them for a month. Maybe they're not ready to run off to Vegas yet, but it was more than the sex. I'm sure of it."

"I'm sure of it, too. And would they be so carefully avoiding each other if it was nothing but a breezy fling? It hurts them, seeing each other here."

"Idiots." Cat left the window and started pulling desserts out of the fridge.

"Speaking of stubborn idiots, how are you leaving things with Russell?"

Cat set a bowl of Jell-O salad on the table and stared at it. "I don't know."

"Do you love him?"

"I don't know." She sighed. "It doesn't feel like it did when I fell for John. And we haven't been seeing each other very long."

"I'm not surprised it doesn't feel the same. You're sixty-five years old, and what's important to you—what you want in a man—is different now."

"I enjoy his company. I know that sounds lame. I'd probably enjoy the company of a golden retriever, too. But I *like* him. I like being with him."

Mary took over, taking the plastic wrap off the Jell-O salad and sticking a spoon in it. "But you're afraid that's not enough."

Cat laughed. "You're very good at this."

"I raised four children, plus had a hand in the raising of four nephews and a niece. Throw in teenage grandchildren and I've seen my share of love woes, trust me."

"His life is here."

"A one-bedroom apartment in senior housing? The occasional Sunday dinner with Dani and Roger?"

"Have I known him long enough to ask him to move to Florida with me?"

Mary slid the bowl toward Cat and moved on to slicing Keri's store-bought chocolate cake. "I don't know. Have you?"

The door opened before she could answer and Stephanie walked in, pulling her earbuds out and shoving them into her pocket. "Mom told me to come in and help."

"You can start carrying things out to the table," Mary told her. "Make sure you keep the dishes away from the edge of the table if Lily's cruising."

They finished preparing the desserts in silence and then it was time to drown her uncertainties in copious amounts of sugar, chocolate and whipped cream. She laughed as Sean and Keri played best out of three Rock-Paper-Scissors for the last blonde brownie, and at Beth, who had her hands full trying to stop Lily from sneaking whipped cream from anybody she turned her blue eyes and dimples on.

They were such a wonderful family, she thought. Having them as in-laws would have been a pleasure.

When she couldn't possibly eat another bite, she threw her paper plate in the trash and headed toward the double-wide swing hanging in the shade of the big maple. John had built it from scratch and she'd spent many an hour there, gently swaying with a four-year-old Emma on her lap. The picture books and stories they'd read together in the swing had helped them both leave their grief behind for a few minutes.

She sat and nudged the ground with the toe of her shoe, giving it a little swing. The wood was warm and smooth under her hand, worn with time but meticulously cared for by Emma.

Russell crossed the lawn to join her and she scooched to one side, making room. "I can't believe how much food you ladies made. I'm going to waddle for a week."

Their hands were on the seat between them and he threaded his fingers through hers. She sighed and rocked her feet against the ground, from heel to toe and back, making the swing sway.

"This time tomorrow, you'll be back in Florida," he said, and it was just a statement. No hint of how he felt about it or whether he was getting around to saying something else.

"Come to Florida with me."

Russell locked his knees and stopped the swing. "What?"

"Well, not tomorrow, of course." Now that she'd

made the leap, she wondered if she should have thought a little more about where she'd land. And how much the landing might hurt. "When the hardware store's closed and you get the property sold, don't move into senior housing. Pack up your car and come enjoy my company in the warm sun."

He just kept looking at her, his expression not giving anything away. Taking a deep breath, she forced herself to give him a smile. "It was just a thought."

"When I was a boy, I read a book about the building of the Hoover Dam. I was obsessed with it, really, and if not for the store I might have thought about an engineering degree. I always wanted to see it for myself, but I gave up on that dream a long time ago. Recently, though, I've had a snapshot in my head of you standing in front of Lake Mead, smiling at me. You're making me dream again, Catherine."

Russell blurred as tears filled her eyes and she blinked them away. "Then, when you're ready, you come on down to Florida. We'll relax on the beach for a little while and then we'll borrow Martha's RV and go see the Hoover Dam."

He leaned forward and kissed her. "I won't be far behind you."

"I'll wait for you."

CHAPTER TWENTY-ONE

"FOR THE GAZILLIONTH TIME, Gram, I'm going to be fine."

And for the gazillionth time, her grandmother gave Emma a very skeptical look. "You just don't seem like yourself."

Emma summoned every bit of acting ability she could muster and smiled. "I'm going to miss you, that's all."

"It probably won't be very long until you see me again. Russell thinks it'll take two or three months to wrap things up. I might fly up and then drive down with him when he's ready."

"Maybe you can stop and see a few sights on the way down," she said, careful to keep the smile bright.

The fact was, it hurt a little that Gram had the guts to put her heart and her pride on the line and invite the man she loved to be a part of her life and Emma didn't. She'd let Sean walk away without even taking a shot. Probably for the best, though. Judging by the way he'd shut her out at the barbecue, she would have gotten nothing by confessing her feelings but humiliation to add to her pain.

Gram looked at her watch. "I'm going to have to go through security in a few minutes. I hate leaving you alone."

"I have so much work lined up, I won't have time to be lonely."

"You can always call me. And make sure you visit Mary. I know she'd like to see you. And feed you."

Somehow she doubted that. "I will. And you call me when you get home."

"I won't forget. Are you sure you don't want me to stay longer?"

"And miss the big bingo tournament? You promised Martha you'd be there."

Gram rested her palm against Emma's cheek. "You're more important to me than Martha."

"And I'm fine." She covered Gram's hand with her own. "You're worrying already and you're not even on the plane yet."

"Maybe you should get a fake dog."

Emma laughed and wrapped her arms around Gram. The laughter turned to a few tears, but everybody cried saying goodbye to loved ones in an airport, so she didn't feel out of place.

Gram kissed her cheek and gave her one last squeeze before picking up her carry-on bag. "I love you, Emma."

"I love you, too." She stood there until she couldn't see her anymore and then she made the long walk back to her truck.

She took the back roads instead of the highway since she wasn't in a rush to get home to her empty house. Nothing waiting for her there but paperwork to catch up on and the echo of her own voice.

Her phone rang as she was unlocking the front door, and her thumbs hovered over the buttons as she tried to gauge whether or not she was in the mood to talk to Lisa. She wasn't, but she hit the talk button, anyway, just because the caller was her best friend.

"Did you get Cat off to Florida okay?" Lisa asked.

"She should be in the air right now."

"Then you should come over tonight for dinner. After the little ones go to bed we can crack open a bottle of wine. Or two."

It was tempting, if only for the company, but there were enough similarities between Mike and Sean in both looks and mannerisms that she wasn't sure she'd make it through the evening. "I think I'm going to throw on some raggedy old sweats and plop myself in front of the TV."

"Uh-oh. A pity party. Do you want me to come over there?"

"It's not a pity party. I'm fine. I swear." Even though she really wasn't, she was afraid if she fell apart over Sean, Lisa might let it slip to Mike and then it would eventually make the rounds and get back to Sean.

A self-pity party was one thing. His pity would be too much.

"Call me if you change your mind," Lisa said.

"Okay. And, hey, see if you can sneak something good out of Mrs. K.'s cookie jar for me."

Lisa laughed. "I will. Call me tomorrow."

Once the conversation was over, Emma stood in the hallway and listened. The house was so quiet. And it was different, too. In the two years before Gram and Sean had descended upon her, the house was always quiet. But now the quiet wasn't the same, as if a joyful song had suddenly been cut off in the middle of the chorus.

Rather than stand around listening to her own thoughts, she grabbed her iPod and—after making sure the playlist she was looking for didn't have a single sad song on it—she stuck her earbuds in her ears and grabbed the cleanser from under the sink. Maybe cleaning the bathrooms would wear her out enough to sleep.

SEAN PUT FIFTY MILES on his truck cruising around town, waiting for his aunt and uncle's driveway to be free of miscellaneous vehicles, before he finally pulled in and killed the engine.

He had soft and hazy memories of feeling sick or

scared or tired and crawling into his mother's lap. She'd hold him and rub his back until all was well in his world again. He needed that now. But he wasn't a little boy anymore and his mom was gone. He had his aunt, though, and maybe if he looked pathetic enough, she'd wrap her arms around him and give him a good hug.

His uncle opened the door. "You look like hell, boy."

"Thanks, Uncle Leo. That helps."

"Guess you're looking to go mooching around in the Cookie Monster." Back when Danny was little, he'd pleaded with Lisa to buy a Cookie Monster cookie jar for his grammy for her birthday. On any given day, the blue monster was full of delicious, melt-in-the-mouth baked goodies.

"Is Aunt Mary in the kitchen?"

"Have you ever known her to be somewhere else? I'll be out in the shed if you want to talk after."

"Thanks."

His aunt was at the counter, hulling strawberries, when he walked into the kitchen. She gave him a good looking over. "Blonde brownies."

One of his favorites. He grabbed two from the Cookie Monster and pulled out a chair at the table. She washed her hands and then poured him a glass of milk to go with them.

"What's got you looking like something a dog dug up in a backyard?"

Since she was wearing her apron with the ever-present wooden mixing spoon in the pocket, he swallowed the smart-ass retort that came to mind. "Not sleeping, I guess. After being in the middle of nowhere for the last month, being over the bar in the middle of the city's taking some getting used to."

She whacked him in the back of the head with that damn wooden spoon and he rubbed the spot. That might actually leave a knot. "Ow!"

"You look at me, Sean Michael Kowalski." He looked in the general vicinity of her face, and she took his chin in her hand and jerked his head up. "You look me in the eye, young man, and don't you dare lie to me. Do you love Emma?"

"Yes," he said through gritted teeth.

She released his face and he rubbed his jaw. "Well, that's a start. And I'm going to guess you didn't tell her that before you packed your stuff and moved out."

"I don't know what I'm doing. Other than not getting any sympathy."

"If you're looking for sympathy—"

"I know. It's between shit and syphilis in the dictionary." So they'd all heard. Many times. "The brownies are good, though."

She pulled out a chair across from him and sat down. "What makes you happy, Sean?"

Emma. Emma made him happy. "I didn't even get a chance to figure out what would make me happy. I was going to go do…something. Travel, maybe. Find a place I wanted to call home. And, yes, I love Emma, but she's so…rooted. She has that house and her business and that's *her* life. I want to live *my* life."

"You've been sharing a life for a month now. And you were happy. Don't deny it or I'll whack you again. And now you're not sharing a life and you're unhappy."

"She didn't ask me to stay." There. He'd said it.

"Had you given her any reason to believe you would?"

He felt himself clenching his jaw and forced himself to relax. "How could she not know?"

She leaned forward and covered his hands with hers. "And how could you not see the way she looks at you? How could you look at her at the goodbye party and not see her heart breaking?"

"I… She was sad her grandmother was leaving."

"You two are so busy trying to hide your own feelings because of your stupid arrangement, you're not seeing each other." She got up and pulled out the bar stool she used to sit at the counter when her feet got tired. "I'm too old to bend over and you boys are all too tall, so come here and sit."

He did as he was told and was surprised to find, when she stepped in between his knees, he was at the perfect height for her to wrap her arms around him. Sighing, he locked his arms around her waist and rested his head on her shoulder.

She kissed the top of his head and stroked his back. "If, a year from now, you were stuck on the tracks and a train was coming, what would you regret? Not taking a road trip to the Grand Canyon? Or not spending that year with Emma?"

He gave a short laugh. "Trust me, Emma *is* the train."

"That's love, honey." She squeezed a little harder and he felt some of the crappiness he'd been feeling slip away. "Think about it."

He took a few minutes to compose himself with the help of another blonde brownie, then kissed his aunt goodbye. "Tell Uncle Leo I'll join him in the shed another time, okay?"

It was quiet at Jasper's when he walked in, and Kevin was nowhere in sight, so he sat at the bar and asked Paulie for a beer.

He stared down into the gold liquid, even swirled it in the glass, but no Magic 8 Ball answer popped up.

Shit. He knew the answer. If he was about to become a bug splattered on the windshield of a runaway freight train, his last thought would be of Emma.

So what if she couldn't cook and couldn't drive worth a damn? And she came with a house he didn't help pick out and a business he didn't help her build. He could live with that. The family they'd make together would be *theirs*.

If she even wanted him.

There was a pad of sticky notes in his back pocket, but he had nothing to write with. He checked all his pockets, but the Sharpie was gone. Hopefully, that wasn't some kind of omen.

"You got a pen I could use?" he asked Paulie as she walked by.

She tossed him a ballpoint and he peeled off the first sticky note. Without letting himself think too much, he started to write.

THE SIGHT OF SEAN'S TRUCK pulling up her driveway hit Emma like an emotional wrecking ball and she backed away from the window, trying to will her heart into submission.

He'd probably forgotten something, she told herself, even though he'd been pretty thorough in removing all traces of himself from her life and her home. Except for the stupid army mug she couldn't stop herself from using, but she doubted he'd make the drive for an old, secondhand coffee cup.

He rang the doorbell and she stopped in front of the hall mirror to see if she looked as much like a train wreck as she felt. She did, but there was nothing she could do about the puffy eyes and pale cheeks. At least she'd thrown her hair into a ponytail, so there was only so bad that could look.

Emma pulled open the door with what was probably a sorry excuse for a smile on her face and froze.

Sean stood on the porch, his face set in the expression she recognized as the one he used to mask uncertainty. But her gaze only settled on his face for a few seconds before being drawn to his chest.

He was wearing a button-up dress shirt and it was pink. And not a tint of pale blush, either. It was *pink*.

"Hey," he said, handing her a small bouquet of pink-and-white gladioli, the stems tied together with a length of pink ribbon.

Her breath caught in her throat as she took them, her mind racing to make sense of what she was seeing. What did it mean? Why was he here, dressed like the man of her ten-year-old self's dreams?

"I, uh…made some revisions to your owner's manual." She hadn't even noticed the journal in his other hand, but when he held it out, she took it.

"Okay." Her voice was as shaky as her hands.

She opened the cover and found a bright pink sticky note stuck to the first page. *I miss you.*

"I miss you, too," she whispered, and slowly turned the pages.

You don't take any crap from me.

You make me laugh.

Missionary is my favorite position now because I

can see your face. That made her laugh, even as the sweetness of the sentiment warmed her heart.

I'll let you drive. She gave him a doubtful look and then turned the page. *Sometimes.*

Yeah, there was the Sean she knew and loved.

When he pulled a small velvet box out of his pocket, one of the tears blurring her vision broke free and rolled down her cheek. And when he got down on one knee, a few more followed. He lifted the lid, and nestled in the box she saw a shimmering ring with a central diamond nestled down between two bands set with smaller stones. It was gorgeous.

"I know I already bought you one of these, but that one was always hanging up in your work gloves. This won't catch on the leather or twist around too much." He tilted his head up to look at her. "This whole month was crazy, with all the pretending, but somewhere along the way it stopped being a lie."

"Did you go getting ideas about me, Sean Kowalski?"

"I did, and it was one hell of an idea, too. I love you, Emma. I think, deep down, that's what I wanted to write on that blank sticky note I left on the mirror, but I wasn't ready yet. I'm ready now. I love you and I want you to marry me. For real."

Words were flying around in her head, but she couldn't seem to get them into any kind of coherent thought. "I don't... I... Are you sure?"

"I'm wearing a pink shirt."

"I love you, too," she said, because that seemed like the most important thing to get out there. "And I want to marry you. For real."

He slid the ring onto her finger and then stood up so he could kiss her breathless. As a little girl she'd imagined she would shed pretty, feminine tears during this moment, but she was too damn happy to cry.

"I was thinking," he said when he was through kissing her, "that if I do some odd-job carpentry, like that deck remodel, and you do your landscaping, maybe we could coordinate our work so we wouldn't have to wait too long to have kids. We could switch off days, maybe."

"That sounds perfect. But will it make you happy?"

"It will." He kissed her again and a happy sigh escaped her lips when it hit her she was going to get to kiss this man for the rest of her life. "But most important, *you* make me happy."

She threw her arms around his neck and—just to be different—she kissed him this time. And then she reached into the back pocket of her jeans and pulled out the blank sticky note. It was a little tattered now, but she held it out to him.

"Wondering what you were going to say has been killing me."

He took it from her and then pulled out a pen that

said Jasper's Bar & Grille from his back pocket. *I love you,* he wrote, and then he stuck it to the front of her shirt.

"So you won't ever doubt it," he said in a husky voice.

"Let's go inside and get started on this for-real thing we having going on." She took his hand and tugged him toward the door. "And, because I love you, I'll start by stripping you out of that pink shirt."

* * * * *